THE SILVER SPITFIRE

A LOVE STORY
by
ROGER HARVEY

When two young Englishmen visit Nazi
Germany and one of them marries a
German girl, events are set in motion that
will affect all their futures. Romance,
nostalgia and gripping drama combine in
this tender and haunting love story set
against the horrors of battle and the
unsettling peace of post-war Britain.

To Demelza

ABOUT THE AUTHOR

Roger Harvey was born in 1953. His published works include the novels *Percy the Pigeon*, *A Woman who Lives by the Sea*, *Albatross Bay* and *River of Dreams*. His *Poet on the Road* is an intimate travelogue of literary adventures in America. He has won many awards for radio writing and for his audio-book poetry collection *Northman's Prayer*, made poetry-reading tours of Germany and the USA, and directed a film version of his play *Guinevere-Jennifer*. His poems, articles and stories continue to appear in British and American magazines and there is more information about his work at roger-harvey.co.uk.

THE SILVER SPITFIRE

"There isn't a particle of you
that I don't know, remember, and want."
NOËL COWARD, *Private Lives*.

ONE

Christmas Eve, 1953. We are warm
and together in a little German church.
They are singing *Es ist ein Ros
Entsprungen,* and at this moment, it may
be the most beautiful music in the world.

Rich colours, white vestments, yellow light from bright candles; and, as if pressed against the windows, a wonderful, luscious, midnight blue. Lisa beside me in her fur coat and tight black gloves; her perfume very strong. The voices of the choirboys float up and around us and through us while we stand like children with bright, expectant, Christmas faces. I love this woman...I have loved her for twenty years. Now we are warm and together, and I feel like a boy on his first date. But something is not right--perhaps it never will be. Perhaps that is the lesson of life: that there is always something not quite right. It is certain that I am no longer a boy.

Before all this began, I used to believe that hardship and suffering somehow made you a better a person; that to go through pain and grief was a sort of education. Now I know it isn't true. It was a young man's belief that had nothing to do with life as it had to be lived. Suffering doesn't enrich your life, it destroys it. Fear and loss and guilt do not help you understand the world, they condemn you to a poverty of soul, deflower kindness, and shrivel love. I want no more of them-- I want it easy, I want it beautiful, I want it to be like this for ever. And now, because I am telling the truth, I suppose I must admit to having lost my youth. I smile to myself. Let it go, I think, this is better. We are kneeling now, the Pastor leading his people in a prayer. I never used to go to church; now I like it. I'm not sure if I believe in God--this God or anyone else's God--but I believe in goodness and purity of spirit, and I believe these people are doing their best to celebrate these things. I know I believe in evil and in Hell. I've seen it, done it, and been there. Hell is right here on Earth, in our everyday lives, in the actions and sufferings of ordinary people--just like these people, slightly drunk on a cosy, innocent-looking Christmas Eve. I know Lisa has been there too, but I don't believe she is evil. Of course that could just be because I love her; I was always prepared to forgive her anything. I find that I still am--and smile again to myself. More perfume, more warm fur coat. She would make any man smile; I feel lucky it's me. But something is still not right. Lisa's black gloves remind me of Werner, and Werner reminds me of the War. I see Spring sunshine, hands on a steering-wheel, white faces, blue sky, fear: a soaking fear I didn't wish to feel again. I remember that keeping to the much-vaunted rules of life is no guarantee of success, that breaking them is no answer either, that no-one is free from the tyranny of themselves. The prayer is over--more fur, more perfume, a girlish cuddle. I remember that even in the most desperate hours, the flame of humanity burns brightly and will not be extinguished. Most of all, I remember that nothing can destroy true love. In the end, it's all we can be proud of, and it may be the only decent reason for doing anything--all the others are fake, or apologies for selfishness.

We are out into the freezing air now, in front of the church as the midnight bells are rung. I am shaking hands with people I don't know. "Froliche Weihnacht. Froliche Weihnacht." Lisa is in front of me. "Froliche Weihnacht to you too!" I shake her hand and kiss it as if I had just met her, and she laughs. We step into the brilliant darkness, like swimmers moving out into a numbing sea. Crunch, crunch, crunch. Deep and crisp and even all right. I try to whistle *Good King Wenceslas*, but my lips won't work. Our breath steams and spurts in the frozen air. The other people are going home in groups; we set off under the crackling moon and are swallowed into silence, emptiness--only the crunch of our boots in the furrowed snow, only the steam of our breaths, only the clasp of our hands. If I once knew Hell, this could be Heaven--right here in the midst of our ordinary lives. Well, perhaps not so ordinary. We both came a long and curious way to find this.

A new sound reaches my ears. Instinctively I stop and look into the sky, studded with stars so bright they almost hurt.

"Jets," I say. "More than one. They must be our Vampires--heading North."

"What?"

"Vampire jets. Our boys have had them out here for a while now. Funny looking aeroplanes." Despite her silent impatience I continue to crane my neck and look into the sky. I don't think she ever liked aeroplanes; she had every reason to hate them. So had I. But I was different; I was a natural; everybody said so and I knew it was true. I can't give up my search of the starlit sky. The roar grows louder, deafening.

"There they are! Look, three of them!"

Three sets of coloured lights race overhead, each stabbing out a fiery orange tail. Instantly I am up there with them: stick, rudder, compass, horizon, throttle, stick, rudder... the night is cracked with noise.

"They're belting it," I say.

"Home for Christmas." Lisa's voice, usually so soft and dark, sounds thin below the roar. They are leaving us...the beginnings of a frozen silence folding slowly down again.

I say: "Behold a throng of angels." My own voice sounds weird.

Lisa does not answer. I take her hand again, and we go crunch, crunch, crunch over the snow. I have loved this woman for twenty years...but the jets have swept me back to another time.

TWO

The four biplanes growled overhead--and I hurried from my perch at an upstairs window, down into the front garden for a better view. I recognized them at once. They were big, heavy-looking machines, each with a flat-nosed radiator and long exhaust pipe running down a slab-sided fuselage: Bristol Fighters, the same type which had been so successful in the Great War--the war in France, which seemed to have been more exciting than anything in the history books, a war in which modern knights had duelled, not in shining armour, but in fantastically painted flying-machines; the pilots of each nation equally heroic in my imagination. For some reason I can scarcely remember, but perhaps because of their romantic-sounding names, the French aces were my favourites, and the daring careers of Nungesser, Fonck, and Guynemer were the stuff of my vivid imaginings, against which the current exploits of peacetime flyers like Cobham and Lindbergh seemed tame: adventures without the deadly sting of combat or the high gallantry of war. In my innocent, childish enthusiasm I felt cheated by Fate that I had been born in the year of the Armistice and had missed all the excitement. In my fascination with aeroplanes all I could do was read the stories in the magazines and watch the newly-painted de Haviland Moths nosing down to the Flying Club, away over the landward horizon on the London road.

The 'Brisfits' came in low from the sea, heading for the Club field, and for a moment their massed engines seemed to rattle the tall buildings in front of me, filling my head with a shocking noise. I sensed that some of the other people, watching from the windows and gardens of our seaside town, might think they were ugly aeroplanes: noisy, dangerous, and a reminder of tragic times which everyone told me had changed the world and killed three of my uncles--but to me they were beautiful, and from that day onwards, more than anything, I wanted to fly.

I was ten years old: a shy little boy in a seaside hotel. Its proper name was *The Promenade Hotel*, and a tawdry sign proclaimed the fact, creaking in the ceaseless wind and streaming rust in the rain, but it was always known locally as *Dellow's*, in much the same way as if it had been an Irish bar. My parents, who ran the place, had no Irish blood as far as I could tell, although my father's devil-may-care open-handed generosity of spirit seemed to proclaim a Celtic ancestry. "Run away to sea, lad," he would whisper his whisky breath into my nervous ear. "Take a tramp steamer to the South Seas, where the girlies wear no clothes and there's rum for breakfast.

You'll come to an island where the natives'll think you're a god. They'll put leaves on your head, wives in your bed, and you'll live like a king on tuppence a week...or join the circus when it comes to town--not that it ever will, not in this dump. Best run away to sea, when your mother isn't looking." Then I would notice a wetness in his eyes, which frightened me more than any of his tales of the sharks and pirates and murderous Chinamen I might encounter when I made the break he never made and ran away to sea. Next to drink and dreams of South Sea island girls, his great relief from the tedium of his run-down life was playing the ukelele and singing in a flat voice. He sang miserable and sometimes meaningless songs from the Music Hall days that I didn't understand then and have never heard since. "Stop that bloody racket!" my mother would yell--and it was back to worrying about the leaky roof, the butcher's bill, and the dubious couple in Room Six.

My mother managed this lacklustre life better than her husband; *managed* was the right word. She was the boss: of the hotel itself and our curiously public life inside it. She used to complain that the War had ruined the seaside hotel business, and ruined England into the bargain. We might have beaten them in the end, but not before "those bloody Huns" had killed all the gentlemen-- including my three uncles, suddenly invested with posthumous nobility--and left the scum, idling about in corners, drinking whisky, and fiddling the cash. She never failed to add that there was no justice, since even the uncle who had been commissioned in the field and won an MC in the trenches had been killed-- leaving a family of 'wasters', as she called her surviving menfolk. These angry outbursts would signal a period of her 'not speaking' to my father, while her monologue was directed at me. Why, the third-rate commercial travellers and pathetic honeymooners we had to put up with these days weren't a patch on the gentlefolk her mother had entertained.

That was when jolly King Edward had been on the throne; he'd known how to enjoy himself, so everyone else did. There'd been real style in those days, the big hotels freshly painted along the sea-front and the nice iron railings properly kept. There'd been real money too, and toffs coming down from London drinking Champagne on the promenade and a French Count with his yacht in the bay. Even the weather had been better: long sunny days, and all the pretty girls with their hats and parasols. And now look at the place--this is what you got after four years of war and ten years of hardship and a waster of a husband.

Yet curiously, just as my mother's lamentations grew most bitter, a stir of change could be felt. New buildings had appeared in our town: bungalows along the sea-front fields, and smart semi-detached villas in the London suburban style stretching inland along whole new streets. There were more motor cars and more guests. My father said Wall Street had crashed (I thought he meant it had

16

fallen over: shops, rooftops, gutters, front porches, the lot, all in a long pile of rubble somewhere in America where the gangsters had Tommy-guns), and he warned that the family finances would be tighter than ever; but in the same year money was found to send me as a weekly boarder to a better school where I like to think I acquired some polish without becoming a snob...but I suppose I must have been insufferable for a few years, I was so pleased to have escaped the dull seediness of my home life. I had expected to be forlorn and frightened in this new world of difficult lessons and superior accents, but I wasn't. I liked it. It was everything the dreary seaside town could never be. When I came back at the week-ends with my grey flannels and school tie and new haircut, telling smutty jokes and boasting about my new friends who had fathers in London and motor cars and sisters who had married the Honourable So-and-So, I saw and despised what I felt was the numbing stupidity and desperate boredom of my family.

"Oh we are la-di-da, aren't we?" my mother would say. "It'll be Oxford next I suppose, then Prime Minister with a little bit of luck."

I detested being shown off to her gossiping friends who were "in for a cup of tea, and be a nice boy and pass the biscuits to your Auntie Vi"; but I knew my father was curiously proud of me. He never hesitated to give me money when I pleaded for a special book, a new jacket, or the pair of gloves I wanted to be seen in when my new friend Alex Fitzgerald took me driving in his father's car. Alex was only two years older than myself, but he looked twenty, and seemed to live like a lord. I was ashamed of my parents, ashamed of the Promenade Hotel, and ashamed of the seedy start in life I thought the three of them had given me. Now, I am just ashamed of having been ashamed.

But, as Alex breezily put it, things were definitely looking up. By the middle of the Nineteen-Thirties I was leaving the Sixth Form while Alex had gone on to

College. Perhaps surprisingly, I moved easily between school friends and a set of much older College boys led by Alex himself. With these young people I enjoyed myself as never before, the process made easy by the money which seemed to flow effortlessly through Alex's hands and those of his elegant friends: young men who wore suede shoes, knew or pretended to know about wine, borrowed their fathers' cars, or had their own. My own mother and father knew little of what was happening. This was a world far removed from that of my own boyhood, an even further from that of my parents; yet they showed no disapproval and did nothing to hold me back when I might reasonably have been considered 'far too young' for this sort of company and its outlandish goings-on.

Alex had a plan to take a crowd of his friends to Loch Ness in the first year of the Monster's fame, but like the creature itself, this never materialized--but the scheme was typical of what excited us. We did make a trip to London to see the shows: everything from *Felix the Cat* cartoons to a Cochran revue. And for the first time in my life there were girls. None were my own age; all seemed rarified, sophisticated creatures with bright eyes and coloured cigarettes. One of them wore bracelets above her elbows; we called them 'slave bangles' and thought her wonderfully decadent. She and all the others smelled of powder and silk and Worth and Pimms and fell regularly into Alex's more experienced arms. Envious of his charm but without real jealousy, I was romantically in love with all of them. None, I might add, showed the slightest interest in me. I thought about sex, and liked to think I knew about it, but never imagined how and when I might actually 'do it'. In reality, at that age, I knew little about sex, and next to nothing about love. Only vaguely, in these bright young people and in my own life, did I sense the lack of it. Yet I was blind to that void, and did not care that I was blind. I was excited enough as I was and felt fulfilled, for I had found myself among something else of which there had been no trace in my background: glamour. Alex and his set, the girls and the motor cars and the parties, brewed a seductive atmosphere without--for me at least--the reality of sex. And delightfully, effortlessly, almost incredibly, they provided the best thing of all: flying.

"Come down to the Club this week-end," Alex had said. "It's not far from where you live--oh, but of course you've known that for years, haven't you? Well, I'm already qualified--on a Puss Moth actually, but I can handle just about anything--but I've had to keep it under my hat or all the girls would be begging joyrides. Just a few of us are in on it. It can be rather expensive but I'll see you in all right. Just watch it in the Clubhouse and--well, er, lie about your age. You know all about aeroplanes anyway, don't you? You'll be a natural, I can tell. Actually, it's easier than driving a car... but don't tell any of the other fellows that. I say, you will come, won't you?"

I was speechless…but of course I would go. I had dreamed of this all my life, and Alex seemed to know that I had, without ever having to say so or embarrass me with the sudden realization of my hopes--but he did seem like a god, nonchalantly handing out favours at the birth of a mortal. And in that way I felt re-born, as if my real life could now begin. I was going to fly, and so partake of the magic I had longed for all through the years of my boyhood. It was to happen so easily, so ridiculously easily.

"Come on Saturday," continued Alex. "If the weather's decent I'll see you go up with the Chief Instructor. If it's a rotten day we'll just soak in the bar."

The sun shone. We never set foot in the bar, and that is how I came to enter the world which had for so long been unreachably above my head, yet was now at my fingertips. By the following Summer my familiarity with flying was such that I could stand on the edge of the field on early mornings, watch Alex take off, and know every beat and pulse of his flight as if it were my own. I would hear his engine drown the birdsong, feel the great propeller blasting backwards the diamond-shedding turf to lift him lustfully into the air, the mist a streaming chiffon from his wings. He would think he was alone, never guess a fellow flier stood across the field to share the swell and clamour of his Earth-parting, to see and know that girl-given talisman pennanted and fluttering between the struts. I would soar to the sun with him, take down into my laughing lungs the ice-cold ether-blast, and wait for that heart-lift when the sun would seem to hurtle from behind a cloud to dazzle and enrich him. I would climb with him high into the blue and venture into far-flung purple valleys of the clouds, feeling all the time his pulse and squeeze against the wind-stiff stick, the ecstacy of a loop, and at last his safe and quiet sinking to the warm ground, smelling the heat of the engine as he trundled in, checking the canvas and the wires with a practised eye. I was a natural all right--even on the ground.

Yet beneath all these delights I remained the shy boy from the seaside hotel; the poor boy too, at least compared to Alex and his friends. My parents were not rich enough to send me to College, and when it came down to it, I wasn't clever enough to earn myself a scholarship. I went to work in the hotel, hating it, knowing it was a backward step from the seductive liberty I had been given, but having to be thankful for a ready-made job in a world where any job was difficult to find--for a young man from my background, anyway. I knew, in that pre-War English way, that I had moved beyond my own class. Now I felt I had fallen back into it. It was depressing when I thought about it; more depressing when I contemplated my constant lack of funds--but I chose not to contemplate that very deeply. I had regular days off and the use of my father's Morris. Indeed I felt rich and lucky: rich in time, lucky in opportunity. In some ways old beyond my years, I realised how fortunate I had been, and that I should be well satisfied with the odd ways in which my young life had turned out. Whenever I could, I drove away from my old home and into that new world above the Earth and the darkness and the miseries of the Earth, miseries I scarcely knew but sensed well enough. And as it said somewhere in the Bible, the Earth might be ready to pass away, and deservedly so, but surely the sky would remain free and pure.

THREE

A hot Sunday at the Flying Club. The gramophone was out-of-doors on a table, a sickly little tune playing over and over again, as if the crooner might languish away in the heat. Members and guests were in deck-chairs with drinks on the grass--a spattering of pale flannel *bags* and straw hats across the green. A couple I didn't recognize were dancing between the tables. Beyond the paddock fence, blue and silver Gypsy Moths stood like great winged lizards basking in the sun.

I noticed all this from the car. I was sniffling with a cold and reluctant to get out. It was not the day to have a cold. My customary sweep of the sky and well-tuned ear revealed that nobody was up, at least not in the vicinity of the field, and there was no sign of Alex in the paddock. Perhaps he would be in the Clubhouse. I did not want to leave the cool shadows of the car, and wished he would come. Why was it still so difficult to face a few people? Why was it still agony for me to do what seemed so easy and natural to Alex and his friends? I had known them all long enough, yet still felt shy and awkward. Perhaps it would be better if I could light a cigarette, shove one hand in my trouser pocket, and stroll across in that lazy, debonair manner of his. I felt for the cigarettes, but threw the packet on to the back seat. No good; I hated the things. Nothing for it but to barge in.

I sneezed in the hot sunshine. Heads turned from deck-chairs and swung away again. On the Clubhouse steps I stood aside to let a throng of giggling girls burst out: white clothes fluttering, coloured drinks in their hands, heels rattling on the steps then swishing away over the grass. That was something else--I was nineteen and had to admit I was still ignorant of women; but I knew enough to realize that Alex was not. Alex had girls around him all the time. Alex was twenty-one.

It was deliciously cool in the Clubhouse; dark, and hung with photographs and old propellers. I loved that room, and was tempted to linger in it, looking at the photographs of the Schneider Trophy aircraft, but Alex was not there, and there seemed no likelihood of finding him indoors. I nodded a reply to the barman's greeting and passed on through the lounge--filled with light from its long windows, more dreamy girls with drinks on a leather settee, a sudden view of the paddock, chairs, and aeroplanes-- and on into the office. The Major, an R.F.C. veteran with just the magnificent moustache one would expect, was poring over a map. A large whisky held down its curling corner.

"Hullo," he said, looking up. "Come for your maps?"

"I'm not flying today, Major. I'd blow apart."

"Ah, spot of cold, ay? Well, have a Scotch."

"Not for me, thanks. I'm looking for Fitzgerald, actually."

"Fitzgerald? Now let me see." The Major went over to a wall-map and consulted the coloured crayon lines on its glass surface. "Ah yes, Fitzgerald. Yes, he is up. He's doing a big dog-leg down here." He loosely indicated a large yellow triangle then tapped the *A. Fitzgerald* printed in the same colour below the map. "Crafty fellow, your friend. He's got all his turning-points over lakes or crossroads. I'm told he never looks at a map once he's out of here. Heaven knows when he'll be back. He's up in the Bulldog."

"Thanks Major."

I knew the Bulldog meant aerobatics, performed well away from the field, and I strolled out to wait in the paddock, collecting a Coronation tumbler of ginger-beer from the bar as I went. The bubbles and the sunshine cleared my head; I began to feel better. I might be the youngest and most callow member of the Flying Club, but I was one of the best pilots. I settled in my chair to study the very pleasing lines of the Moths as they stood perkily on the grass. A pity more 'planes were not up. That was the trouble with this place, I thought--most of the members were here for the social advantages: the drink, the parties, the girls, the dancing. I did not scorn these things--I had enjoyed them with Alex and his crowd of friends, or at least pretended to. But they did not truly move me; I had discovered they were not part of my soul. More than half these people had never even sat in an aircraft: they had the ludicrous word *observer* stamped across their membership cards, and that, to me, is exactly what they were. My natural reserve did not stop me from feeling very proud to have *pilot* stamped across mine. There were times when I felt that word set me apart for ever from the others and their kind; and that, in my easy practice of a skill discovered rather than learned, I would transcend their gaping silliness. Youth may be arrogant, but it is not always certain--yet by now I considered myself old enough to admit that my most perfect relationships were with sky and clouds and wind and sun and the thundering engine beyond my feet, partaking of a high communion inexplicable to those on the ground. Only Alex bridged the gap between the others and myself, moving as he did with moneyed ease from cockpit to dance-floor, a sure player of his game, dice loaded to be likeable and fortunate...and, somehow, friend to me.

A faint singing in the grass, like a sudden chorus of insects, woke me from this reverie. In a moment it had become the shrill note of wind in the wires and a little biplane whooshed low overhead, the pilot gunning its idling engine to life and banking steeply away across the field. Alex was back.

Chairs emptied, drinks were put down. Figures lined the little fence like spectators at a race meeting. Alex was already well beyond the field, his wings flung up like a ladder as he turned. His aircraft made a poignant sight in the softening afternoon: dark blue against a paler, more translucent sky--almost too glorious, too delicate, like a beautiful girl seen once and lost for ever. Then the sun flashed off his wings, the stub-nosed Bulldog cocked its tail, and here he came, very fast, in a throttle-bending sweep towards the Clubhouse. Everyone ducked as he roared over our heads. Then people recovered, laughed; girls adjusted their hats. Our Bulldog was an ex-R.A.F. machine, of the type so popular at the Hendon displays, and was perfect for aerobatics. Stripped of its armament, its enormous Bristol Jupiter engine reconditioned by our club mechanics, it was faster than ever. Painted in our smart blue and silver, it provided us with very zestful flying, and made our club the envy of many another. In short, it went like a rocket... and now, away beyond the village and the London road, it was being hauled up the sky in spiral turns.

"Burning it a bit, isn't he?" The Major had come out to watch. "But I must say he does it well."

Alex did it well. Elegant swoops and dives are easy, since it is natural for an aircraft to lose height. To gain it beautifully is much more difficult. Alex did not fight with gravity, he used it to swing from stall-loops into last-minute Immelmann turns, let it give him speed for the next pull up. He danced up the sky, and I was with him all the way: lying on my back with him as the Bulldog hung on its propeller, letting the stick knock over, feeling the lift in his stomach and legs, pushing open the throttle for more height, easing it back, watching for a sign of overheating from the straining engine, flattening out for a second or two, then pulling her up, up, and up again. That was how I wanted to spend my life.

"Beautiful," said the Major.

Alex was very high now, and directly above us. The throb of his engine seemed far away--then it faded altogether, and we could hear the birds singing. The Bulldog seemed to stand still, then quiver, as if a shock had run through its stiff little body. I knew what was happening, felt everything that Alex would be feeling in the dreamy beginnings of a spin. The ground-colours would be swinging and racing and blurring, the eerie weightlessness would come and go, and now he would be battered upwards into his straps, the wind howling in the wires, the stick slammed hard across his knee. Down, down, down, down! A swelling, bursting pressure behind his eyes, a sickly smell of oily tortured metal blasting in his face, a crazy terror sucking and swallowing him down, down, down!

In the awful hush I heard the Major cough uncomfortably.

"Time he was out of that, " he said quietly.

"It's all right Major," I grinned, "he knows what he's doing."

"So do I--and it's time he was out."

The Major is right, I thought to

myself. You must pull her out now. Come on, pull her out, now!

I felt rather than saw that little twitch of the wings: Alex was pushing the stick forward. It was the only way out of a spin like that and it took some courage. Full throttle--there she went with a roar--stick right forward--down, down, still going down…now up, up.

"Come on," I muttered under my breath, "get her nose up. Come on."

People were shouting, clenching their fists, willing him, praying him up. It was going to be terribly close. Here he came, dragging that nose up, faster, faster…!

The Bulldog screamed overhead, still on full throttle. Unable to stop ourselves, the Major and I bent double and covered our heads.

"Bloody fool!" I heard him say. "Bloody fool!" The Major was dusting his knees and elbows, running his fingers through the remains of his hair. "He knows damn well that's the only Bulldog we'll ever have!"

I laughed--a loud, silly, nervous laugh. I wanted to speak, but no words would come.

"You're a cool one, I must say." The Major was still re-arranging himself. I could only laugh again.

"He's safe enough now," I smiled. "You'll still have a Bulldog in one piece."

Alex was bringing her in, around the field in a wide and gentle curve, friendly sunlight shimmering through the propeller. The ecstacy was banished, the divine was gone.

"Bloody fool," said the Major again. "Now what the Devil's he doing?"

"I think he's going to land," I replied evenly.

"Well he's too high."

A tinge of fear wormed in my stomach. Alex *was* too high, and approaching too fast to cure it. Still drunk on the dive, was he too exhilarated to have noticed? If he kept this line he would overshoot, straight into the paddock...but no, here came his oldest trick: a shocking drop-like-a-stone sideslip right on to the middle of the field, snapping back to straight-and-level for a perfect three-point landing and a short run up to the fence. The spectators clapped. He cut the engine and gave a little bow behind the windscreen, a boyish grin bursting inside his helmet. Then he was out and vaulting the fence towards me, looking more than ever like the man who broke the bank at Monte Carlo.

"Clever Dick," I said, receiving his hot handshake. There was a faint spatter of oil across his white overalls--on his jaw it made him look unshaven. The sunlight was rich and golden now; it caught the dark gleam of his pressed-down hair and threw deep shadows on his throat and temples. There were times when Alex looked like a messenger from Heaven.

"The Major says you're a bloody fool," I told him.

"Then the Major knows a thing or two," he answered mildly in that light, thin voice one never expected from so tall a man. "The Bulldog's like a ton of bricks in a dive," he whispered. "Took everything I had to get her nose up." Alex was combing his hair with the look of someone who has just crossed a busy road in the rush-hour. "Come to think of it, it's lucky you're not scraping me off the grass. Anyway--I'm off to Germany for the hols. D'you fancy coming?"

Germany! I was taken aback.

"Will Lisa not mind?" I asked.

Alex laughed. "Of course not. We'll be staying at her parents' house--it's a very big place. You'll be more than welcome. They're lovely people."

"Yes, but they don't know me," I protested. "Won't I be in the way?"

"Rubbish. You've already been invited--they expect you to come with me." He patted me on the shoulder and led me off to the Clubhouse. "Anyway," he bent closer to my ear, "I especially want you there. You see, I'm going to ask Lisa to marry me. You can be Best Man."

This, then, was the real thing. I had known about this girl, how Alex had met her two years ago when he had been with his parents in the Alps, how other holidays had been shared, and how she had come briefly to London--but I had not guessed that Lisa had meant more to him than any of the other girls he knew, nor that his trips to see her had been any different from the other extravagant gestures he made. (Once, he had driven to Edinburgh in a day, just to deliver a Birthday present to a Scots girl. She still wrote to him.) Now, in the weeks before we left, I came to know a different Alex. He still took girls up in the club Moths and appeared at the ceaseless round of parties--but now more soberly, as if nursing a new and secret responsibility; and he did not dance in his old and carefree way, however passionately the girls might look into his face or clasp his hand. His conversation was now all about Lisa, her family, what we would do in Germany, and how they had fallen in love. In the hard bachelordom which used to mark English adolescence, such things were not always easily discussed, even--perhaps especially--between the kind of adventurous and carefree young men Alex and I liked to think we were. Yet here he was, wanting to talk about nothing else.

"Look what I had made for her," he said one day.

He drew out a slim morocco case. Pearls, I thought at once, pearls--or some enormous diamond necklace. That's what he's done: he's blown half his inheritance on a diamond necklace, and it's going to look like something from a whodunnit story. But when he opened the case, all I saw was a gold medallion nestling in dark blue satin.

"Go on," he urged me, "take it out."

It was thick and heavy and had a pattern of vines in frosted relief around the edge. On one side was written *I Love You* in Copperplate; on the other *Ich Liebe Dich* in Gothic Script. As I let the chain run through my fingers and the cool gold weigh in my palm, I knew my friend was now caught up in the oldest, finest, simplest story of them all. It made me happy, but it made me sad too, in a way I had not felt before.

"You never met Lisa when she was over here, did you?" Alex fiddled with his cigarette.

"No," I said, "and I'm rather peeved. You've never even shown me a photo of her."

"Best keep it that way, 'til you meet her in Germany."

"I know," I joked, "she's a fat monster with a moustache, and you daren't let me see a picture of her 'til it's too late to save you."

We chuckled at this, and Alex polished up the medallion with his handkerchief.

"I'm sure she's going to like this," he observed, admiring the fine relief-work. "You see, it's quite marvellous: I understand her taste perfectly. It's as if I've always known it, without having to ask. She knows what I like, too."

"Well I'm glad she does. But since you're going to marry her, remember what Oscar Wilde said: *The only basis for marriage is a mutual misunderstanding.* So you're off to a bad start already."

"Oscar Wilde was a nasty old queer, so please don't quote *him* at me."

"She sounds very pretty, anyway," I said.

"Pretty?" Alex snorted. "Is that your word for it? Pretty? Well she's not pretty," he went on with smoke in his eyes, putting the case back in his inside pocket. For a moment I was confused by the serious tone of his voice, then he took the cigarette from his lips. "She's absolutely gorgeous."

FOUR

It was the birds that woke me: the twitter of little finches, and behind it, the muffled cooing of a woodpigeon. The birds--and a cool, blue and green light, a light of cloudless sky and tall trees. The light--and a soft whiteness in the room; the big bedroom windows open, and the long white curtains stirring gently. The whiteness--and a moment's wondering where and why and how and is it a dream? Then the feel of the bed and the shape of the room and I was awake with bright sunshine streaming in. My first morning in Germany!

I threw off the mountainous *steppdekke* and lay thinking how strange and exciting it was to be in this great house and to have all the holidays ahead. A new smell came faintly to my nostrils. Coffee? Lavender? Cigars? Not quite. I got up and padded across thick blue carpet to the window. It reached to the floor and opened easily, inviting me out on to the balcony. A warm and sunny morning revealed a spectacular view. The house was set in a breezy, park-like area atop a long rise, so I could look beyond the trees and see the town, a mile or so distant. Other houses, just visible amid the foliage of their gardens, poked tall roofs above the green. We were in a wide and airy suburb, neat and trimmed, but broad and rich too: masses of flowers, young trees, pale and shaven lawns--and beyond the town, a rolling landscape merged in the morning haze to a stain of forest and a dark-edged horizon. Closer to the house, behind an old stone wall, there was an orchard stretching down the hill with rows of trees, some still in blossom. The woodpigeons were cooing in there. That teasing smell again--and a sound of footsteps! Down below on the garden terrace Alex was smoking a foreign cigarette: its aroma curling up to me.

"Oi!" I shouted down.

"Morning," he smiled up. "You've slept in."

"The bed's too comfortable, and that big snuggly thing sends you off like a baby."

"Werner's gone to the station to fetch Lisa. They shouldn't be long. Come and have breakfast."

"Right-o."

Shall I ever forget the Odenwald's bathroom? I had never seen anything like it. You opened a white door and stepped in on to black marble--miraculously warmed from underneath. The walls were clad in gleaming glass of midnight blue, and every so often you could look at yourself from a different angle in the vast mirrors. Choose either of the two white marble wash-basins and you could have a gush or a trickle of water through modern chrome taps. The hot water was always instantly hot and the cold always icy. How did they manage that? Approach the huge bath up marble steps, lie in the deep hot water, and you could stare endlessly at the geometric patterns in the white plaster ceiling, then see them echoed in the long, uncurtained windows. I thought it was a wonderful bathroom, and felt like a film-star every time I went to clean my teeth.

Twin beards of water thundered down into the bath and I lay looking at the steamed-up windows. Frosted triangles emerged from clusters of semicircles, mounting over themselves in a series of impossible perspectives. Only one night here, and already I loved this place, but how would I fit in as guest of this strange family? I had met Herr Odenwald and his bony wife when we arrived. They had welcomed Alex and myself with an open, broad-minded largesse I had not expected to find in Germany; but they were packing for a holiday in the Alps and had left to catch a midnight train to Innsbruck. Their son Werner was said to be away on business-- I had no idea what that business might have been and it hadn't seemed polite to enquire--but would apparently return during the night and collect Lisa at the station when she arrived from finishing-school in Geneva. There was a silent little maid too, and Frau Zeller, the enormous cook who spoke no English but who seemed to take an immediate fancy to me. Amidst the bustle of our arrival she handed me a plateful of sugary cakes and went clucking away like a grandmother goose. "She says they'll fatten you up a bit," translated Alex, taking a cake for himself. The chaos of international comings and goings--wildly exciting yet at the same time disturbing to me--did not seem to ruffle the Odenwalds. It was all casual and easy, as if they were charmed and amused by Alex but scarcely interested in the fate of their daughter with him. With me they were polite and distant, speaking a too-impeccable English and wishing me a pleasant holiday; but they spoke to Alex in German, Herr Odenwald laughing a quiet, tall man's laugh as he shook Alex's sunburnt hand and patted his lean shoulder. Everyone seemed to agree it would be a good holiday and a good marriage, and off they had gone, leaving their magnificent house to the younger generation. The casual manner of all this had surprised me--at the time it seemed rather daring, even risqué. Now, of course, it wouldn't raise an eyebrow.

I lay back in the bath, studying a bank of chrome pipes which ran around the room. They gave off a comforting warmth, and curved into the wall like the gleaming exhausts of Werner's Mercedes. I had seen neither the brother nor the car, but a photograph of it hung in the hallway, and Alex had immediately pointed out the great black and silver monster, saying he could not wait to drive it and show Werner a thing or two about handling a car. It was as if this enchanted foreign pleasure-palace was already his own; as if his passport to another world had already been stamped, and that he might appropriate its riches whenever and however he liked. I felt no such ease; all the less for sensing it in him.

"Rich!" I heard him rapping on the bathroom door. "Stir your stumps, old chap. Werner's here with Lisa."

"Blast him. I'm all wet!"

"Put on a dressing-gown. Nobody minds here. Come straight down--we must welcome them properly."

He ran downstairs. Damp and rushing, I followed quickly after him.

The Mercedes, revving into low gear, ploughed up the gravel drive as I came to the door--two golden heads beyond the massive bonnet. Needles in my stomach now: armies of anxiety seemed to march upon me with the remorseless tread of that huge car. How would I fare with these two? I could not see them properly for reflections in the rakish windscreen, but the girl was waving: a little white hand and a clean blue sleeve. Gravel spattered from the wheels as Werner turned in front of the house and Alex waved and ran.

The engine stopped its pounding; bass notes died in those brutal exhaust pipes. Werner stood up behind the wheel. He had bright yellow hair swept off his clean, bony, suntanned face. He gave us a cheery salute and leapt out of the car--tall and lithe in a dazzling white shirt and black trousers tucked into riding boots. I waved back, but Alex was already at the other side, talking to Lisa and opening the door for her.

"Come on you clot!" he shouted at me, and waved me over. Feeling ludicrous in dressing-gown and slippers, I slapped across the gravel. A bell of golden hair swung up and out of the car--giving both her hands to Alex now--pale blue blouse, grey skirt--he kissed each hand in the continental way--clean white knee socks, grey lace-up shoes--then drew her to him, kissing both her cheeks--

Werner laughing, shaking hands--she had tiny sunburnt fingers, a soft round face-- "Richard, this is Lisa"--warm hand, bright teeth and wide pink lips, every shade of gold vibrating in lovely hair, deep brown eyes, dark eyebrows, soft and laughing voice--all this under a brilliant blue sky, lighting up the day so I could never forget it. Were ever eyes so brown, or sky so blue?

I gasped, I muttered, I felt a fool. The three of them were all talking at once.

"How was finishing-school?" I managed.

She turned the brown eyes on me in something between a smile and a haughty stare.

"Finished!" she laughed.

"My sister hates school," stated Werner. "She likes only playing tennis." Little sinews moved inside his open-necked shirt. He looked between us all, as if searching for confirmation. "That is true, yes?"

Alex picked up a suitcase. "Take Lisa's jacket, will you Rich?"

I fished into the leather-scented seats, drawing out the linen jacket and a sporty-looking hat.

"What a lovely hat with a feather in it," I said.

"O--oho--ho!" Lisa laughed with a voice so deep and soft that she might have been murmuring asleep. "Then you shall carry it for me!" She thrust it on my head, and Werner led them giggling into the house.

That first day was still beset by comings and goings. Werner drove back to the station to collect the rest of Lisa's baggage which had somehow been delayed... so I got a ride in the big Mercedes before Alex, and answered Werner's incessant questions about the King and Mrs. Simpson and Mr. Baldwin and the Coronation and the Flying Club and English beer. I saw the town, too: bright in the cloudless windy morning. Werner took me through the *Markplatz*, where stalls and buckets of flowers were spilling everywhere, and nosed the car into a warren of old streets where gabled houses tumbled towards one another and quaintly carved and painted signs hung low across the pavements. Flowers blazed and trailed from every window; back in the centre of the town it was the blood-red banner with the black and twisted cross.

That night I stood on my balcony and looked out once more across the town. It was a lake of lights beneath the sky: still dusty pink in the West, ice-blue in the East, with the first few stars appearing. Below me in the darkened garden Alex and Lisa whispered together as she poured him coffee, and the smell of those foreign cigarettes rose again to tease my senses. More coffee, soft footsteps, the creak of that old chair...I could not hear what they were saying. But her deep laugh floated up to sting my hot young face with passions I could scarcely name, then was lost into the blue and velvet night.

FIVE

The world used to be so big and full of secrets. In Germany that Summer, they seemed to be pouring out, letting me taste them one by one, giving my senses no respite. Everything excited me: the smell of the town, the foreign landscape, the undreamt-of thrills of the *Autobahn*-- where else could you drive all day on a race-track?--the big new buildings in sheer white stone, this enchanted house with its great black staircase, the brash new Germany of which Werner was so proud. But older, softer things enraptured me too: the rich old orchard, full of mystery; the squirrels I would sometimes see there as they darted from branch to branch; the luscious colours of the sky; and the charming manners of my hosts. On one of my first mornings, I found a little box of sweets on my dressing-table. Peeling off the golden foil, I discovered a chocolate beetle, and, mystified, brought it down to breakfast.

"Your *Maikafer*," Lisa explained with a slow smile. "It is a great German tradition to place one in the room of a new person in the house. Aren't you going to eat it? It will bring you luck."

There was music, too: music everywhere. Werner would play his gramophone each night, and the house would be filled with great symphonies, folk-songs, and sometimes a harsh, new, jangled tune from the night-clubs or cabarets. Lisa would play the piano and sing in her astoundingly deep voice. They were sweet, lilting songs: *Schloss Linderhof so Wunderbar, Wo die Alpenrosen Blühn,* and her favourite, *Bist Du bei Mir,* sometimes sung to Alex standing silently in a corner with the lamplight falling across his handsome face.

So this was the real thing. He was in love with her--but then so was I. Who could not have been? She was so beautiful, every part of her, so effortlessly, gleamingly perfect, like a constellation of film-stars rolled into one unbelievable girl--but I had to believe in her. Here she was, right next to me at the dinner table-- and talking with her mouth full, too. There she went, laughing through the house, passing me things, asking me to help her lace up her tennis-shoes, holding me round the waist for a photograph in the garden, jokingly scolding me, correcting my German; one moment giggling like an amused sister, the next cool and sophisticated like a Society hostess, always breathtakingly gorgeous yet right here, reachable, looking into my eyes every day. Of course I was devoured by desire, and the most elaborate sexual fantasies began to take over my being, occupying my dreams and my waking hours with equal insistence. To hold her, to be held by her, to roll into an all-consuming physical love…but surely that could not be possible when Alex was going to ask her to marry him and the three of us were on holiday together. Surely she would refuse me, sharply and coldly, if once I dared to even speak. How could she ever be interested in me, the shy boy from the seaside hotel who had somehow tagged along into this glamorous world of foreign friends, big cars, wealthy fathers, modern houses, fast aeroplanes, and beautiful girls?

I was not especially aware of

jealous feelings, or would not admit them. If I envied Alex, I did not want it to spoil the idyll. For the moment it seemed enough to love Lisa in this boyish way, feeling I might never win her but at least, without risk of losing her, bathe for ever in her dazzling presence. Sometimes I just laughed to myself, it seemed so extraordinary that I could be so lucky, trapped in the same exotic house as a goddess cast in flesh. Yet when she sang or played the piano, or music floated through the house, my passions would quickly get the better of my reserve. One evening, the strains of an open-air concert blew softly through our windows from the town.

"What is that wonderful music?" I asked.

"That is Schubert's *Unfinished Symphony*," said Alex.

"Let's go there at once!" I almost cried, grasping Lisa's hands, finding them warm and soft and rippling with tiny bones. "Let's go there and hear it."

"No," she said dreamily, turning

from me to rest her elbows on the terrace balustrade. "It is better from far away."

Early each morning we came down to an English breakfast--but with strong coffee instead of tea, and a selection of jams instead of marmalade. Werner still insisted on calling it an English breakfast however, since he always served bacon and a rack of toast, and would proudly say: "Every morning in London this is eaten, yes?" looking to Alex for confirmation of his expertise in foreign affairs. Alex only smiled--but always ate the toast. Outside, the woodpigeons would be cooing--although now I had learned to call them *Ringeltauben.* Werner would bustle about, giving orders to Frau Zeller and the maid, but Lisa and Alex would sit quietly on the sunny terrace with their coffee, or if it was raining, stand together and look out of the long and streaming windows. Her bright, gleaming clothes, her shiny hair and creamy skin: they all seemed to shimmer round her warm curvacious little body, as if she were indeed some kind of angel sent down to scorn all other women and make every man stop and stare and fall instantly in love. Alex, dark and languid, quite unlike his brisk and English self, seemed sunk in a perpetual dream, as if nothing could happen or matter any more... and into my impassioned excitement crept a new boredom.

Sometimes Werner would go out by himself, leaving us to play tennis or walk into the town for lunch at a café; sometimes we would all drive into the countryside with a picnic, or to another town where Werner would show us the sights. In the evenings we might play tennis again, or cards--at which neither Lisa nor her brother liked to be beaten. There were times in those card games when I had never felt more uncomfortable and never less sure of myself. She was lovely, but sly, and I knew she tried to cheat. Werner, much more volatile, was in some ways easier to deal with. He had a kind of mad certainty about everything that made his decisions swift and binding, and by grimacing and clenching his fists when he was losing, could unwittingly defuse the situation by making everyone else laugh. He never saw the joke, of course. But for all these moments of tension and flashes of amusement, I felt we were drifting in a pastel-coloured mist, like the rain-clouds which would sometimes float across the house and garden, drenching this new world and trapping us in it.

"How are you and Lisa getting on?" I asked Alex one night when we were alone together.

"Wonderfully," he beamed. "Isn't she gorgeous? I told you she was gorgeous, didn't I?"

"Well--when are you going to ask her to marry you?"

"Already have, old chap."

A darkness settled upon my spirit. I didn't know how to say what I felt.

"Naturally she said yes," continued Alex with a smile, "just in case you were wondering."

"Well, you lucky old devil," I managed, taking his hand and shaking it.

Now his smiling shrug seemed so casual. I wanted him to make more of it.

"When will it be then?"

"Not for a while yet," he explained quietly. "We'll sort all that out when her people get back. We might have to do the whole show twice, you know--once over here and again back home. You could be in for two tremendous parties."

"Congratulations Alex. It's wonderful."

At last he laughed aloud and slapped my shoulders. Muscles worked in his face, tears almost came to his eyes.

"Yes, isn't it?" he grinned, shaking my hand again. "It's the best!"

Despite my seemingly hopeless love for Lisa--or perhaps because of it--there were days in Germany when I was indescribably happy. The radio or gramophone would play, the sun would shine, and I would sit in the garden or wander through the orchard to the delicious music of Mozart or Schumann. The orchard was a place of absolute peace and I never tired of walking there or stretching out with my friends along the twig-strewn aisles between the trees. Sometimes Alex would bring a bottle of wine, and we would drink from tall glasses when he had drawn the cork with the practised ease of a lounge-lizard. Years later I would come to despise these accomplishments, but then they seemed unaffected, lovely, and wonderful, for they were as natural as the stirring of the leaves or the singing of the birds around us. One day, after drinking and lying on the grass, we decided to decorate the house with leaves and branches, 'to bring the Summer to our table' as Lisa put it. So, beneath a sky of massive white clouds piled high against the blue, Werner stood on tall ladders and handed down the boughs to Alex, who passed them on to me. They bore a freshness of the open sky, bathed in windy sunlight all the Spring, and now carried home in Lisa's smooth brown arms. I wanted this sweetness to course through me all my life.

While Lisa was changing for dinner that evening, Werner brought cocktails on to the garden terrace: Alex's was cherry red, mine a violent green.

"Port and Starboard," quipped Alex.

"No, no," replied Werner. "Gin. So, tonight we must go to the cabaret. *Zum Wilden Hirsch.*"

"*The Wild Deer*, ay?" said Alex. "And what goes on there?"

"It is an excellent place. They have the best band in town. Hallweg the illusionist is appearing tonight--and there are dancers." A gleam came into Werner's eye. "Sometimes, there are naked dancers."

A faint flush came to my cheeks. When Alex turned to face me, the back of my neck began to prickle.

"D'you fancy a night out with a stageful of naked women?" he drawled. It was the way he said *naked women* that did it. I felt myself go scarlet.

"Not really."

"Richard doesn't want to go," said Alex airily. "Can't think why." At that moment I hated him.

"You really should see it while you are here." Werner's voice had none of Alex's dry mocking in it. Perhaps he had not noticed my blush. Just then, Lisa glided out on to the terrace, luscious in a purple dress.

"What are you fellows talking about?" she smiled. I noticed with amazement that her painted lips were exactly the same colour as the dress.

"Your brother is suggesting we should go to a cabaret and see the naked dancers," said Alex blandly.

"And are you shocked?" she smiled her most disarming smile.

"No," Alex's voice had lost its sureness, "but I think Rich is."

"I...I've never been to a cabaret before."

"He means he's never seen naked women before--but it's really time he did, don't you agree? Yes," he turned to me, affecting a breezy nonchalance, "you really should go, old fellow. Part of your education and all that. Mind you," he glanced at the others, "you'll soon be bored. When you've seen one pair of tits, you've seen the lot."

"I'm disappointed in you Alex," smiled Lisa. "I thought you were a connoisseur."

They all laughed at this--Lisa as easily as the men. I was appalled that such things might be said so casually between them, and hardly knew where to look.

"It is something to see, I suppose," continued Lisa, but suddenly without enthusiasm. I knew she had seen my face.

"I know personally," Werner carried on regardless, "that one of the girls wears nothing but a top-hat, a cane, and a pair of high-heeled shoes."

"Ach, that's nothing," returned Lisa. "In Berlin they wear nothing at all and wrestle in mud."

"Perhaps we should go to Berlin," observed Alex drily.

"And now dinner is almost ready," announced Werner, ushering us off the terrace.

"You do look lovely tonight," said

Alex to Lisa, and they took each other's hand.

"Shall we go to *Zum Wilden Hirsch*?" persisted Werner.

"No," breathed Lisa, looking between Alex and myself, "I don't want to go. You men go if you wish--I have been out all day and should like a quiet evening. Perhaps I shall listen to the radio-concert.

She is like the falling of dusk, I thought to myself, a soft-falling gift of peace, wrapping me up in her beauty, banishing pain, awkwardness, and anxiety. Pure, welcoming peace. Loving her was so easy; it was impossible not to love her.

"Another time, Werner," said Alex.

I came up behind them, plucking up courage to take Lisa's other hand.

"You know," I said to her, "if they ever need an angel in the pictures, they should have you."

"Dear Richard," she snuggled for a moment into my side, "what a lovely thing to say."

The meal was brought by Frau Zeller and the little maid. Werner--perhaps feeling cheated of his night at the cabaret--ordered them about with a harshness I had not seen before. I could never be like that, I thought, although part of me wanted his cool assurance for my own. Werner was cruel, but not deliberately or perversely so. Cruelty was quite natural to him; he bore it with the nonchalance of smiling blue eyes, practised it without guile or deception. Lisa, on the other hand, was crafty. For all that I loved her beauty and marvelled at her grace and glamour, I could see her shamelessly simpering and wheedling and fluttering her eyelashes and tickling Alex's ear with her nose until he--or indeed anyone else--would be unable to refuse her anything. And, for the first time, I saw Alex as a child: as childish as myself, perhaps more so. Here in this great black palace of a house, he was no longer the carefree daredevil Flying Club hero. Here he was a toddler in a glittering playpen; taken down from the clouds, robbed of his marvellous machines, no longer free to press into his hands that means to taunt the gods. Here he was fed the goo of sentiment on silver spoons, clutching now at friendship, now at love. My moment of revulsion passed, and I saw again my happy friend, his lovely girl, her bright and handsome brother. But the nameless worm of new anxieties had been born, to stir and burrow into futures none of us could guess.

A light rain blew across the lawns, blackening the soil around the linden trees, blearing the long windows of the *salon* where I stood. Amidst the sodden blankets of cloud there were occasional foamy pink and golden billows. Behind me, Lisa was playing Schumann on the great black piano. She seemed to be coaxing the music over a lump in my throat.

"You play wonderfully," I told her without turning round.

"Does it make you feel good?" Her voice was quiet; she played more softly than ever. "Does it make you feel as if you were a little boy again, sitting on your mother's knee? Does it make you feel as if you were floating above the clouds in your aeroplane, or standing on a mountain, or looking out across a deep dark forest?" It was her voice which held me as much as the music: the deep lilt of it, the dreamy warmth of it, the low liquid vitality of it, wrapped up in fluffy, pearly, sibilant smiles.

"It makes me want to cry," I confessed

"Ach!" she declared, "we'll make a German of you yet!"

And she dashed off into some lively Mozart, laughing, pouting, and tossing her golden head. So much was stored up in my heart...I felt it might burst at any moment. I turned away from the window and leaned on the piano.

"Let's go to this rally," I suggested, "you know, in the town. They say there'll be bands, and dancing afterwards--and we can surprise Werner. He told me he was in the organizing group."

"It's raining," she said, and

stopped playing.

"I think it's going to stop."

"Where is Alex?"

"He's making himself a drink. He'd like to see it, I know he would."

At that very moment Alex came into the room carrying a gin and tonic.

"Anyone want a drink?" he asked.

"Too early for me," I answered. "I was just saying to Lisa, why don't we go to this political rally and see what Werner gets up to?"

"No," Lisa's voice was suddenly cold, "I don't want to go. I cannot bear to see him playing soldiers with all those stupid men. We'd only argue."

"Argue? But why?"

"I do not agree with his politics."

"Oh," said Alex breezily, "we never let politics stop us enjoying ourselves in England. Stuffy old men making up laws; half of them asleep in the House of Lords. Who wants to be bothered with it? It's all a lot of nonsense anyway."

"You know it is not nonsense in

Germany," she stated flatly. "And your amusing English picture of the sleepy old men at Westminster is not exactly true to life here, Alex--you ought to have realized that by now." Her English was so precise, he accent so faint and teasing--I always loved listening to her. Yet now, in this speech, she sounded hurt and angry as she shuffled up the music and closed the piano.

"I know nothing about politics at all," I admitted, hoping to relieve the tension with a chuckle.

"All right then," Alex sounded calm enough, but a little troubled that Lisa had been so inflamed. "What *are* we going to do today?"

I felt it had all been my fault.

"The rain's stopping," I remarked, desperate to say something. "I knew it would."

"I could beat you both at tennis again." Lisa's voice was soft and sly.

"I'm sick of playing tennis," said Alex, "and anyway, it's no contest. You only have to look at Rich with those eyes of yours and he misses the ball."

"Even from the other side of the net?" she murmured. They were sharing some sort of private joke.

"I'm afraid it's true," I laughed, hoping to cover my embarrassment with a smile. But I could not bring myself to look at them as they kissed.

"If Werner hadn't taken the car," said Alex, "we could have gone out and I'd have shown you some real driving."

"Let's do that!" Lisa sprang up from behind the piano. "Let's take the car this evening when Werner comes back. I have a new scarf--I shall wear it!"

"All right," he decided. "D'you know," he added to me, "that thing does well over a hundred?"

"Werner wanted to be a racer," said Lisa, "but he gave it up to go into politics."

"Well there you are, you see," replied Alex. "Politics is nothing but a damn nuisance. Instead of standing on a soap-box, talking nonsense to people who don't want to listen, he could have been a racing driver: much more fun."

"And killed himself no doubt," I put in quietly.

They did not seem to hear. Lisa was glowing with the idea of going out in the car. "When my brother hears of this," she told Alex, "he will challenge you to a driving competition."

"Oh, will he now?"

They cuddled in the curve of the piano.

"Politics might be safer," I muttered.

"Politics is rot," said Alex, not looking at me.

Werner drove fast, stirring up the great brute of a car with a none-too-gentle foot, making the humps and troughs of the country road into a madman's switchback. Alex drove just as fast, but caressed the throttle and the wheel, so that all was smooth and dreamy and the shriek of the wind no more than a distant song. Werner was still too excited by his day of marching and music to notice he had been outclassed--or surely his pique would have been intolerable. He sat beside Alex shouting: "Faster, faster! It is necessary to be hard with the pedal!" Weary of these incessant orders, Alex gave me a wry look through the mirror and stood on the throttle down a long straight. The engine howled, the car leapt up, Lisa and I were pressed back into the leather seats. Werner whooped with delight; his sister laughed and thumped his shoulders and put an arm round Alex. These people are drunk, I thought, drunk on love.

At length we pulled up in front of an inn, Lisa taking off the dark blue scarf and shaking loose her hair as we climbed stiffly out of the car, somewhat battered by the wind and now astonished by the sudden quietness of the balmy evening. Werner pulled off his tight black gloves and rested against the bonnet, giving us all a sunburnt grin. "So," he said to Alex, "you drive well."

"Thanks." Alex lit a cigarette, and I watched the blue-grey smoke rise into the sparkling air. It was indeed a beautiful evening, enlivened with the fresh smell of damp earth, darkness just beginning at the Eastern edge of that translucent ice-blue sky. Away to the South, great pink-edged mountains of cloud were floating, more perfect and more thrilling than the castles of a fairytale. Werner said they had been formed over the Danube or the Alps. "The Alps," I murmured to Lisa, imagining her high in the eternal snows, beautiful and proud in furs. The car crouched on its sooty tyres like a monstrous animal of molten lacquer; Werner flicked dead moths and flies off the bonnet and the headlamps. From a little wood behind the inn came the distinctive drumming of a woodpecker.

"Do you hear that, you fellows?" smiled Lisa. "There is an old saying: she who hears the *Schwarzpecht* must have Kirsch."

"You make them up," said Alex, "but I'll see you have a full bottle."

"Go inside," commanded Werner. "It has been such a good day I shall buy you as many bottles of Champagne as you can drink!"

"You're on," said Alex.

A delicious smell of cooking met us at the door. At a table lit by candle-dripped bottles, we sat down to pork pies, great slabs of brown bread and fried onion, smoked sausages by the plateful, and an enormous apple pudding. Outside in the beer-garden, a cool and dusky breeze began to stir the tablecloths; but in here everything was warmth and light. Werner bought us the Champagne and Alex bought Lisa the Kirsch; soon we were merry and toasting everyone else. Everyone else toasted us. The little bald waiter grinned like a ruined cherub; soft, silly music came from an ancient gramophone; it seemed that nothing could ever again be wrong with the world, nor that anyone could ask for greater, simpler happiness. Yet I watched the others with a kind of dazed detachment. My oldest most cherished friend and this laughing, golden, round-faced girl were caught in a shimmer of light, an impenetrable glory which spoke in the flickering candlelight, the tinkling glasses, and the hot aromatic flavour of the baked apples--but which had its being far away from me. I told myself it could never really be part of me. The meal carried on; I never betrayed my innermost feeling. None of the others knew that in these apparently carefree moments I had resigned myself to a life without Lisa. It was almost a relief--I could afford to laugh and raise my glass. I could now be happy in all sorts of ways except one. All I had to do was admit that she could never be mine.

Hot, laughing, glowing with wine, we piled into the car. People crowded at the door to see us off. The engine roared, the lights of the inn fell away behind, and in moments we were rushing through a dark forest: Alex wearing Werner's cap, cold gaps of sky between the trees, a spangle of stars.

"Werner! Take us to the lake!" Lisa shouted from the back seat where she clung to Alex's arm. "Take us to the lake! I want to show them the moonlight on the water!"

And suddenly, as her words were lost into the wind, I realized how close and loving they were, and how far beyond my world they had already stepped. They had grown, through love, into a new and composite entity, so that one would be forever incomplete without the other. Ironic, I thought, that I should now find greater ease with Werner's busybodying, his confident chatter, and his cavalier handling of the big car than with my old friend and the lovely girl who now claimed his heart. They had embarked upon some golden journey where I was sure to get lost, had already entered some paradise where I would be a dark and clumsy stranger...but here I was, with them, yet without them.

We arrived at the lake. It was a chilly sheet of black water surrounded by dense conifers, and so absolutely still in the Summer night that the moon and a few stars were perfectly reflected in its glassy surface. We stood on the gravelly shore, whispering and listening to the night. I knew, as so many men at one stabbing poignant moment come to know, that this was the woman I would always love. I might never touch her, might woo or marry a dozen others, but would always love Lisa beyond them all. I was filled with misery.

"What a place," breathed Alex.

Lisa put her hands in the pockets of her jacket.

"Sometimes I used to swim here when I was a little girl," she said huskily. The thought of it refined my torture. Her eyes were huge and glistening in the darkness. I wanted her golden presence to last forever.

"...and sometimes I used to chase my little sister around the trees." It was Werner, speaking in a sharp-edged voice to cut through all this night-magic. "She would shout at me so loudly I would have to run away to save my ears."

The spell was broken. Alex ruined it completely by trying to howl like a werewolf and by throwing stones at the moon's reflection until the lake thrashed up into gleaming shards of light and the stars were extinguished in the leaping, shattered water.

Drunk and tired, Werner slumped in the passenger seat while Alex let the car cruise back to town. Alex drove wonderfully, as if he were stroking the mighty heart of the engine, allowing it to swish and beat along at its own pace. Drowsily I watched the headlamps cut their pale yellow swathes down the road, illuminating now a dead grey hedge, now a gaunt telegraph pole, now a lonely house. Lisa fell asleep in the back beside me; her head rolled on to my shoulder. She was relaxed, oblivious, but my heart beat faster. I could feel the tickle of her bright hair at my neck, see the long dark lashes lie against her peach-soft skin. A faint but gorgeous perfume rose from her, even in the open, windy night. 'That is all I shall ever have of her,' I thought.

SIX

Werner's cocky cheerfulness, which had been so evident during the last few days, was eventually explained: one night at dinner he disclosed his plans for a garden-party to celebrate the engagement. It was to be held at the house just before we left for England. There would be everything, he promised: a special marquee, crates of Champagne, and a dance-band. It was not long before Alex and he were in busy chatter about all this while Lisa drank her coffee and looked at me with her dark eyes. In a few moments the garden-party had developed from a pleasant surprise into a campaign for enjoyment, and Werner was already planning it with military thoroughness. It seemed he had left nothing to chance and that everybody would be entertained all day and all night. I began to dread the event, not only as the first of several rites which would mark my loss of Lisa to Alex, but as a public display of forced gaiety under her brother's relentless baton. I had visions of Werner providing naked dancers on the terrace, but neither the maturity nor experience to relish them. Yet for all his fussiness and his tireless arranging of other people's lives, there was something splendid and fun-loving in all this, and his enthusiasm became infectious.

"It'll be wonderful," I said, looking beyond the windows to a brassy sky, "as long as it doesn't rain."

The night grew heavy with approaching thunder. Werner, intoxicated by the imminent fruition of his plans, was determined to bring a foretaste of raucous merriment into the house. He sang songs while Lisa played the piano; he brought up four bottles of Austrian *Dunkelstein* and commanded us each to drink one. I had no head for a night of wine, but he and Alex soon became very drunk and went down to the kitchen where they terrorized Frau Zeller into making more and more coffee laced with brandy and with *Schnapps*. A dangerous contest developed between them and they careered around the house putting on all the lights and drinking wines and liqueurs in every room. Uncomfortably sober, tired, and oppressed by the thundery night, I made for my bedroom.

Lisa was standing at the top of the stairs, fiddling with her bracelet.

"Ah," she smiled, "you also are escaping."

"Yes. I'm tired. Where are they now?"

"I have no idea," she said, still looking at her wrist, "but it will not be long now. Soon my brother will fall over with wine and we will have peace."

"Will he be all right?"

"In the morning, yes. He will force himself to get up early, take a cold bath, and then at breakfast he will eat twice as much as normal and tell us all what a strong fellow he is. I am not worried about him. It is Alex. He is not good at drinking, I think."

"He's an expert," I smiled, "I promise you. He's drunk more whisky than I've even seen."

"That is why I am worried. Can you help me with this?" She thrust out her arm. The safety-chain of her heavy gold bracelet was tangled in the clasp. I could not undo it.

"Come," she said, moving away. "You cannot see here."

She led me into her bedroom, flooding it with light. It was a large room with a massive bed and pale wooden wardrobes in the modern style. The windows were open and the hot night air came in to mingle with her perfume and the scent of make-up on the long dressing-table. She sat on the bed and rested her arm on the eiderdown. I bent over her creamy wrist and made a show of labouring away at the tangled chain. Despite my resolve to let her go to Alex and my belief that I could never win her, I was devastated by having her so close beside me, warm and full of life in the luscious purple dress. Far away, the first faint rumblings of thunder could be heard.

"You are very gentle," she said, and when I made no reply, she added: "Alex is gentle too."

"I should hope so," I muttered.

"What?" she chuckled, shaking her wrist to make me look up. "What do you say?"

"I mean…he should be gentle with you." I stammered, looking into her shimmer of golden hair. I loved her now and would say so, or try to. "You are so lovely. I… think you are so lovely."

I had somehow expected her to shake off my words with a laugh, but she smiled and lowered her eyes. For a moment the whole world seemed suspended in the little warm wrist I held: the drunken fever of the house, the distant rolls of thunder, the beating of my heart--all, all of it pulsing through her flesh so close to me. Behind her spread the rich covers of her bed, and the delicate embroidery of the pillow-cases with their edgings of white lace were like something from a fairytale, beautiful but melancholy. And she seemed stranger than ever, yet happier too, as if she held the secrets of quietness so few are given. I bent again to the knotted gold chain.

"Alex is a lucky man," I said.

"And I am lucky to know you both," she answered, and just at that moment, the bracelet came away. Her arm looked very bare without it. "Dear Richard," she took my hands and kissed them, "how clever you are with things. Come, sit by me here." The great soft eiderdown sank and rose about me.

"I'm not clever with people," I moaned.

"Ach," she smiled, and slapped my leg in an unexpectedly mannish way, "do not be ashamed to be young. Soon you will laugh to remember how embarrassed you were by things which are quite natural."

"You mean I'll soon be old?"

"No," she laughed. "You are a rotten philosopher!" *Rotten* was a word she had learned from Alex. Somehow it seemed out of place on her lips. "But do not worry about that either," she went on. "I put fliers above all philosophers: they know the truth of the world by looking down on it."

"I've hurt you!" I exclaimed, noticing a patch of redness where the clasp of the bracelet had been, and took up her wrist again. "I'm sorry." The truth is, I was so in love with her then for her beauty and the things she had said, that I did not want to let her warm hand go.

"Then you will fix it with *Kölnischwasser, Herr Doktor,*" she grinned, passing me a bottle of cologne from her bedside table. Doing as she asked, I splashed and stroked it on her wrist, then, intrigued by its cool fresh scent, wiped it on my cheeks and chin. How easy it could be with her; how easy to be natural.

"If I'd just shaved," I smiled, "this would be good and sharp."

"I see you have *lebenslust,* my friend."

"When you come to England I'll take you up in a 'plane--then you'll know all about *lebenslust.*"

"That will be good," she smiled again, sweeping her feet up on to the bed and putting her hands around her knees. "Ah, if only the world was a better place for such things."

"You don't like it?"

"Oh, I like the world well enough--

it is the people in it. I fear they are going to spoil everything unless we take great care."

"Now you are the philosopher."

"One has only to read the newspapers. Not everything in Germany is good. All this trouble we have now, it came about so strangely--sometimes I wish I had been born many years ago, when my father was a young man: that seemed to be a good time; perhaps far in the future will be better also. When I was in Switzerland I read the French and English newspapers, even the American ones. There is a lot of trouble in the world. I tell you, if the world was run by women, it would not be such a stupid place."

She was perfectly serious, and I believed she was right, but we both laughed aloud at our sudden images of female politicians, female generals, and female industrialists. Then we listened to the thunder for a while. It came closer, but no rain fell.

"We are going to have a storm," I

said, moving over to the window.

"Yes. My Grandmother died in a thunderstorm. I always remember that, but I always love the storms here. Nothing else matters in a thunderstorm but all the noise and rain. I like that. I never feel I can get close enough to the middle of it."

"Me too. Perhaps this will be a really good one."

She had come to stand beside me at the window and was looking out: changed, excited, vital. "Yes," she said, "here are the first drops of rain." Dark pennies of water could just be seen on the illuminated balcony. "Let us find the others and all watch it together."

"All right."

"Before we go, Richard..." She stopped at the bed, where twin hollows still held the memory of our silent loving, "...take this, please." She held out the bottle of cologne then put it in my hand, placing both of hers over mine. "You like it, don't you?"

"Yes," was all I could manage to

say.

She drew my hands up and kissed my knuckles.

"You are such a fine fellow," she said, and walked out of the room.

Noise and confusion reclaimed the night. Werner was on the stairs, Viennese glass in hand, shouting in German and leading a very drunken Alex up to see the storm.

"What's he on about? What's he say?" muttered Alex, clutching a bottle.

Lisa hurried down a few stairs to meet him.

"Only that the Storm Bird is flying. Are you all right, my darling?"

"'Course. 'Course. Where the Devil's he taking us?"

"Follow me!" cried Werner, his face aglow with drink and a wild gleam in his eyes.

"I think we are going on to the roof," said Lisa, taking Alex's arm.

"On to the roof? But it's the middle of the bloody night!"

A peal of thunder echoed

overhead, and rain lashed down upon the house. Werner had broken into raucous song, and was leading us past the bedrooms to a door that opened on to a little roof-terrace where sometimes we would sunbathe. But the world of light and Summer seemed far away, and this wild night the only reality. Werner stood for a moment with his hand on the door, swinging his glass and shouting the refrain from some heroic anthem--then he flung it open. Rain poured in, making Lisa squeal with shock and Alex stagger back. But Werner strode out boldly on to the roof, singing and shouting in a towering ecstacy. A flash of lightning seared down across the trees; moments later a tremendous crash of thunder split the night. We huddled cold and shocked in the doorway, but Werner plunged on into the blackness, pulling off his shirt and shouting, yelling, singing to the storm. His gleaming torso streamed with water, his bright hair spiked across his forehead, veins stood out upon his throat.

"See?" he cried, turning back to

face us. "To the North the East the West and the South--all of Europe is before us!" Another flash of lightning cast a frightful, livid glow across his face. "Will you stand like cowards in the corner? Come out!" A boom of thunder drowned his words....and still we crowded together at the doorway, rain lashing our legs and faces. Werner dashed his glass against the wall and flung his arms wide. "Come out!" he screamed--and suddenly there was a movement at my side. Lisa marched out, her shoes splashing through pools of water, her hair and her dress soaked in a few seconds. She took her brother's hand, and together they sang the chorus of his song: deep and wild, lovely, tragic, pure, and happy. Her bare throat and shoulder caught a flash of blue, making her seem for a moment like a marble statue, a white goddess cruel and cold, the golden hair a crown of steel, mad and beautiful, utterly foreign to everything I had known and to her own time and place, unreachable, dangerous... then her own skin-colour returned and she was lovely again, more lovable than ever, more lovable than anyone could ever be: so beautiful, so close, so nearly mine.

Huddled out of the cold and blinding rain, I watched as if in a dream, knowing that Alex loved her, drunk and on his knees beside me. He loved her in whatever way was his own; I had no right to criticize it, but I did, for I knew I loved her with the mad ecstatic spirit which was the same as hers, but not like his. I turned my face to the rain and heard her singing the very music of my own soul. For all that, who was to say I loved her more than Alex...who but my own wild heart, and hers?

Werner had his way with the garden-party. He embarked upon a tireless campaign of organising the like of which I had never seen. Orders were sent by telephone and by post. Little groups of military men began to arrive in the afternoons, along with others who looked like special policemen. Werner would take them round the garden, pointing out different places. On one of these visits, a group of brown-shirted boys measured the lawns, and notes were made in little books. He was obviously on easy terms with the senior-looking officials who accompanied them, and I began to sense his influential position. When they caught sight of me watching from an upstairs window, a curt show of bowing and heel-clicking was made from the terrace, which I returned with a smile and a little bow of my own, made informal by a cheery wave. I felt like the Prince of Wales on a European tour--but I was never introduced to any of these visitors. That was the most infuriating of Werner's traits: one moment he was brimming over with camaraderie, the next he would make me feel like an unwelcome foreigner.

Alex and Lisa let him get on with it--not that they could have stopped him had they wanted to. But, as the time for her parents' return drew nearer, they became more and more wrapped up in each other, leaving Werner and myself to our own devices. Now, in the long Summer evenings, I would be left alone to try my hand at pistol-shooting in the garden, learning kitchen-German under Frau Zeller's matronly direction, or reading one of the few English books in the house.

On the evening before the garden-party I sat late on the terrace, watching rich sunlight creep up the wall and out of the garden, where wooden trestles and the long canvas rolls of the unassembled marquee lay like the wreckage of a strange ship, and festoons of unlit party-lights cobwebbed between the trees. From Werner's room came the sound of his gramophone: wild and melancholy Bruckner, Mahler, and Beethoven. The music made me restless, and I could not read my book. Instead, I paced about the darkening garden. Here I was, I thought, just about as lucky as I could get. If ever I had wanted to escape the seedy hotel, surely I had done so now. I had gone in search of glamour, and most certainly found it. But in the morning, the

Odenwalds would return; in the afternoon, the garden-party would take over. I experienced an end-of-term feeling as well as the torpor of a calm-before-the-storm--but there was nothing to do, nowhere to go. I could be self-satisfied, but I couldn't be happy. It was strange to feel so lost in this magical place. From tomorrow, time would no longer stand still: this idyll would be over, and the rest of my life would have to begin. Suddenly wanting the activity of the house around me, I went in to take a late bath.

Up there at tree-top level with the windows open, I lay in the steaming water and watched the luminous sky grow steadily darker as night crept down. Werner still played his gramophone--but now the music was even more haunting and more tragic. At last relaxed and sleepy, freshly powdered with talcum and wrapped in my dressing-gown, I set off for my bedroom...but as I passed along the landing, an odd gleam caught my eye. Looking across the indigo gloom of that massive stairhead, I could see that Lisa's door was open. A soft pink glow suffused her room from a bedside light, and I could see right through to the windows, open to the stars and the scented air and the faint cold movement of the benighted trees while inside all was warmth and luxury. I stopped and listened: soft, coaxing, murmured laughter came to mingle with the music; then I saw Alex and Lisa. They stood just inside the doorway, holding each other's arms. She had taken off her shoes and looked smaller, but her whole figure seemed to burn and shimmer with light in her pale clothes. Alex stroked her hair; she kissed him on the chin--then slowly, slowly she put her hands inside the collar of his shirt...and tore it from his chest. She flung back her head, tossed her bright hair, opened her mouth in a wide smile I had never seen before--and they moved out of sight. I crept away, half in wonderment, half in fear. This display seemed to signal the end for me. I shuffled along like a little boy banished from adult pleasures. I felt that Lisa would never want to tear my shirt off and stroke my chest, and for the first time I wasn't sure I actually wanted her to. Nor did I believe that I had truly escaped my old life of shabby uncertainties: I could hear my father telling me there'd soon be another girl who would want me to tear *her* clothes off, if only I'd stop moping about and come down to the pub...but suddenly in the darkness a new sound distracted me. The music had stopped, and a faint gurgling noise replaced it. I was shocked to see that Werner's door was open and that he was coming out towards me. His face was white and tears streamed down from hollow, reddened eyes. We stumbled into each other.

"What on Earth's the matter?" I exclaimed, catching hold of his arm.

He wrenched himself free.

"I have been listening to Wagner!" he cried, and blundered on into the bathroom.

I had been right enough: nothing could be the same once that hectic day was upon us. When the Odenwalds arrived, Werner was already marshalling a troop of servants in and out of the newly-erected marquee. Their busy chatter and the clinking of plates and bottles put up a stir throughout the house--a constant distraction from Herr Odenwald's tales of mountain walks and his wife's descriptions of lake-steamers and Alpine flowers. They had brought presents for Alex and Lisa: a matching pair of Swiss watches in rich red gold. Tiny diamonds were cunningly placed on the numerals of Lisa's, while Alex's showed the date as well as the time. I had never seen anything so magnificent, and they seemed to me the height of almost decadent luxury. But when I saw what the proud parents had had engraved on the backs of the watches, my heart soared as if my own soul were gaining the happiness which shone so brightly from my friends. In a heart-shaped border on the back of Alex's watch ran the words *Bist Du bei Mir*, and on Lisa's the English *Be Thou with Me*. Then there was a flurry of kissing and shaking hands, and I thought how wonderful it was to be with such people. I had not been forgotten either: a slim package was thrust into my hands, and I found I had been given a watch too. It had a stout steel case with a thick black strap. The clear numerals stared up at me; the big pointers had luminous paint on them. "Good for flying," said Herr Odenwald, shaking my hand again. I was thrilled and honoured, but visited by a keen misery. The back of my watch was bare, cold, stainless steel.

The afternoon was bright and sunny: Alex making the joke that Werner had even organized the weather. The party began with a cold luncheon and went on until the lawns were trampled, the flowers were spattered with wine, and nothing seemed to matter any more as over one-hundred brilliantly dressed strangers thronged in and out of the house, spilling across the lawns and flocking round the marquee: a wonderful thing gaily draped with flags and pennants like a pavilion from a medieval tournament. Inside was the shock of grass beneath one's feet and a noisy assemblage of partygoers already intent on getting drunk. At the other end of the garden a little band of soldiers, decked around with banners, kept us entertained with stirring military music, to which some couples would strut and dance their heavy polkas.

Lisa appeared in a dress like a waterfall, made from a thousand shimmering ice-blue pieces. Her hair was caught up loosely at her neck with a ribbon of dark blue velvet.

"My sister is the *Lorelei* come to life," said Werner proudly, presenting her to everyone he could find.

"Oh yes?" retorted Alex with a smirk. "Remind me to pass on any shipwrecked sailors we find in this lot and she can entertain them on her rock."

Lisa poked him in the ribs, big-sister fashion; Werner carried on as self-appointed Master of Ceremonies. He was not in uniform, but his black trousers, white shirt, and scarlet cravat did look splendid. Alex and I sported blazers and flannels, and must have looked rather incongruous amongst all the black and grey and silver uniforms, the bow-ties, and the cocktail dresses. It suddenly struck me, as I beheld this froth of enjoyment, that Alex and Lisa were already playing the parts of a married couple. That they loved each other could not be in doubt; that they were happy was not in question. This was a queer sobriety, a public playing-down of the private wonders I had seen and almost shared. That seemed a shame to me, in ways I couldn't have expressed then, but which are now all too familiar.

At eight o'clock the lights came on and made the whole place look like an amusement park. Girls whooped with laughter, wine was poured anew, and still more merrymakers squeezed through the house and out across the gardens. Members of a special orchestra--special even in an era of special orchestras--took up their positions to provide more music for the already ecstatic dancers. Their repertoire ranged from Strauss waltzes to

American jazz and all the way back again. Lastly, under moon-yellow lights, a group of *schrammelmusikanten* assembled to play zithers and accordions and to sing our old favourites like *Almenrausch und Edelweiss* and *Wo die Alpenrosen Blühn*. All the people at that party--men and women, young and old, soldiers and schoolgirls-- stood in silence or sat together under the illuminated leaves and listened as the music carried our spirits to an older Europe of mountains and flowers and stories buried deep in memory. Dazed with wine and sentiment, I thought I had never seen anything more beautiful nor heard anything so sweet.

Now I was sprawled in a chair as they sang their last song. A tall figure blocked out the coloured lights of the bandstand: it was Lisa, holding a bottle of wine. She looked big and dark and my eyes were dazzled by the lights flaring from behind her hair.

"My poor Richard," she seemed to speak from miles above me, "you have been all alone here and not enjoying our big day."

"No, no." I scarcely recognised the sound of my own voice. Was I shouting or whispering? "I've been dancing for hours. I'm just tired."

"Don't you mean you are a little drunk?" All I could do was smile up at her. "And who was that pretty girl I saw you dancing with?"

"Oh," I blushed, "one of Werner's friends."

"He did not mind you stealing one of his girl-friends?"

I made some silly answer while she rested back against a garden table and crossed her feet, a gently mocking look in her eyes. But soon she had become serious again: very gentle and dark-looking, the light showing up creamy, down-soft skin on her neck. How could I ever have decided I could live without her?

"It has been a lovely day and a lovely time," she said. "You and Alex are so kind to me. Soon we will be married, soon we will be back in England." She said it in a bright excited way, as if the end of my adventure would be the beginning of hers. "Soon we will be married," she repeated. Was she just ordinary then? Just a girl blessed with good looks but a spirit like anyone else's? Just another woman who wanted a husband? Was it really so desperately ordinary, all this wonder I had been through? Had I just been drunk all this time, drunk on her beauty? Surely not-- surely it could not just be ordinary. She turned her head, golden against the midnight blue. No--this was Lisa, and I loved her.

"Lucky Alex," I breathed.

"Lucky Lisa, too," she smiled, and stood up suddenly against the lights. "Here, my good young friend…" she said this in a voice which made me feel not quite so boyish "… have some more wine." She bent down from the sky and poured a golden stream into my glass. "The party is nearly over."

SEVEN

There remained the ordeal of the

weddings--ordeal indeed, for by this time I had admitted to myself that I was completely in love with Lisa and worse, that she was not in love with me. Worse still, I believed what I felt was something greater than a young man's anguished infatuation with a beautiful woman who was going to marry someone else. That might fade or be outgrown. This pierced me to the very middle of my being and felt as if it would stay there for as long as I lived. Thus stricken, I had to be Best Man, and appear to like it too--for I sensed that if Alex were to know the truth he would snatch Lisa completely away from me and I should never see either of them again. At this point I would quite willingly have never seen Alex again, but I could not bear the thought of losing sight of Lisa. I even talked myself round to accepting a kind of second best on the principle that something was better than nothing: if I could somehow hold on to my friendship with Alex, I might at very least be able to bathe in Lisa's beauty from a distance. This, after all, was no less than I had already been able to enjoy. I hardly dared think how I might progress from there--or imagine how I might fail.

The wedding in Germany was almost an extension of the garden-party and Werner took it over in much the same way. I really had very little to do beyond looking the part and producing the rings on cue. Very unusually for those days--at least in English marriages--Lisa and Alex were to exchange identical wedding rings, but the continental flavour of their union was to introduce their English friends and relations to many charming German customs, of which this was only one and in which I already delighted. Now, of course, it was spoilt for me by the simple fact that Alex was marrying Lisa and I was not.

In my newly-admitted mood of jealous disappointment, I vowed I would speak the truth to Lisa, or if not the whole truth, then at least a half-truth to let her know something of my love for her. Of course I lacked the maturity to admit that she had probably guessed my predicament, that she might find it comic, and that in years to come I might find it comic also. The resolve burning inside me, I desperately wanted to catch her alone and to speak like an ardent lover in a play, but I was forever foiled by Alex's continuous and infuriating presence. If this was funny, I did not appreciate the joke. It was doubly difficult when I found Lisa's spare time being taken over by her mother and her two ten-year-old cousins who had arrived to be bridesmaids. They paraded about in their Tyrolean costumes and exchanged hats and giggled English at Alex and it all might have been pleasant and charming if I hadn't considered it a prelude to my emotional ruin. A tiny part of me sought action: a sexual conquest of Lisa which would surely end this misery. I wanted to take her in my arms and find her white and unresisting while I kissed her lips, made wild love with her, stroked her magnificent body from her hair to her toes, told her the desperate truth, and took her away with me to hide in

England. But the rest of me, the part that might have done these things or even a less boyishly dramatic and more likely version of them, was utterly frozen. I could and would do nothing like this. It was hard to admit I wasn't old enough or lucky enough. I was useless and immobile. Suddenly, I was like a boy again faced with the adult world of older people getting married--which now seemed to have more to do with money and family arrangements and social standing than with being in love. I had no money and no social standing and no-one to make family arrangements: all I could do was be in love. It no longer seemed enough. I might rave and moan and nothing would change, except that everyone would be deeply embarrassed and I would look even more foolish than I already felt. So I would do nothing, be nothing, admit nothing. And to match my mood, the wedding itself seemed a strangely empty event.

It was both a civil and religious ceremony. With their wealth and influence, the Odenwalds had arranged for the *Burgomeister* and his staff and a flurry of priests to perform it in the vast marble-clad entrance hall of the house, which, for this occasion, was made to look even more like the foyer of a cinema. Werner had arranged for spotlights to follow Alex and Lisa throughout the ceremony. They were worked deftly by his Brownshirts who had been ordered to appear in white caps and belts. White banners had appeared around the hall too, emblazoned with a device of Werner's own design: the entwined letters *L* and *A*. Alex declared himself deeply impressed and made Werner's day by telling him he could nicely go to Hollywood and become a great director. A few weeks ago I might have loved this spectacle; now I was just too sour to admire it. Even Lisa herself seemed unreal, and myself no longer capable of appreciating her beauty. She wore a long dress of snow-white satin cut in the close-fitting modern style, made all the more startling by the simplest veil on a pearl chain head-dress. She looked as if she had come from a German myth, perhaps equally set in medieval times or far in future centuries. Her golden hair was timeless, but her silver shoes were hard and modern and they rang on the floor as she walked past me, a beaming Alex beside her. In the glare of the spotlights she looked cold and metallic, a cool goddess not to be won by any mortal lover, an ice-maiden not to be melted in marriage. This flung me a beam of reflected solace: she would be hard, cold, unlovable, and a bad wife to Alex, myself, or anyone. It wasn't worth my being so upset. But I still felt lost and impotent and, most curiously of all, as if nothing had really happened.

The wedding in England affected me much more deeply. Strictly speaking it was only a church blessing of the marriage conducted largely for the benefit of Alex's mother who was said to be very religious. Suddenly, we were back in England where everything seemed smaller and more pathetic. Without the tireless Werner, everything seemed less organized, too. I was officially regarded as Best Man but again had little to do, and I found myself sitting glumly in a village church near Alex's home in Sussex. His parents and members of his family whom I scarcely knew made up most of the congregation, with a few of his College cronies and friends from the Flying Club. As might have been expected, these people were smartly turned out, but it was hardly a full-dress affair: Alex wore a sober grey suit. Enlivened as it was with a flashy tie and big carnation buttonhole, it still gave him an air of new austerity, while Lisa looked rather severe and businesslike in a matching grey and maroon costume. The atmosphere was almost bleak, and not helped by a high wind that moaned and battered around the church windows. The service was very 'high', and the vicar went on and on in that Anglican drone I found difficult to tolerate at the best of times and which now annoyed me almost to madness. But the gods, I smiled to myself, had sent her a storm: a wind to drown out all this nonsense. It rattled the roof and beat at the stained glass and set up an uneasy draught over the chilly stone floor--a stir of panic beyond anyone's control.

All this combined to raise desperation in my spirit. I was losing Lisa for ever now. I did not wish this marriage to be blessed, I wished it to be cursed. 'I want you to be very unhappy,' I thought, watching their backs and the ravishing curve of Lisa's body, discernable even through her dull costume. 'I want you to be wretchedly unhappy, hopelessly unhappy, so that this marriage falls apart and Lisa comes to me. I love her better, I love her more deeply; for God's sake, I even appreciate her piano-playing more! I understand her German character; I glory in it. What is just a continental oddity to Alex, something exotic and charming, is to me the discovery of a matching romantic soul. Alex does not understand Romance; if anything he scorns it. For him, Romance is what goes on in a cheap novel or a nightclub song; for me it is the whole experience of living, of being alive to the World and everything in it; seeing, feeling, sensing everything around me, in me, and in Lisa too. She has understood me and looked at me in a way that told me she should be married to me and to no-one else. So I curse this marriage and everyone here who is part of the conspiracy to take her away from me.'

As the vicar droned on and the wind lashed the roof, I was by turns angry and ashamed of my anger. I told myself I was just being silly. This was boyish petulance run wild. Lisa didn't love me, had never loved me, could never love me, and would be perfectly happy with Alex. Why not? They made what everyone would regard as a splendid couple, and we could all continue to have such fun if only I would grow up and find myself another girl. What could be simpler or more natural? Thousands of other people must have managed it. The stained glass rattled furiously. Behind it, no sun gleamed--only a cold white sky. 'I want you to be very unhappy,' I thought in tune to the grim scuffle of the wind.

We were outside now, deciding who should go in which car. There was laughing and chattering and a holding on to hats in the wind. A photographer appeared with an ancient-looking camera, so different from the sleek Leica Werner had used only a few days before. Already, with the strange quality of having woken from a dream, that day seemed years ago. Behind all this was a scream of trains running somewhere quite close in a dark wooded valley, up to London or down to Brighton, I could not tell which--but the sound cut into me with the cruel knives of departure, longing, and loss. Like that she would go from me--with speed and power and a scream of engines, hauled away to a better life in London or a house in the country with money and parties and the kind of pleasures which I had only tasted on someone else's generosity and which I knew could never truly be mine. Another train, screaming in the other direction, would take me back to the wretched seaside hotel and my grumbling parents and a shabby world waiting for a war. It was all over, every bit of it--what a fool I had been to think it had meant anything at all. But I still cursed the marriage, and wished it would dissolve into a new love between Lisa and myself, however difficult or unlikely such a thing might be. I hated everyone here for strengthening and perpetuating an arrangement that already seemed to be destroying me. Then we were all shaking hands and kissing cheeks. Of course I hated myself more than anybody for my ability to tell a lie and then to live it.

"I hope you'll be very happy," I smiled.

EIGHT

After the weddings, Alex and Lisa went to live in Kent. I remember my first of very few visits. The house was small but well furnished and beautifully warm. It wasn't the chic London flat they might have chosen, nor the big country manor in which I had naïvely imagined they might live--it was a real marital home: practical, affordable, and delightful in ways I could not have foreseen. It smelled rich and peaceful, secure and happy; I felt poor, edgy, and unwanted. Perhaps for the first time I realized that Alex and Lisa, romantic and cuddlesome with each other, could be brusque and cold to an outsider--which I had now plainly become. Their love appeared to be watertight, my chances of disturbing it were nil, and my old wish to do so now seemed obscene. I retreated into a new resignation. Other people might have called it growing up.

Depressed and lonely, but somehow freer of spirit, I returned to my parents' hotel, now duller and more hopeless than ever. I saw Alex and Lisa growing inexorably away from me. It must also be said that I grew away from them, which to any observer might have seemed a healthy and a fortunate thing. Yet as inevitable war approached, Alex and I began to meet in London. I found it quite easy to take up the threads of our friendship again, so long as Lisa was not there, but of course everything was different, and not only because of the coming war. It was as if neither of us wanted to take up the old fun of our escapades in case we should find it unbearable, or no longer fun at all. In any case, fun, and the escapades that might have produced it, hardly seemed possible in these grimmer days.

We usually met for a drink in a favourite pub off Shaftesbury Avenue. Here we would sometimes see theatre people, some of whom Alex seemed to know slightly, and I was introduced to a new circle of acquaintances: actors from the revues, dancers, singers, and stage-designers. They lent a determined gaiety to the tense atmosphere as we all watched the newspapers for Hitler's next move. It was as if *the show must go on* in spite of war, with even a hint that there might be a better show than ever because of it. The women dressed 'to cause a stir', as we used to say, while the men tried to look clever and intense. Underneath the posing, they were warm and friendly. I had never had anything to do with showbusiness or the Arts and like so many people of my era and experience had imagined them to be filled by effete and homosexual men, false and vindictive women, and an affected insincerity. Now I came to know better, and began to envy the comradeship of these people, spiced as it seemed to be by their constant love-affairs and their overriding commitment to artistic endeavour. That commitment, their genuine concern to create something new from resources within themselves, impressed me most of all. If I had had any talent, I began to think, I might have gone into showbusiness and enjoyed life much more. It would have been like belonging to an extended family. They would have cared. I should have had lots of girl-friends, all 'easy' and loving and warm and I should have lost my crippling shyness so much sooner. I should have had a great career, or if I had failed, at least found something to do and somewhere to go with people who understood me. Some of them might have stabbed me in the back, but others would

117

always have seen me through, or so I thought on those afternoons in Shaftesbury Avenue. But at the same time I realised I didn't have any talent, and that it was too late anyway.

Alex steered me away from the bar into a quiet corner. He had bought me another drink and pushed it towards me.

"Rich," he began, "I want to ask you a tremendous favour." He eyed me with a mixture of helplessness and suspicion. "Will you do it for me?"

"Well of course--if I can." I felt I owed him one ever since he had seen me into the Flying Club, and I genuinely wanted to help--but it had been a long time since I had seen Alex look so serious. I began to feel nervous.

"You might find it rather tricky," he added.

"Come on," I snapped. "What's up?"

"Well you know your parents' place on the coast..."

"Yes." Alex usually never referred to the hotel. He knew my background of course, but one of the reasons I liked him so much was that he never embarrassed me with it. I always felt he had understood perfectly how I loathed the seediness of my childhood and how grateful I had been to escape it into his exciting company. That was another reason for doing this favour--but I didn't like the sound of it so far, or the tiny quiver I detected in Alex's voice as he took up his drink. "Yes. What about it?"

"Well, I thought... Lisa and I thought...that, er, she might be able to stay there." He took a drink without looking at me. "You know--while the war's on." He lowered his glass and spoke into it. "I mean there's going to be a war now, isn't there? Everybody knows that."

For a moment Alex's request seemed perfectly reasonable--then all the implications of what he was asking burst upon me. I actually broke into a sweat.

"You'll do this for us, won't you?" he went on before I had time to speak. "Shouldn't be a problem for your people. I daresay they could do with a hand in that place. She'll muck in, you know--she won't be proud. It'll be like having an exotic chambermaid. I'll tell you one thing: she'll bring in the chaps on leave like moths around a flame. Your father's bar'll do better..."

"Alex," I interrupted, "Alex--you realise what you're asking?"

"Yes of course I do," he said with annoyance. "I want you to hide Lisa down there 'til the war's over and not tell anyone she's a German." Now he looked directly into my eyes. "D'you follow? Or are you half-witted as well as scared?"

"No, no," I answered swallowing a drink and forgiving him the rudeness of his anxiety, "I see exactly what you're driving at--but I'm not sure it's a very good idea." A riot of indecision was running through me: of course it was a good idea. I should have Lisa all to myself in the hotel; Alex would join the Air Force and be posted miles away; he might even be killed in the first raids. It was a perfect idea. It was also quite impossible--wasn't it?

"Look," Alex was speaking again, "all you have to do is make sure no-one finds out she's a German."

"Oh well that'll be easy won't it?" I laid on the sarcasm. "No-one will ever supsect she's German, will they?"

"She can pretend to be Czechoslovakian--it's been done before."

"Oh yes, and I can be a Polish refugee, can I? Just to add a bit of realism? Come off it, Alex. It's a long time since I've heard anything so ridiculous."

"We've worked it all out."

"I don't think you have. They'll try to intern her--isn't that what happened the last time? Look, I'm not sure about the rules on this sort of thing, but there has to a way through. Your family and your father's friends must have some influence. Tell the truth and it'll be all right."

"No it won't. And never mind *my* father, *her* father's very big in the Reichsbank, you know that. Visit the family and you'll bump into a top Nazi round every corner. One of her uncles is friendly with Himmler, and you've

121

already seen what that bloody Werner's like. It'll all go against her. She'll be locked up or shot or something."

"I can't believe that," I said--but I was beginning to.

"She'll pay her way, you know," Alex put in with a sudden wan smile.

"For God's sake, it's not the money. Think of what would happen if she were found out. She'd be arrested as a spy or something."

"There you are," he smirked, "you're beginning to see what an awful mess it is--and why you'll have to take great care of her."

"Look," I said grimly. "Think."

"We have thought," he said darkly. "We've thought of every bloody thing; back and forwards, the whole way through. This is the best way, the only way. If Lisa goes back to Germany our own lot'll be dropping bombs on her, just wait and see."

"But if she stays here we'll all be in the muck."

"Ah so that's it, is it? We'll all be in the

muck--that's what you're afraid of: what'll happen to Mammy and Daddy if they're caught harbouring a German spy. They'll be shot as traitors and you'll be all over the papers. From what you used to tell me I'd have thought you'd be glad to be rid of them."

"Now look here," I told him. "The whole idea's bloody mad. If you're not going to tell the truth to the authorities here, Lisa will have to go back to Germany and sit out the war somewhere safe. That shouldn't be too difficult to arrange with her family, so long as you do it quickly."

"That leaves us a couple of weeks to sort it all out," he said bitterly.

"You should have thought of it earlier." I did not really want to hurt him so, nor did I want to throw away the chance of having Lisa living so close to me, but I knew I had to do both.

Alex stood up.

"I told you we've thought of nothing else since this nonsense started."

I made no reply.

"So that's it," he said, "You won't help me." There was an agonizing pause. "Won't you even speak to your parents about this?"

"I suppose I shall," I snapped. "You've asked me to. I don't own the place, it'll be their decision. But I know what they'll say: that it simply can't be done. I'm sorry, but we both know it's wrong."

"Rich," he sounded very humble, "I've got nobody else to turn to." Then he stood up, arrogant again. "All right. I'm going back to Lisa now. You can let me know by telephone."

It was July. Everyone was waiting for news of what Hitler would do next and whether or not it really would mean war-- but the dire situation in Europe had not prevented the usual Summer rush to the seaside and the promenade was full of visitors. Indeed there was a particular sense of holiday this year, as if everyone knew perfectly well there would be a war and were determined to enjoy themselves in spite of it. I was in no mood to watch the British at play, much less join in, and all the talk of Hitler and Chamberlain mixed with seaside chatter about teas and ice-creams and the weather just irritated me. I had met, known, and lived with real Germans--not the bogeymen of these innocent people's imaginations. I reckoned that if we had to fight the real Germans, we would come off very badly indeed, but I didn't want to talk about it. The subject was a closed one with my parents, but now more than ever it was clear that they disapproved of my curious relationship with a German family. I made sure they did not know how deeply the whole experience had affected me and that they should remain ignorant of my true feelings for Lisa. I restricted my comments to wondering exactly how and when war might be declared, and discussing with my father how quickly I might get into the Air Force. I was keen to fly professionally, and did not imagine I would have much difficulty in doing so, but for the moment I felt I had to stay and help in the hotel. Through sheer cowardice I did not keep my promise to Alex and ask my parents if they would take Lisa. I did not telephone him with the invented answer that they had refused. He did not telephone me either, and with the passage of every day I hoped with increasing certainty that the terrifying issue had been dropped.

Yet even with this threat receding daily, life was anything but easy. Everything was a chore, and I particularly hated Fridays, when my mother insisted on a general tidy-up before new guests arrived for the week-end. Friday was also 'bin day', when the refuse collectors--we still called them dustmen in those days-- growled around the streets in their green lorry...and here I was bringing bags and boxes down the back stairs ready for collection from the back lane.

It was warm, and the sky a soft blue, but seagulls crying above the fire-escapes lent a bleak and wintry aspect to the back of the hotel. I wondered vaguely how we would all be when Winter came this year, and paid little attention to a revving engine and a squeal of brakes somewhere in the lanes--but the sudden honking of a horn made me look up just as a large and powerful motor car rounded the corner and snarled to a halt in front of me. It was Alex in his father's Ford V8.

I saw Lisa was with him, wearing light-coloured clothes and sitting in the back as if she were being chauffeur-driven. A huge cabin trunk was propped up in the front seat where I might have expected her to sit. There were suitcases beside her in the back and another large trunk tied on the roof. Before I could wave or acknowledge her properly, Alex climbed out, unsmiling and determined.

"Found you at last," he stated loudly, giving me no chance to open my mouth. "And you were right: this is a dead-and-alive hole even in the holidays. All the same, I didn't really want to catch you round the front of this place."

I was shocked. Alex had never visited my home. My life here had never been part of our relationship, I had never wished it to be, Alex had known and respected that--until now. I felt embarrassed and vulnerable, a thousand times more so with Lisa sitting in the car, somehow unable to look at me. I knew it was anything but a social call.

"Let's go inside," said Alex harshly. "Lisa's surrounded by bags, she can't talk to you. Let's just go in here."

I found myself steered backwards into the rear entrance of the hotel with its smell of old food and dusty mats.

"What is this?" I found my voice. "What d'you think you're doing?"

"I'm giving you a last chance to help us." Alex spoke in a flat staccato. I knew he was pleading, but could only make it sound like a stream of orders. Suddenly, I knew exactly what he was going to say-- and worse, what I was going to say.

"Before you start, Alex, before you upset yourself, you know I can't do any more for you."

"You can bloody well listen!" he snapped. "Now, I'll not bore you with details here, but if you'll agree to take Lisa in and let her live with your people,

I'll see there's plenty of money and no shortage of anything you all need. We're all ready--she's got everything with her. Just a room and a job." The strength and certainty ebbed from his voice. "Just agree to it, will you? Just let it happen, it'll be all right..."

"I can't, Alex. You know I can't."

"...just think," he carried on as if he had not heard me, "you'll have Lisa here, for the whole war." A cocky cheerfulness crept into his words. "She'll make you schnitzels when you come home on leave. I could think of uglier people to spend a war with." He paused, a curious sneer on his lips. "Don't think I don't know exactly what you think of Lisa, what you feel for her. This is your chance and a good one, lover-boy."

"Don't say that."

"It's time somebody did."

Our eyes blazed into each other's faces.

"Well?" he growled at me. I realised he had hold of my jacket. "We haven't got all day--the bloody war might start!"

"Alex, I can't do this."

"You mean you won't. You're afraid."

"Yes, in a way. We're all afraid. You're afraid, or you wouldn't be saying such things. You wouldn't be here at all. My mother is afraid too. I discussed all this with her, just as I said I would. It was no good. If it were up to me you know I'd find some way out. But I don't own this place--my mother does. She's the boss and she's said no. Everyone would be arrested, it would be a terrible mess. You must see that."

He just stared at me--while I writhed inside. I did not know how I had got through the lie; could not have explained exactly why I told it. I saw him start to believe it.

"Mammy's boy, ay?" he sneered. "I bloody well knew it."

"Look," I managed to continue, "if--if you can't somehow keep together and you want Lisa to stay in England, why can't she go to your people? She'd be much better off there and you know it."

"That's quite out of the question." He

dropped his hand from me.

"Well so is this--and for the same reasons, I imagine."

"My family just won't hear of it. Your mother might come round if you can find the guts to try her again. It'll be easier with your lot."

"My lot? Oh, it'll be easier with my lot I suppose, because my family doesn't matter. They can have all the danger of keeping a German girl under wraps while the whole country goes to war just because they're not so high and mighty as *your* lot!"

"That's not the point."

"I think it is the point." At that moment I didn't care how pompous I sounded, I felt it was true. At the same time I realised I no longer had any business with the truth. "If she is to stay in England at all, it should be with her in-laws."

Alex seemed to look beyond me, and spoke quite calmly. "They say she should go back to Germany."

I drew a deep and shaky breath. I had

just told a lie, a double lie that I didn't think Lisa should stay with me and that my mother had put a final ban on the scheme. Now I was to throw away my friendship with Alex and my love for Lisa, throw away a last, queer, unrepeatable chance to win her. Of course I wanted to accept her, to let her come in not only to the hotel but into my whole life. I would confess the lot to Alex; he said he knew it anyway. I would woo her, she would come to me, my dream would come true in a totally unexpected way, and to Hell with the consequences...but I was just terrified. I don't know where I found the strength to say the words, but I said them.

"I say that too," I spoke hoarsely. "I think Lisa should go back to Germany."

"Right." At last Alex knew it was no good. Suddenly, he was almost jovial. "Lucky there's a plan B. You know where we're going? Paris. After that, the Reichsbank itself is laying on a special 'plane to Berlin...God knows how with all this brewing. And she's got a safe conduct out of France if war's declared before then. I get out too--but in the opposite direction of course. There's a father-in-law for you."

"War won't be declared for weeks yet," I said, suddenly recovered and eager to reassure him. "You'll make it."

"Thanks," he gave me a grim smile. "You seem to have European politics well under control."

"Hardly," I gave a ghost of a smile. "That's your department."

He turned on his heel to go back to the car. I stepped forward to say: "I must wish..." but he spun round and stopped me with an outreached hand.

"She doesn't want to speak to you," he stated, resuming his walk to the car.

"But I want to speak to her!" I cried.

"Tough luck!" This time he stopped me with a fierce expression. If he had been holding a gun he could not have looked more deadly. He turned once more to get into the car. "You're a weak bastard," he shouted down the lane, "you know that, don't you? She's not right for you. And you won't do well in the war either--you're too much of a coward!"

I sank back against the cold brick wall, heard the car start and the tyres squeal away. I never saw Lisa's face as the car turned out of the lane. I remembered how Werner had driven her towards me that sunny day so irretrievably lost in my past; now Alex was driving her away from me. In a moment my life seemed to have been transformed. All I had left was a pile of rubbish at the back of a run down hotel.

NINE

I picked up the telephone, spoke to the operator, and was connected to Alex's number. I listened to its ringing with a quickened heartbeat. I disliked telephones at the best of times; their insistent drama and jangling disturbance seemed only to bring bad news. Now I was making a call that could stir up more trouble. I imagined the telephone ringing through the distant house in Kent; I had noticed that it had rested on a sunny windowsill, so different from this dull table in the dark and musty hotel office. Surely Alex would be back by now--it had taken me long enough to work up my courage to speak to him and if he wasn't there I should have to go through it all again. All of my own doing too--it always was. If I had told the truth I wouldn't have felt like this, could have faced Alex more squarely, would have felt I had lost Lisa through circumstances beyond my control instead of turning her away myself without even trying to put the scheme to my mother. Once more, I rehearsed what I was going to say--but could only remember his turning on me, the car driving away, Lisa not looking at me. Weak--that's what he had called me and I knew he had been right. All the same, he could not have imagined the strength I had summoned up to make this call.

"Hello?"

"Ah, hello Alex…thought you weren't there for a moment. It's Rich. Look--I just wanted to make sure you and Lisa had got away all right…and to apologise for being such a pig when you came down here."

How Alex took this would colour the rest of our lives. I had imagined the scene long enough, but could not predict his reaction. My words had come out all wrong, anyway.

"It went all right." He was cold, perhaps even unfriendly, but neither angry nor cruel. "Good of you to ask." Was that a hint of forgiveness? "I've been back a few days now--wondered what you were doing." I had not expected such concern. Did that mean a renewed friendship?

"Frankly I've been worried sick and felt awful. I should have done more." Of course I should have done more; I should have told the truth. Yet to confess to the lie now would surely destroy our fragile truce, if truce this was. "I should have done more," I repeated.

"Perhaps you should," returned Alex, the coldness still in his voice, "but we'll try not to let it come between us."

He might have been forgiving me, he might have been asking me to drop the subject, but I plunged on, unable to stop myself.

"And how is Lisa? Is she safe."

"At the moment she's in Berlin but I don't expect she'll stay there." Something in his voice made it very clear that Lisa was definitely a subject not to be pursued.

"Right."

"I'll see you soon." That was unexpectedly cheerful. "Can't be sure when, I haven't decided if I'm closing this place up or not, or I may be staying with my people for a while, see what happens. We'll keep in touch."

"Yes of course. Thanks."

"G'bye then--and watch out for Mister Hitler and his Nasties."

"Will do. Cheerio."

War was declared. It was almost an anti-climax; the truce between Alex and myself seemed just as important--and for that matter just as incomprehensible. We met for the last time in our London pub, crowded with his disbanding actor friends, and it could not be the face-to-face confrontation I had feared. Like everyone else we talked about what was going to happen, but did not seem able to reveal our own plans. Then we were invited to a farewell dinner at the Flying Club. It was being taken over by the R.A.F. Trenches had already been dug and windows taped; sandbags had been piled outside the Clubhouse and grey lorries stood around the paddock. The dinner was a sad affair--and sadder still was the new mood of violence and worry. Everything was rushed and disordered, as if all that had been easy and fun must now be put away for a harsh and loveless endeavour. Yet there was suddenly a new feeling of excitement, the promise of a kind of freedom, and I could not help but be drawn into it.

"So, what are you going to do in this bloody silly war?" said Alex, propping up the bar.

"Join the Air Force, I suppose. In fact I've already applied. I'm pretty sure they're going to take me in as an officer right away, even though I've never been a cadet. It's all those hours I've done on different types."

"Nothing to do with that uncle of yours getting his MC in the trenches?"

"I'm sure it isn't," I laughed.

"Well, I wouldn't be too definite about this officer business. You may have to go in as a Sergeant Pilot or something--and I wouldn't worry about it either. You'll get a commission soon enough."

"I just want to fly again," I confessed. "This is the best opportunity for years."

"Oh, is that what it is?" Alex sounded very bitter. "Well, I can see you're *eager for a crack at the Hun,* as they used to say...just like the rest of these poor pathetic johnnies. God knows what it'll do to you all."

I was rather drunk, my head was full of my own heroic ideas of war-flying, and I was about to say: "Nonsense--we'll have the sausage-eaters for breakfast." Then I remembered that one did not say such things to Alex, and that I of all people should have known better than even to think those stupid and insulting words. What I actually said was: "I'll try to keep out of the worst trouble."

"Keep out of it?" Alex snorted. "You're dying for it! And the tragedy is, it's all pointless anyway. It's quite ridiculous that grown-up people should be behaving like this. Civilisation is supposed to have outgrown war. Eminent thinkers have explained there's no need for it--and they're right, there isn't."

"No need for it?" I retorted. "What d'you mean? If we don't stop Hitler and his mob they'll be marching down Piccadilly. These aren't the sort of Germans you and I know: these are all gangsters and madmen. We can't have them taking over the world."

"Oh for God's sake don't talk that rot to me! I've been hearing that sort of rubbish for weeks now; I don't want you pushing it down my throat as well. War's a stupid waste--all war. Look what happened in Spain. This one'll be no different--only worse. It'll be longer and nastier than all the others put together. Don't you see that? Or don't you care?"

"I just think it has to be done," I said.

"It has to be done."

"Well there must be a better way of doing it than this." He swallowed his whisky and thumped the glass down on the bar. A kind of glum fury burned out of him, leaving me surprised--and angry, too. I had not expected any of this from Alex. He wasn't finished either. "Why d'you think I never went to Spain when those fellows came round the aero clubs trying to recruit pilots?"

I cast my mind back two years and could hardly remember the event.

"Because you're not a card-carrying Socialist?" I grinned.

"That's not the bloody point! The point is, it meant dropping bombs on poor innocent people in towns and villages we'd never even heard of, one side or the other, you'd never know who was who, and I wasn't prepared to do that. The rest of you just thought it would be a lark."

"But we didn't think that," I said as soberly as I could, recalling the incident now. "As far as I can remember only one

141

of our chaps went--Ronnie Hepworth, wasn't it?"

"Oh yes," retorted Alex mockingly, "well Ronnie Hepworth would, wouldn't he? He was a mindless killer. He'd been to Spain before and he liked bullfighting. He was the sort who'd set cats on fire when he was a schoolboy. He wouldn't care a tuppennny damn who was down below as long as he got his bombs off all right and navigated his way back to the bar."

"So you think anyone who joins up now is a mindless killer?"

"Yes!" he yelled into my face. "Yes," he announced loudly to the air in front of him, "that's what you'll all have to be now: mindless killers, making sure someone else doesn't kill you first. Ever been in a butcher's yard?"

"You want to be careful what you say," I pleaded. "These fellows might think you're a Conshie. I say," I added with a sudden befuddled horror, "you're not a Conshie, are you?"

This enraged Alex. I saw his knuckles

go white around his empty glass; his whole body stiffened, as if a coiled spring were inside him. He did not look at me, but stared straight ahead. Then suddenly he relaxed.

"No," he sighed, "no, I'll fight...but I wish I didn't have to."

Then he laughed, but it was a bitter laugh.

"Well," I said, slapping his back, "you'll probably enjoy it: knocking enemy fighters out of the sky and all that." But as soon as I had said it, I could have bitten my tongue off with regret.

"Don't be stupid," he snapped with real anger in his eyes, "don't be so bloody stupid! All that's finished. All those R.F.C. tales the Major used to tell: playing football in No-Man's-Land, shaking hands, pilots waving at one another before they opened fire--that's all over. There'll be none of that this time. Don't you realise that? Don't you see? There's no decency left, and you're a fool if you expect any."

"I don't expect any."

143

"You do. You're like a twelve-year-old before a rugger match." He fiddled with his glass again, then pushed it away. "Some rugger match this is going to be." He looked at me. His eyes were full of sorrow. "I'll drive you home," he said, "you poor stupid sod."

In the cool privacy of the car, I sobered up.

"You must tell me about Lisa," I said.

"Must I?" Alex fumbled the gears. "I'm not sure there's any point in that."

I winced. How much of my love for her did he know? My love for her: another man's wife; my friend's wife. When I thought of it like that I was appalled. Yet I could never tell how much it really mattered to him; how much he might hate me for it, or how much he might laugh.

"At least let me know where she is."

"She's in the wrong country at the wrong time." He gave me a thin smile. "Well, one of us would have to be, wouldn't we? It might not be all bad," he softened. "She's with her own people;

they'll do everything they can to protect her, I know that. Can't get away from it though: it's damned awkward whichever way you look at it."

"How will *you* manage?"

"Very badly," he muttered. A long silence fell. My thoughts were very confused. At first I was relieved. He wasn't outwardly furious with me, he was making grim jokes: shreds of the banter that had once flowed between us. Then a slow, deep sorrow crept to the surface and made me huddle lower in the seat. Alex drove on, locked in his cold composure. Waves of tenderness welled up in me--how much I wanted to make things better for my old friend, but all the words I wanted to say would have sounded wrong. Yet I was ashamed of myself for not saying them.

"I'm sorry," was all I could manage. Alex made no reply. If he had forgiven me for allowing Lisa to go to Germany when I might have tried to save her from it, he did not say so. Neither did he blame nor rebuke me. I had attempted an apology but made a bad job of it; in the same way I knew had tried to forgive me, but would still regard his separation from Lisa as my fault. Our predicament had fallen into the Great Unsaid of English life, and with war upon us it seemed unlikely that we would drag it up again into open debate. Yet after a few more miles I felt I had to speak, and asked him what he was going to do now.

"I've already joined up," he said flatly. "Fighters."

TEN

After training--a period memorable for its uncomfortable beds and shouting sergeants--I joined my first squadron to fly Hurricanes from a miserable station in Scotland. As if the new rigours of service life had swept away his animosity, or at least buried it, Alex wrote to me in what looked like a new spirit of friendship. He was in Wales, then Bristol, then Hampshire, training on the new Spitfire, the wonder-'plane we all wanted to try. He joked that he could outfly my old bus of a Hurri any day, and said we should meet up over Yorkshire to prove it. My soul was teased by the image of the friends whose bodies had become two aircraft, whose voices had become distorted words in each other's earphones, and whose paths might only cross in this stolen, furtive meeting in the sky; and the idea of our secret, eerie contest high over the middle of England haunted and disturbed me. But of course it never happened. I pushed the memories of Alex and of Lisa far away.

In those first few months it was easy, for there was always the strain of new surroundings, new people, new anxieties. Then came a sudden slackness. It was war, but there was nothing to do. We began to feel that we faced not a blazing Europe, but a damp squib. My thoughts strayed back to Alex, and of course to Lisa. What would happen to the two of them, the three of us? And did it really matter? Did anything really matter any more? I seemed to have shown to myself that I wasn't in control of anything in my life. I had loved Lisa, yet been unable to do anything about it. I had resolved to stop loving her, yet had not done that either. Then, when I had been unable to act, unable to save them or myself, they had both gone from me and beyond my influence--if I had ever had any. The only thing I could control with any degree of satisfaction was an aircraft. It would be easy and delightful to concentrate on that. Then the 'phoney war' ended, and the Squadron was posted to Norfolk. There, over the big flat fields, the wetlands, and the iron-coloured sea, we fired our first shots in panic or in anger as the Germans came in their grey and green and sky-blue aeroplanes: big, fat, noisy machines bristling with guns but easy to hit. There was no contest. In our nimble fighters we outclassed them at every turn. The C.O., who had a taste for history, said it was like the Spanish Armada all over again. It was very easy to get cocky, and most of us did.

I admit it now: for a long time I enjoyed the war. It was both a freedom and a closed certainty: a delight for cruel men, thoughtless men, weak men, and moral cowards. Perhaps I was all those men. The enjoyment it allowed came not as an appalling truth about war, but as a simple discovery within myself.

Each year as I had grown from boyhood, my life had seemed less certain, and I less confident to deal with it. Now, at a stroke, its complexities were stripped down to black and white and it had a marvellous, simple purpose. I was effortlessly good at it too. I was a natural pilot. Certainly I developed and refined my skill, but it was a proficiency for which I could scarcely take the credit: everything came so easily, as if I had been doing it since the cradle, or was merely taking up an activity of which I had been a master in some previous life. And it was what I wanted to do. While other men had nursed ambitions now ruined by war, had wanted money or families or great careers, I had wanted to fly. To be doing it now every day was the greatest gift that Fortune could have flung me. To climb into an aircraft, to lift it from the Earth and make that beautiful noise between the clouds--that was a magic at which I never ceased to wonder, a drug of which I could never have enough. Where other aspects of my life had been glum or shabby and, more recently, sullied with shame and weakness, flying was sweet and strong and pure and glorious...or so it seemed to me in those early days. Of course I was frightened--but on the whole I felt fulfilled, not diminished by war.

A burst of energy had been released within me and the other young men with whom I served. We were not ashamed to fight, to be called to clear the skies. I learned very quickly that all is not evil in war. Now, of course, it seems almost shameful to admit it, but I learned also the splendour of possessing an enemy; and that the stronger and more vile and more determined he became, the finer it was to be pitted against him. At the same time I learned that the constant pressure and fear of war eats into the soul and is more destructive than bombs and bullets; that these heady joys exact a terrible, appalling cost; and that the people on both sides would have been better occupied learning the more subtle arts of peace. But these were the lessons of later years. For the most part we were happy: flying every day, flying for our lives. Little wonder then that we dressed for battle with a devilish élan; little wonder we were proud that the names of our aircraft were on the lips of every schoolboy; little wonder that our hearts should swell as we flashed over the farmers and the housewives, the cyclists and the tradesmen waving us on from field and lane and village below; little wonder that our principal emotion should be glee. Of course there was terror, too. It came in odd ways, at odd times: not always just before the firing began, not always alone in bed; sometimes in the face of a friend, in a sunny teashop, in boarding a train at the end of a few days' leave. But it was always pushed away. We had such weapons, such skill, such power, such arrogance at our disposal that being killed seemed a ridiculous notion. Of course we wouldn't be killed: neither would we be burned and broken, smashed and flayed, nor turned into monsters, cowards, or madmen. That was the talk of Conshies and people we dismissed as 'stupid bloody civilians', people who didn't realise that flying was a piece of cake. We made sure it remained a lark: a serious lark, but a lark nevertheless. When moments came which told us otherwise, we kept them to ourselves.

As the weeks passed I grew better at flying in a team, more hawkishly observant in the air, more adept at shooting. I did not consider myself cruel or brutal and had never wanted to kill anyone, least of all people like myself, my fellow airmen, whose passion for flying had taken them into the skies and who were my enemies not by nature, but by vile circumstance. But in the air, and about this deadly business, I had no thoughts of my idyllic time in Germany; did not connect these fliers with Lisa and Werner and the country where I had been so happy. They seemed to come from another dimension. And in any case, I did not think of my adversaries as men--none of us did. We were shooting down an aircraft, an enemy aircraft bent on dealing death and misery to all we had known and cherished, to those who had borne us, and to those we loved. How quickly, once it was all over, such words became unfashionable; but when we were together in the squadrons, most of us held this unshakable belief without guile or cynicism. Apart from patriotism--which was very real to us--we were compelled to live by the simple maxim of the soldier's life: the enemy in its machine had to be destroyed. If we did not destroy it, it would surely destroy us--for all that in happier times we might claim its pilot as a brother of the air. But this is the language of reflection and of stories told after the event. At the time we rarely talked like this, and never reasoned out what we were doing. We did our job and exulted in doing it well. When one of our number was killed, we mourned his death but briefly, for deep down we knew--but never would admit--that in the morning any one of us might be the next. So we would do our job with even greater dash and ardour. And at first, before the horrors came, it was astonishingly easy.

Then, with little time for us to adjust to it, the real trouble started. I was posted to Cambridgeshire to train on Spitfires. They were wonderful to fly, with amazing speed and handling so fluid that it felt possible to control them as much by thought as by movements of hands and feet: a pilot's conceit which contributed to their legend. Most impressive of all their characteristics was a kind of dreadful strength distilled into a sweet little body, as if the resources of a god were being granted to a mere mortal, as if through the slender controls we were being handed a unique and awesome power. At length the squadron postings began to come through. I telephoned Alex, knowing he was stationed on the South coast.

"Any chance of wangling a posting to

your mob?" I asked him.

"Don't know." His voice was very clipped. "It's certainly hotting up down here. Some of you boys'll be sent this way, no doubt of that. Seems no reason why you shouldn't be one of them. By the way, they've made me a Section Leader."

While he spoke, it was as if I forgot the last shreds of the troubles between us. They seemed to be over, as if war had finally made them unimportant. I had been foolish and weak and made mistakes, but he had been sensible and understanding. Now we were both about a harsher and more clearly-defined business in which a new comradeship might be forged...if only we could fly together!

"Nothing I can do officially of course," he went on. "Speak to your C.O."

I did. He said he could not cater for the whims of individuals, and that I would go where I was sent and think myself lucky just to be put on Spitfires. So I went glumly up to the Midlands, feeling far from the battle and from any hope of joining Alex. But within a few days the *Luftwaffe* turned their fury on the Southern airfields. We began to hear of waves of enemy aircraft, and of appalling losses. The C.O. had me in his office. He was not normally stern or unkind, but now he regarded me with a granite expression.

"I have to send half my boys to the Southern squadrons," he said bleakly. His voice was full of regret, like a headmaster at the breaking-up of school. "I'm told you want to go to Kent."

"Yes, sir. May I ask how…"

"Never mind that. I'll see you get the posting you want." The 'God knows why you want to go' there remained unspoken, but was clear enough in his face. "You're lucky," he continued, "if you can call it that. I'll not be able to pulls strings for much longer, not in the middle of all this."

"No sir. Thank you sir."

"That's it then. Good luck."

I thanked him again, saluted, and made for the door. Without looking up he added: "I don't know if you ever pray, Dellow, but if you do, pray for more pilots like yourself... or pray for bad weather."

Blue skies and brilliant sunshine above the South coast of England: cool green Downland grass rolling over high chalk cliffs, and far below, the swill and suck of the Channel beaches. Behind the grassland, rich golden fields swung up into the Weald of Kent, the orchards and the farms, the trees and hollows and the great swathe of lush countryside. There, beyond the cornfields bathed in Summer haze, there lay our airfield. There, beneath the innocence of skylarks, engines ran and roared; oil spilled, fuming and heady, to be drunk by the parched earth or to leave great dark patches on the scorching, tyre-streaked tarmac, like the shadows of clouds on a sunny afternoon. It did not feel like war on the languid day I arrived. But this airfield was only moments from the Channel coast, only minutes from the enemy, and directly on the bomber-route to London. This would be very different.

Alex came out to greet me. It was the first time I had seen him in uniform. I was shocked. It made him look thinner than ever; older too. Against regulations, he had trimmed his moustache to a neat black bar, and had taken to sweeping his hair back more severely. Within a few minutes of meeting him, I realised his old languor had gone. He shook hands with genuine affection and patted me on the back, but he was crisper, sharper, colder... and, when speaking, he had begun to look beyond my eyes, as if his attention must always be straying to something above and behind me. As soon as my paperwork had been completed, he walked me across the field to a Spitfire parked on the dusty turf.

"Now you can strap this to your backside," he grinned. As he showed me over the aeroplane, all the old enthusiasm of our Flying Club days returned. Here was the huge propeller, ready to claw at the sky: once it was spinning, all ungainliness would be lost in the perfect shape of dagger wings and pointed nose. Here were the rows of snorting exhaust-ports, sooty with use; here the glinting canopy with its tiny, secret world inside; here the neat little tail-fin. But under the wings the eggshell blue was streaked with oil, and there were aluminium patches all over the fuselage.

"By the way," Alex put his hands in his pockets, "nobody here knows about Lisa."

A shiver ran through me, and something like a lump came into my throat.

"I mean," he went on, kicking dry soil through the grass, "nobody knows she's a German." He paused and put on a brilliant smile. "Couldn't have these chaps thinking I was married to Jerry, could we?"

"Very wise," I answered as brightly as I could. Did Alex want this dismissed in the silent understanding I was prepared to give, would he begin to unburden himself out here on the naked airfield, or was his manic jokiness part of something completely beyond my experience? Already I could sense the enormous strain of his secret--and suddenly I didn't want to cope with any of it.

"My wife's in Canada," he said. "That's the story."

"It's a good one."

"Right."

We took another look over the Spitfire. This is safer, I thought. I'll get through this if I can just stick to the flying. For God's sake let it just be flying. Alex was running his finger along the wing where camouflage was flaking.

"Could do with a coat of paint," I observed.

"You can forget the Red Baron stuff here," a curt voice broke in at my shoulder. I turned sharply to find a little tubby figure with sandy hair and a round, pugnacious face. It was the C.O.

"Good afternoon, sir," I said stiffly.

"Showing him round, are you?" he said to Alex. Every word sounded like a rebuke.

"Yes sir. Can he go for a test-flight sir?

This will be his machine."

The C.O. eyed the Spitfire. "Belonged to Williams, didn't it?"

"Yes sir."

"Well I hope this young man keeps a better look out for himself."

I felt like a schoolboy whose nameless misdemeanours were being discussed by prefects.

"About that test-flight sir," persisted Alex.

"What's the point in that? Burning fuel for the fun of it. No bloody point at all." The C.O. turned to me. "You've done your hours on these things, haven't you?"

"Yes sir; of course sir. I've been operational with number..."

"All right. No need for joyriding about then. If you need any practice you'll get it in the morning: coastal patrol. Incidentally, Forrest is your Section Leader."

"I had hoped you'd put him with me, sir." Alex had obviously tried to keep disappointment out of his voice; the statement sounded flat and impotent.

"You've got your hands full with Cooper, Howard, and Clark--and you know perfectly well there'll be others by the end of the week." The C.O. turned to me once more. "Do exactly what Forrest tells you and you'll be all right--but don't expect a picnic." With that he stumped off in a cheeky, belligerent gait.

"What a charming fellow," I droned. "How d'you put up with him?"

"He's not so bad," said Alex, leading me back to the huts. "Truth is, we're all a bit pushed at the moment. Had a few losses. He takes them very badly."

Alex steered me towards the cluster of chairs outside Dispersal. There was a window with a telephone on the sill and a Sergeant writing busily behind it; everyone else was outside wearing flying-kit. Some ignored me; some watched me intently, others lazily, others with mild amusement. At once I sensed the horrible expectancy enveloping these men. It bristled in the air; it churned my stomach.

"This is Richard Dellow," said Alex, and I extended my hand towards the group, wondering if I should greet each man--but instead I was met with a choric "Hello Dellow". I grinned as best I could.

"We're on stand-by at the moment," Alex put in, sensing my embarrassment.

"Sit-by, actually," said a genteel voice from one of the deck-chairs.

"Yes," came another. "Resting the old rump, what?"

"Better than having it shot at, you'll see."

"But don't let the M.O. sell you his tin pants--they can ruin a chap for life."

"Been over to France yet?" It was a serious question from a ruddy-faced young man clenching a pipe.

"Not yet," I answered. "I'm to go on coastal patrol in the morning. I thought you fellows let them come over here rather than go looking for trouble."

"Oh, we poke our noses over there once in a while, just to let them know who's boss. By the way, I'm Geoffrey Forrest. I'll take you over in the morning."

"Thanks a lot," I replied. Someone chuckled bitterly from behind a magazine.

"You'll settle in all right," said Alex as I followed him into the hut. I was not so sure. If I could just keep it to the flying--just the flying. I would be good at that; everything else was a nightmare lottery with the odds stacked against me.

Next morning we sat tilted backwards in our cockpits on the dry English grass, warm sunshine swishing through the propellers as we awaited Forrest's signal to clamour into the air. A faint but persistent anxiety crawled in my stomach as I did my checks for the dozenth time, then was pushed away as Forrest gave his signal and we roared across the field. A deafening noise, a frantic bumping--then up, up into the blue. The long, lifting nose blotted out the horizon; the engine thudded deep into my head, drowning out all thought. Forrest snapped us into close formation: myself and a Scotsman called Buchanan on his left, two new Sergeants on his right. They were using more throttle than I had expected, and it all looked dangerously close and hurried.

Higher and higher we climbed, tucked into one another like a school of darting fish, thrusting shark-nosed into the upper air. Once we had burst through the last racing flicker of cloud, a dazzling sky-brightness flooded the cockpit, emptying it of the friendly clutter I had known on the ground. Up here there was no protection save our own speed, no defence other than attack. It was like being strapped naked to a javelin. I turned the ring of my gun-button from *safe* to *fire*: now I had eight machine-guns at my command...and a terrible, mad smile came to crease my cheeks.

The Channel swung up like a schoolroom map, perfect in every detail, and slid away under our wings. Forrest had finished his climb, but there was no reduction in speed--indeed, flattened out, we seemed to rush forward at an even wilder pace. I could feel the delicate poise of this marvellous machine between my hands: she responded perfectly to the slightest pressures. I was drunk with a new and violent power.

"Crack it on!" said Forrest, and we advanced our throttles. The engines blared, the Spitfires leapt forward, shot like bolts through the pure, exhilarating blue. There might be war, there might be terror, there might be death--but I knew I was going to love this.

"Stay together now." Forrest's voice was calm and clear in the earphones. "Keep your eyes peeled. Over we go."

He led us round in a long, gentle bank. There was the coast of France. Would the shooting start now? Would the batteries I knew were down there suddenly open up? Nothing--nothing but a few clouds and the empty beaches far below; nothing but the soaking roar of our engines and the blinding, perspex-crinkled sunshine. Did it hide a crowd of German fighters? The good ones still came out of the sun in that oldest, deadliest trick. I tried to imagine who might be watching us from the ground, to count the minutes it would take for an enemy squadron to scramble up and catch us, but most of my attention was given to searching the sky and listening to Forrest telling us to follow him, turn inland, keep station, watch for AA batteries, and asking each of us in turn what we had seen.

"Nothing doing," came a new voice over the R/T. One of the Sergeants.

"All clear, leader." That was Buchanan.

"Nothing over here." The other Sergeant.

"Report what you see, Blue Three." Forrest doing his drill.

"All clear," I replied, looking at his glinting canopy and trying to talk to that.

"Disappointed?" came his voice, suddenly relaxed.

"Not really."

"The buggers must be sitting at home eating their sausages," remarked one of the Sergeants.

"Aye, we picked a quiet day for you," said Buchanan--then Forrest put us into line astern, pulling us North to Dover.

"Wrap it up then... follow me down...home we go."

And back we came, nursing our engines, seeking refuge under English skies. There were not many quiet days after that.

ELEVEN

The Summer blazed on. I became easier with my fellow pilots; the fighting grew more intense. There was little time for resting now: we spent more and more hours in the air, ordered up to meet wave after wave of bombers and their darting, savage, fighter escorts. To sit at Dispersal was no longer relaxing, it was horribly tense--and every time the telephone rang to scramble us, that lumbering run out to the aircraft was beset by the kind of fear to knot the stomach and turn the legs to jelly.

I didn't want to remember the first time I thought I was going to be killed, then found I could not forget it. A crowded battle over the Channel coast--a glimpse of Pegwell Bay and I recognized the big golf-course at Sandwich--all familiar, somehow safe-looking, my own country just down there--I had done it before and come home, why should this be any different? I fired as a German swam across my sights, fired automatically without skill or relish just because a target was there. Perhaps that's what all the others were doing, perhaps not; perhaps there were fighters up today who were not lazy or tired or ill-at-ease but cunning and sharp, determined to kill me, already looking at me and only me. The German swung away unscathed. It was so easy to miss: so fast, so fleeting, so difficult to hit anything. I'd be all right, I thought, just pull up this way... then shells ripped into my fuselage. I heard them behind me--never saw the attacker-- heard them very close. Then nothing. Another miss. But next time, next minute, now? Instruments all O.K., engine still running, no fire, controls answering, my hands worked, I could see. But next time? How soon? Now? Perhaps there would be no pain at first, just shock like this, then blood and sickness, a kind of whiteness spreading into pain, but just before that, fear--inescapable, terrible fear, closing round my head like giant hands pinning me down to suffer it, soaked in the sweat and muck of it, like drowning in foul water, shouts for help and pitiful tears and the horror of flinching, the shame of fear, the double shame of not admitting the shame, the going on, the doing it again, being a coward, ultimately not caring, not hiding it a moment longer in shrieking terror: white, inescapable, enveloping me, me and only me, no escape. So I would die like that--and soon, if this went on. Any day, quite easily, with an effortless finality. Yet was I not supposed to be lucky--a quick and careful survivor in the air? Everyone said so; I said so myself. Lucky. But luck could run out--I had already seen it too often to believe I could go on unscathed.

When I landed and experienced that slightly drunken feeling of having both feet back on the grass after a head-reeling combat flight, everything seemed just as it always had...and here was Billy Prescott, fat boy of the Squadron, waddling over to look at the ragged holes behind my headrest.

"See?" I joked, poking my fingers through the holes like maggots wiggling out of a pantomime cheese. "Missed by, ooh, a couple of inches."

"Shame," said Billy. "You could do with a haircut."

He waddled off again, the bowsers came up to start refuelling, we ambled back to the huts, re-tuning our ears to footsteps and birdsong. Everything just the same again...except I would now be afraid to climb back in, really afraid in the pink squashy unseen middle of myself.

A few days leave: it was somehow worse in the quiet bar of the country inn. Yet surely not--it had to be better, once I relaxed with a drink. Hot sunshine spilled off tender green leaves beyond the windows and bounced off the chalk-white road. Some things were timeless, would surely survive for ever, and the WAAF who accepted my offer of gin-and-tonic had lovely white teeth and a willing smile. I could go ahead with my plan for London, looking up people who might not be there, dodging air-raids, seeing a third-rate show on my own--but why should I put myself through that? This was a quiet place; nothing to do but buy her drinks. She took off her cap and laughed at my stories--even the ones I made up.

So I made love with Shirley because I couldn't think of any reason not to--but also because I was afraid, because I thought I should never see Lisa again and that she would never forgive me or show any interest in me and that she was lost to me anyway through her marriage to Alex; above all because I believed I was going to die. Apart from that, I felt old at twenty-two and felt I had been a virgin long enough. I never knew why Shirley made love with me, and never thought to ask. I had believed, as a youth, that a man should give everything to the woman he loved, desiring every inch of her body, worshipping her spirit, demanding nothing but love in return: the old, pure, medieval, knightly way: born in me, true to my soul, practised without affectation.

That was how I had loved Lisa, as a boy and as a virgin. Now it seemed I could no longer be either, and it didn't matter how I loved Shirley, or indeed whether I loved her at all. War had made me utterly selfish. I booked a room.

How easy it would be to say it was not love, to paint a picture of crude desire, fulfilling for the moment yet empty for ever, a hollow victory for sex...but that would not be a true picture. It would not admit the hours of genuine love and affection, as real as anyone else's, perhaps better than those in many a dull marriage. It would deny the moment I came into the darkened room and found her sitting in a huge chair as if asleep--but she was wide awake and looking into the lamp, its orange glow across her face. She smiled up at me without moving, her eyelashes heavy and dark in the lamplight, her blue eyes dark in the darkness of the room, her bright hair darkened in the shadows, her blouse open and her smooth body waiting for me, soft and unreal. It was so easy for me to love her as I lay across her knees and took her little head between my hands, brown in the red darkness. I kissed her lips, moist and warm. Was this too easy to be right, too quick? Right and wrong were no longer to be considered-- everything was quite natural in the quiet room where her face was my world and her body was bared beneath my hands, hands she said were gentle, hands she wanted to kiss. She lay back in the chair and I touched her bare waist with my fingertips and began to tell her how wonderfully white she was. She smiled and stroked my hair.

"Don't be shy," she murmured. "I'm not shy. There's no need…"

She rolled her body out of her clothes and pulled mine from my limbs. She called me Darling many times, and told me not to stop, not to stop for anything, to love her as if she were the last girl in the world, knowing she was my first. Her body made me happy and my body was ready to make her happy whenever she liked. There was a curious joy in realising that however mad the world, the bodies were still working…but they were bodies without souls, mine anyway.

Yet to say there was no love would also deny the terrible power of my longing for her as the smell of her cigarettes aged in the cold room. It hung itself between the curtains and the rainy windows, even in my hair, we had been so close. Gone. Was it only last night I had held her, felt the cool smooth skin like gold-dust in my fingers suddenly turn hot and molten? In this very chair, still clinging to her fragrance? How fine were the little sinews in her throat, how alive were the bones in her slender hips, her knees, her ankles. How I wanted her resting in my arms again, melting into my body like the sea into sand. So I shall not say there was no love…but it was easy to hurt her at the end, easy to walk away saying this could not last for either of us and meaning it. It was more difficult to feel noble about it. There was no honour to be retrieved in my admission that since Lisa was lost to me, I would be lost to Shirley. I was tired, ashamed, above all sad. Once again I would seek my salvation in flying, find what purity there was left in the world by lifting myself into the sky--but even that had been spoiled, and spectacularly so. And everything I remembered about Lisa would come back to me, except Lisa herself, who was lost through my own cruel folly. Was Alex lost too? He was an increasing worry to me. We were serving in the same squadron, but we might have been miles apart, so chilly and distant had he become.

His closest friend now was Howard, a pilot who had been with him long before I had joined. They went on drinking bouts together. Howard would come back drunk and happy, singing stupid songs and telling jokes. Alex would come back silent, with a little smile around his lips and worries in his eyes. Whenever I tried to help him, he laughed it off or snapped at me; and sometimes to try and help seemed useless. What power to help had I? And anyway, we were in a sense already dead men, or so near to death that we were beyond redemption. Sometimes, seen running out to the aircraft, or high above the grey unfriendly sea, our bulky figures in helmets and 'Mae Wests' did not look like men, but like ghosts. Our existence was not proper life, but a kind of purgatorial suspension. We would be killed--if not today, then tomorrow. So what could possibly matter? Why bother to interfere in the simple business of death and make things more difficult? But sometimes, as I sniffed the morning mist, or listened to the distant crackle of engines across our dewy field, or rode the great oceans of wind, or coasted down under glorious golden clouds, I desperately did not want to die, and I thought: No--life is here, it will go on. Our fears are born of loneliness and abnormal strains, and all around are wonderful things. One day the fighting will stop; one side or the other will have won, and there will be an end of it. The politics will cease to matter. A time for life will come again. The ghosts will put on the clothes of ordinary men; peace will breathe the souls back into their wasted bodies. A time for joy will come again, for music, for simple pleasures, and for love. We will live, we will see true happiness one more. So I shall help my friend, tell him he will see Lisa again, tell him he is loved, tell him not to drift into despair, tell him always to be watchful and to hold on to hope.

It was no use. Alex would not let me near his private grief or terror. I watched my old friend sink into a waking nightmare.

I too was changing, had become harsh and loveless, had lost my innocence in bullets and in flames. Yet this had happened in the most beautiful world I knew: the ravishing world of the sun and the clouds, the only place in which I felt truly at peace, though death might stalk it and horrors stain the blue. Man is surely the strangest creature on this planet, and the most perverse. There were days when I was perfectly happy, days when I quite shamelessly wanted the war to go on for the rest of my life--so that I might forever have our country airfield as my home, where the engines roared and raced and lifted the Spitfires up on dagger wings above the madly tilting Earth, where the cool green Downs and the broad wheat lands beyond were bathed in a light so rich and golden that it might have slipped on a sunbeam from Paradise. Within minutes of dodging enemy shells or sending a bomber and its helpless crew into a ball of fire, I might be sliding home across the patchwork quilt of England, flinging back the canopy and whistling a merry tune to the Summer wind. Surely it was madness--yet who shall say the mad cannot be happy? Who shall tell the monsters not to wear the skins of ordinary men?

Towards the end of this crazy time we were vectored up over the Channel to meet a large formation of bombers. The whole Squadron was airborne, split into sections with the C.O. leading one and Alex the other. It was one of the very few times I flew under his direct command.

"See anything?" snapped Alex as we

roared up into the blue.

"Nothing at my side, Leader," I replied.

"Nothing over here." It was Howard's Northern voice. Already this was quite a show: Alex had all his friends around him, tucked in neatly below and behind his wings. Spirits were high, and there was a lot of excited chatter in the earphones.

"Cut it out, Blue Section." The C.O. took over. "We can't hear ourselves think over here. What do you see Blue Leader?"

"Not a thing, sir." Alex didn't sound too disappointed; he was still taking us up in copybook formation. Ground Control broke in with a new vector.

"That's mucked it," Alex growled in my ears. "Look where they're sending us."

As we made the turn I saw a huge mountain of cloud sailing towards us like an iceberg. There were a few other big piles far away over France but nothing to equal this one. It was magnificent: a smoky, boiling, giant's castle in the air. I searched desperately for the tell-tale glint of perspex or the cluster of specks which would betray the enemy formation.

"Your plots coinciding now," said the Controller in the maddening voice of someone playing draughts at home.

"Where are they, Control?" The C.O. sounded weary of this already.

"It's a joke," said an airborne voice. "There's nobody here."

"The buggers'll be in that cloud!" That was Howard.

"You couldn't hide forty-plus in there," came another voice.

"You bloody could," said Howard.

"This is Knightsbridge Leader to west End Control," the C.O. was formally taking over now. "Check your plots. We have nothing here."

There was further chatter from the ground, an inexplicable French voice drifting in from somewhere, then the C.O. split us up around the massive cloud, now filling our windscreens.

"Take a look, everyone."

"Red Leader, we're going over the

top," announced Alex. "Blue Section, up we go!"

"Watch it then, Blue Section." There wouldn't be much help from the C.O. now: he was taking Red Section round the back.

"Blue Section--Buster for height!" That was Alex ordering us to push our throttles through the gates for full power. We hurtled upwards. Once more the sun burned into the cockpit, as if the light itself were being smelted and poured down over us. Lulled by the engine's roar and lifted through the topmost frothing pinnacles of purest white, memories of aerobatics in the old Bulldog came back to me... then, flattening out, we saw the cloud for what it was: vast, wide, with yawning chasms in the middle--a whole new world. Tingling all over, I stared down, fascinated, as if a dream had suddenly been made real, or all the secret wonders of the sky laid out before me. Somehow, it was a sinful feast: too much, too lovely, too pure to be believed. We dived and swooped and boomed into the amazing caverns of the cloud where the light was grey and tinged with yellow, raced through milky wisps, and climbed again the foaming, bulbous walls.

"Nothing doing," Alex broke in upon my reverie. "Follow me round."

We were rushing round the dark side of the cloud now, Alex calling up Red Section for a rendezvous, the sun dancing along a blinding snow-white ridge above us. It was mesmeric, awesome, fantastic: we were inside the very halls of Heaven. Ahead reared a gigantic pillar, bathed in dazzling sunlight with a great, grey, smoky core. It was a sight of Biblical proportions, and it made me wonder if this is what the Israelites had seen in the desert all those centuries ago, when *the Lord went before them by day in a pillar of cloud, and by night in a pillar of fire...*

A terrible noise sliced through me. Guns! Shouts! Engines! Everyone was yelling and talking at once as out of the cloud burst four Messerschmitt fighters spewing fire and ruin, cutting up our neat formation. Cooper gone instantly; Davis in flames; the rest of us banking wildly away, desperate to avoid the merciless fire. One...two...three...four...they burst around us in a confusion of black-crossed wings and the faint exhaust trails of their straining engines. They had yellow prop-spinners: the mark of a crack squadron. There would be no escape from their deadly intent. Here they came, for us and no-one else, ready for another kill, raking us with fire: Lawson spinning away, his engine spouting smoke and oil. As I pulled up I caught sight of Red Section taking on a herd of speckle-backed Dorniers. They were far away on the other side of the cloud. There would be no help from them; only Alex, Howard and myself pitted against these four.

"For Christ's sake!" yelled Alex. I had never heard him so nervous. Had he been hit? No--surely that was his machine sweeping above me. "Get behind him Rich!" I heard him tell me. "The other one! The other one! No, no--pick off that tail-end Charlie!"

It was easier said than done. There

was scarcely time to think, less to be afraid--yet I could feel fear rising in me. I must fight it down, keep my head, pick a target and shoot, dammit, shoot! Soon we had fallen far below the enormous cloud and were whirling and spinning over the coastline. They were superb pilots; would not bunch or let us beat them in a curve. It was impossible to get a clear shot in.

"Two behind you!" I shouted at Alex, and he waggled away, spurting bullets at a third just crossing his nose. This was their new tactic: ganging up behind to share the shooting. While Alex and I spun and wheeled to right ourselves, they had snapped into line abreast behind Howard, harassing him down to a lower altitude, hounding him out over the sea.

"Come on! Come on!" he pleaded in our earphones. "The bastards are behind me--the four of 'em!"

We crashed our throttles through the gates once more and hurtled down the sky, blasting away at the four grey shapes as we went. In moments we were low over the water; then, annoyed by our fire, one of the Messerschmitts pulled up and tried to draw us off. Shells crashed into my wings and a jagged hole appeared in the cowling. I wouldn't be able to take much more of this. Frantic to escape, I spun round and round the sky trying to dodge the bullets, fear and dizziness swimming over me. At last the German zoomed off to rejoin that horrific chase across the sea. I somehow righted myself and got my nerve back to go down and follow him--but they were far ahead now, and flog our engines as we might, we could not catch them.

A fine white smoke now trailed from Howard's aircraft, but they persisted in shooting at him, driving him Eastwards low over the waves, towards Holland, I imagined. I had never seen anything more horrible. More frightful still was his indignant, anguished, boyish voice in my ears.

"Come on--give us a hand! They're knocking bits off my wings now!"

Alex and I streamed bullets at them, but nothing seemed to hit. Howard was crying like a child now. It was ghastly.

"Help me! Help me!" he wailed. "Please God help me!"

The Germans were still firing at him. We fancied we could hear the shells exploding in his cockpit.

"I'm ditching! I'm ditching!" he sobbed, his nose up in a sickening lurch, "I'm..."

His voice was cut off by his impact with the water. We saw the coarse, untidy spray of white as he beat down into the sea, then the lumpy garland of waves around his aircraft. We flashed over him in an eerie procession: the Germans, Alex, myself. When I turned to look for Howard, there was nothing at all.

Then a new horror, stifling and relentless like a hand across my mouth: they were coming for us. One by one they would pick us off. Already they were climbing round, turning, turning, one...two...three...four...banking up and pairing off in a perfect lazy arc, ready again to sweep down upon us. I fumbled the controls. My tongue went dry. I sat like a frightened rabbit, watching their turn. In such economy of movement they would kill me. They were deadly, invincible, they could no longer be avoided. I was going to die; this was it. Sunshine came to warm my eyes--perhaps it would not be so bad. They would get me here; I would burn in the air, not fight water round my face like poor Howard. The fellow on the right would do it: he was ahead of the others and I could foresee exactly the beautiful arc his wings would describe as he grew bigger above me. Here he came now, making little green and blue sparks...

"Come on you stupid clot!" It was Forrest screaming in my earphones, back from the other fight and hurtling underneath me on full throttle. "Come on--run for it. You too, Blue Leader!"

I kicked hard over and slammed the throttle forward again. We bunched together, racing for the coast. The Germans did not follow.

TWELVE

The death of Howard wrought a

terrible change in Alex. He would barely speak--to me, or to anyone. Despite his vast experience, he did not have the facility of tucking his soul away behind a daily armour-plating, so that all the horrors might fall upon a hardened shell. His whole being took their full weight. My attempts at helping him only made it worse, for then the burden of an interfering friend was added to the loss of Howard and the impossibility of improving his predicament with Lisa. But when I saw him sitting in the corner of a pub one night, expressionless, with tears rolling down his haggard face, I knew the end was near for Alex. The others poked his ribs and thought him crying drunk, but I knew he was at the bottom of the pit. Next day, I went to see the C.O. Strange, I thought as I entered his office, that a crucial moment in my life and Alex's should once more be played out before a grim commanding officer.

"What's the matter, Dellow?" He was in truculent mood.

"I'm worried about Fitzgerald, sir."

"And I'm worried about the whole lot of you. Isn't it my job rather than yours, worrying about the men in this Squadron?"

At that moment it would have been very easy to be insubordinate, but all I said was: "Yes, sir."

The C.O. shuffled some papers without looking at me. Here, I thought, is a man completely without the dashing qualities of leadership the general public always believed such people were supposed to display. He was a little, sandy, balding man nursing a bad temper in a bleak office. Why must it be he to whom I should attempt to pour out the complexities of Alex's soul?

"I can see as well as you that Fitzgerald is on the brink," he said blandly. "God knows, we all are one way or another--although I must say you seem particularly resilient, and that's very encouraging for the others, you know. We must all try to stick it out while we have to." It occurred to me that he might say this to everyone; perhaps he was reading it off one of those pieces of paper. "As to Fitzgerald, I'll do what I can, but I'm afraid leave is out of the question at the moment."

"I see. Thank you, sir."

"Does he have personal worries on top of the war?" Suddenly the voice was not unfriendly with its new note of humanity, but it sent a shiver through me. Was this the time to tell the C.O. that Alex had a wife in Germany? God only knew what would happen if it were to come out this way. I guessed he would be grounded, perhaps even discharged. He would get his rest all right, but he would never forgive me.

"Not that I know of, sir," I lied.

"You're particularly close to him, aren't you?" continued the C.O. He was dealing with deeply personal things, yet was as expressionless as if he were talking on the R/T.

"As you know, we flew together before the war." Before the war...had there ever been a 'before the war'? Images of the Flying Club and of Germany came to me like a dream: sweet, innocent days, unbearable now, dissolving into a hopelessly distant past. "We had holidays together," I said. All I could see was Lisa-- her golden hair swinging to a tune I could hardly remember. I suddenly did not want to remember it, but could not help trying.

"Shall I send him to the doctors?....I said shall I send him to the doctors, Dellow?"

"Er--yes sir, if you think it will do any good, sir. I much appreciate your understanding, especially since…"

"All right, all right, don't make a speech. I'll do what I can, but I'm not a magician. That'll be all."

Whatever the C.O. might have done, he never got a chance to do it. He was killed a few days later when the Squadron took on another horde of fighters over the Thames estuary. Forrest was made acting C.O., and we all thought he made a good enough job of it, but a week later Wing sent us a new man. He drove up in a big Alvis tourer with a flashy suitcase in the back, the sort of luggage one would only expect to see in First Class on an ocean liner, and it made me wonder what he had been in civilian life--but now he was a young, cadaverous Squadron Leader with thin white hands and the gleam of decorations on his tunic. He had a high-pitched snorting voice and a disconcerting habit of staring at you when he spoke. He brought with him the spectres of a new and subtle madness from which our airfield could no longer be a haven.

His arrival coincided with a lull in the fighting, so he was able to indulge his love of spit and polish and bull in all its forms. He made comments about our personal appearance and ordered everyone to smarten up. He was finicky in the mess and destroyed the easy-going atmosphere that was our only relaxation. Worse still, he was teetotal, and made no secret of his disapproval as he eyed the rest of us downing pints of bitter. He laid on compulsory P.T. every morning before breakfast, which was nothing less than ludicrous in the middle of our desperate struggle. Those who failed to turn up were ordered to run twice round the perimeter--fair enough in its own way, except that a senior N.C.O. was sent round with them... and that was the signal for the downing of tools and general gossip in the hangars. Some appalling slacknesses came to light, and that vital trust between mechanics and pilots, built up over incredible fears and hardships, was eroded in a few days. The more regulations the C.O. introduced, the more everyone tried to dodge them. As Forrest remarked, it was no way to run a fighting station.

While the rest of us suffered this, Alex was deteriorating in his own way: drinking like a fish and becoming careless in the air; sometimes arguing fiercely with his old friends, sometimes sunk in long and desperate silences. I was determined to do something for him, and I went to see Flight Sergeant Green, who had kept me right in my early days. Green was a plump, middle-aged, good-humoured man who had been with the Squadron since its days in France. He had seen a hundred pilots come and go and he knew Alex well. I put it bluntly to him that Alex was cracking up and that we should see the new C.O. together.

Green selected a chin and rubbed it. He knew I wasn't exaggerating, but he was appalled at my idea of a joint plea to the C.O., and he put on his most severe backbone-of-the-service expression.

"Might not be the time to cause a fuss, sir--what with this new gentleman still settling in and all the rest of it."

"Oh come on, Flight. You know Alex. He's going round the bend. Since Howard went he's been impossible; I can't get to him any more. Together we can make a case and really help him."

"Not strictly my business, sir. It's a matter for the officers. Why don't you see the medicos? They'll fix him up."

"Well, it might not be the best way. He doesn't respond well to doctors--never has. Anyway it's a rest he needs, not a packet of pills...and you know I can't go over this new man's head."

"If you'll forgive me for saying so sir, you've gone over it already in telling me all this. My job's on the ground sir, kicking backsides and..."

"...And you don't want to be seen nursemaiding officers who can't stand the strain, is that it?"

Green looked hurt. "I wasn't going to say that, sir." He drew a heavy breath. "But it might be seen that way. I wouldn't go stirring it up with the Old Man, sir, not if I were you. All the same," a kindly light came into his face, "I have noticed one or two things, 'specially since poor Mister Howard got the chop."

"Tell me honestly--what do you think?"

"I think it's a bloody shame--but ask for a private word, sir; I wouldn't go in with an N.C.O. in tow."

"Right. Thank you. You've been a great help." I could not resist shaking his hand. Somewhat embarrassed, he gave me his mother-hen look.

"Tell me, Mister Dellow. How does a

young chap like yourself take it so well, and poor Mister Fitzgerald is all to pieces?"

"'Cos I'm a better actor, Flight."

The new C.O. was standing at the window, looking past the taping and the sandbags to Forrest's aircraft being refuelled. It was cool and quiet in the office while the sunlit activity of a world at war bustled on outside. How I wanted to be part of it all again: crude and simple, the war which was a kind of peace...but here I was for my friend's sake.

"This is very unusual," drawled the C.O. "I don't care to receive complaints from my pilots."

"It's not a complaint, sir. I am very concerned about Fitzgerald. I've known him a long time, and I believe he's cracking up. I think he should have some leave, sir."

I knew I was in for it when the C.O. turned from the window and stood behind his desk, his thin fingers tapping the edge of it, his chin thrust upwards. I tried to make myself as wooden as possible. Suddenly his eyes stared into mine.

"This really is extraordinary," he whined. "You dare to approach me on behalf of another officer and demand leave for him on the grounds that he's--how did you put it--*cracking up*?" His head and his voice went higher and higher. "Is Fitzgerald incapable of speaking for himself? Well?"

"Fitzgerald is in no state to speak for himself, sir." I tried to be as calm as I could. "He wouldn't ask for leave."

"But you think he should have some? I suppose you want me to ground him."

"No sir. Of course not, sir. No pilot wants to be grounded." I let the 'you ought to know that' hang unspoken in the air.

The C.O. raised a foppish finger. "You realize Fitzgerald is the best pilot in this shabby lot. He has a brilliant record."

"I am aware of his record, sir."

"Yet you persist in this defeatist attitude!" The finger now pointed at me, and the voice had become a manic whinny. "I know your type, Dellow. You're the sort who wants the easy way out, the sort who believed in appeasement before the war, the sort who's frightened to strike hard in case you hurt your knuckles. I have no patience with that sort of wetness...and when I say my door is open to all my men, I don't mean they should all rush in with crackpot theories about one another's mental health. Fitzgerald's performance of his duties seems unimpaired."

"With respect sir, if you cannot see that one of your men is..."

"Silence!" The voice was that of a mad pony. "Don't you dare be insolent with me!" He clasped his hands behind his back and strutted up and down. Reason, or even argument, was impossible with this man. I must have been stupid to try it. Now I gave myself up to his tirade, looking at the wall behind his tossing head.

"Let me tell you your own business, Dellow--so you can mind it. Your business is to kill Germans: lots of Germans, one *schweinhund* after another." He anglicized the word *schweinhund*, somehow filling me with rage. I tried to freeze myself into a solid passionless block so that his words could no longer hurt me. "Shoot 'em down, Dellow; fry 'em in their own petrol, send 'em down into the sea! I have an idea that you think there's something decent about the enemy, that behind all this they're just like us, that you'd somehow like to invite them for dinner and discuss the finer points of aerial combat. But what do you know about Germans? Have you ever met one, spoken to one? D'you think they would spare you a couple of minutes for an amiable chat? Look at them on the newsreels. They're scum, Dellow, scum-- like rats to be got rid of. You want to think yourself lucky the Air Force has given you the finest aircraft in the world to do it with. Think of the other chaps slogging about in the Army, think of men in the Navy like sitting-targets in tin cans. Imagine life in the Merchant Navy, surrounded by U-boats and nothing to defend yourself with but a rusty pop-gun on the rear deck? And what do you think it's like in a submarine? Bloody awful! And you're whingeing instead of making history. So remember your business, Dellow: butchery in smart aeroplanes. If your peculiar friend has lost his taste for it, you can't afford to make it any concern of yours."

His blue eyes stared madly into my face. Things had gone so far in this extraordinary interview that I felt I might as well speak my mind.

"I had hoped *you* would be concerned, sir."

To my surprise, he did not yell at me. He backed away and stood behind his desk again.

"I don't admire your rudeness, Dellow. It will not get you whatever it is you want. Things have been very lax on this station and I'm determined to smarten you all up." The whinny came back into his voice. "I will not have my officers wet-nursing one another when they should be getting on with the job. As far as I'm concerned, you are all fit for general duties until my medical staff tell me otherwise. You're dismissed."

He was, I think, the only man I have ever truly detested.

Outside, I faced a stolid Green.

"It didn't do the trick, Flight."

"I'm sorry sir," he said flatly, "but I could have told you. Don't really know what to suggest, sir."

I was furious with myself and everyone else.

"Right," I snapped at Green. "That'll be all."

Now I was disinclined to speak to anyone about Alex. I avoided Green, feeling I had thoughtlessly embarrassed a man whose integrity I admired, and I could barely bring myself to look at the C.O. after his disgusting lecture. But worse was to come. One morning Alex found me alone in the map-room and slammed the door.

"So who's been telling tales, ay?"

"What d'you mean?" I asked, my

stomach already in knots.

"You know damn well what I mean!"

"I was only trying to help," I confessed.

"You've been a big help, haven't you? Now you've got the brass-hats thinking I'm barmy!"

Apparently the C.O. had had him in his office and asked him point blank whether or not he was cracking up. Dellow thought so. Was there any truth in it? The bitter irony was that after all that, Alex still had not been granted any leave.

"I'm sorry, Alex. I thought you needed a rest. I still think you need a rest. There's no shame in that. You're just not fit."

"Oh, so you think I'm barmy as well, do you?" He was angry, belligerent, frightened.

"Look, old chap…"

"Don't *old chap* me!" he exploded. "You can bloody well stop poking your nose into my life. When I asked you to help me, you wouldn't. Well now I don't want your help. I'll deal with things my own way and I don't need you to tell me how to look after myself!"

"You want to be all right for when this is over, for when Lisa comes back, don't you?" I instantly regretted saying it.

"Don't mention Lisa like that!" His eyes were red and scoured-looking. He had screwed up his face into a mask of hatred and frustration. "Don't mention her name in the same breath as this stinking war. You have no right to mention her at all!" For a moment I thought he was going to burst into tears. Instead he clenched his fists, as a baby on its back might clutch at the air. He brought them gently down on my chest, then turned away. "Just don't mention her. Don't mention any of it, please."

He relaxed his face. He scratched the back of his neck. "I'm all right," he said quite cheerily. "I am, you know. I'm as sane as anyone--or as sane as anyone can be in this bloody nonsense."

"I have been terribly worried about you," I declared. "Ever since Howard..."

"All right!" He had wound himself up

again and spun round to face me as if the momentary lull in his boiling emotions had made way for even greater storms. "Howard was my friend," he snarled, "my special friend. I trained him up, he flew his best with me, he understood me...yes," he blazed into my face again, "better than you! Then those bastards put him in the sea. There was no need for that, you know--that's not in the rules..."

There are no rules, I was thinking, no decency. Didn't you tell me that yourself? But I said nothing. His floodgates were beginning to break, and it would have been cruel and stupid to stop them.

"I could take it when the others went-- it's what you expect, really--but with Howard it's been different." Little wrinkles clustered round his eyes and a wetness gathered in their corners. "Now I have this dream. To tell you the truth, I don't know if it's a dream or something I've just imagined mixed up with what I've seen. Anyway, we're up there over the Channel: you, me, Howard. The Germans come out of that cloud, firing at us--one by one they group behind. We're hit but we're okay; then they go for Howard, just like it was. I hear him shouting at me *Help me! Help me!*--but I'm flying away from him, I can't make the turn." Tears were rolling down his face; he had hold of my jacket. "Then I'm down in the water, but I'm somehow outside Howard's cockpit, watching him inside. It's horrible. It fills up with water...he's yelling and beating at the straps... then there's no air left and he's... he's biting and gobbling at the canopy and I'm breathing water too and he's looking at me and he says...he says..." Saliva had trickled out of Alex's mouth, his whole face was wet with tears. He clutched frantically at my lapels as if he were begging for his life. "...he says *Aren't you coming down with me? Aren't you coming down?*"

He took a great gulp of air and looked, horrified, at his hands. Was this my old friend--once so carefree and so happy? No--that Alex was quite dead. This was some other monster in his body. I hardened myself; met his misery with an iron heart. My tenderness of spirit, my thirst for beauty, my ability to understand: all those were put away for better times. My selfish fear was not for Alex, but that I should not be able to bring them out again. Suddenly he pulled his hands down his face, smearing the sweat and the tears between his fingers.

"All right," he gasped, looking away from me, "all right. I can keep going. But someone's going to pay for Howard, and for Lisa, and for all…this." His voice was hoarse and mad and I didn't know what to do. He straightened up. "You can tell that to your little nancy-boy of a C.O…." he made for the door, "…but mind you don't catch him powdering his nose!"

Over the next few days, as I wondered how I was ever going to cope with these new horrors, Alex actually seemed to get better. I did not properly understand his threat that 'someone's going to pay', but I began to think he might be over the worst, and that his terrible outburst might have signalled a recovery. Then came a period of such fierce and constant activity that there was scarcely time to think of anything other than flying and sleeping. On more than one dawn flight we saw London ablaze. London was burning: that such things were happening seemed hardly credible. But it was real enough, and those of us who survived endured not by skill or daring or fortitude or bravery or any of the much-vaunted heroics so popular with the public at the time--but by luck. Who lived, who died, who got hit, who went crazy, who kept going: just luck. The nightmare lottery I had imagined had come hideously true. It was scarcely to be believed, and not to be thought about too much. Then the Blitz was over, and with it the days of whirling, crowded battles in the sky. The newspapers called us heroes, but none of us took it very seriously. Certainly there was no time for resting on our laurels. After a smattering of leave, a crop of postings, and stream of replacements, we were kept hard at it. Later there were raids over the French coast, taking the war back to Europe.

One of our favourite targets was Wissant: a big *Luftwaffe* airfield famous for its Messerschmitt fighters--but they weren't as good at scrambling as we were, and by snorting across at scant height we could inflict a lot of damage and belt back home before they could catch us. There was an element of fun in this daredevil beard-singeing. It put war flying back on safer, more reasonable terms--and the odds were fairer. It may seem ludicrous to talk like this now, but that is how we felt then. For me it was another taste of my exhilarating early days; and it was a tonic for Alex, making him chuckle again in my earphones as we raced across the sandy beaches and up over the dunes. When these raids started, one section would stay out over the Channel while a 'vic' of three went down to do the job; but as we got away with it so well, the covering section was soon dropped and two Spitfires would be sent over by themselves, always pairing pilots who knew each other well and had flown together in the same section. The hit-and-run technique was successfully applied to railway marshalling-yards, harbour installations, and fuel dumps. Then Alex and I got another Wissant job.

We flashed out over the sea, hugging the waves and glancing down at the water sparkling under a Winter sun. It was a crisp and frosty morning: the sky a vast blue dome without a single cloud. Usually these raids were only done under plenty of cover. Today we would have to be quick.

"Everything okay?" Alex's voice crackled over to me.

"She's running like a dream," I answered. The Spitfire felt light and precise under my hands, like a racehorse capable of anything. It was an irresistible temptation to 'porpoise' her over the waves, exulting in the gentle rocking of my seat and the throb of the enormous engine.

"Right-o. Let's put on some juice and come at them from the landward side."

We advanced our throttles and

whipped over the beaches. The flat countryside lurched beneath us as we made the turn to bring us over Wissant. It was not a good idea. By the time we had the airfield in range the Germans were putting up their 'planes.

"Damn!" said Alex. "Have to be a quick one. Go for the sheds."

I was already firing, ripping up the corrugated roofs with my shells. Then the airfield had flashed behind us, Alex breaking to the left, myself to the right.

"Only one more pass then we'll have to scarper." Alex was enjoying this.

"Keep like this and we'll come at them from both sides." So was I.

We screamed down once more, plastering the field with bullets--but it was too late. By the time we had stopped firing, three Messerschmitts were safely airborne and giving chase.

"Straight for home now!" I shouted-- but they were faster, and beginning to fire at us.

"Bugger it," said Alex.

Half-way back to England we had to

turn and fight.

They were good shots, and did some damage to my starboard wing-tip. By sheer luck I hit one of them and he turned for home immediately, spewing oil and glycol. Alex was luckier: he sent one gliding down into the sea. The third put his nose down and darted back to France unscathed. We let him go: there would be enough to worry about in getting home.

"Well that was easy," remarked Alex drily. "Are you all right?" He swooped underneath me, taking a look. "Mmm-- nothing hanging off, no smoke or anything, but they've made a mess of that wing."

"It'll be all right if I don't try anything fancy," I told him. "She wants to go into a right-hand spin."

"Keep her steady then. You'll make it."

I turned once more for England. About a mile ahead, the stricken Messerschmitt Alex had downed lay floating on the water. I remembered that many *Luftwaffe* pilots were glider-trained;

perhaps that was how this fellow had made a perfect belly-landing after Alex had knocked out his engine--almost impossible on water at the best of times. His aircraft looked like a big green fish basking on the surface. I had never seen one float so well... and there he was, getting out nicely and plopping into the calm water, bobbing there in his life-jacket--just in time too, for the Messerschmitt was slowly sinking beside him. At the approach of my Spitfire he waved an arm. I gingerly tipped a wing and gave him a friendly hand, wondering if his people were as good at picking up survivors as our lads were. Someone must have see the fight from the coast, and he was close enough inshore to be taken prisoner. I imagined him sitting out the war in a P.O.W. camp somewhere in Wales or Scotland, bored but safe. There were worse ways to end a war. I was about to say so to Alex when I heard a tell-tale click in my earphones and the breathy ambience replaced by the hiss of empty static. Alex had turned off his R/T.

"What's up, Alex?" I flicked back and forth from *transmit*. "Alex? Alex?" Nothing. Then he came from behind, turning beneath me, lining up with the German in the water. I could hardly believe I was watching what I saw--but it was plain enough. I was sure, before the asking, that there would be no answer to whatever prayer was in my throat. White spouts plumed along the sea--the little figure jumped and danced backwards like a cork...then there was only the rumpled water, and Alex pulling up the stark and brazen sky, heading for home as if nothing had happened.

My silence became part of Alex's guilt. My bright and simple joy in flying--only just nursed through the long and bitter fighting--was now tarnished by what he had done. I soiled it further by not telling anyone about the murder I had seen, by taking on the worst of his appalling secrets. For murder it was, plain enough-- and Alex went about with all the artificial banter of a criminal covering his tracks. True, at times he looked more harrowed than ever, but I am not sure he wished the deed undone. His action had borne the marks of long deliberation, his stony silence the suggestion of a grim and callous satisfaction. For Alex had crossed the line from war to barbarism.

Some might argue that there can be no such line, and that the so-called rules of war are nothing but an apology for vileness. That may be so--but I am not sure that any of us consciously weighed up these matters. Most of us never thought about them at all. When they crossed our minds, we instantly overrode them with a stern conviction in what we had to do. We wanted to do our job, do it well, and come home in one piece. Above all, we wanted to stay alive--and, in a most curious way, it was that same fierce determination to survive which made us want the enemy to live, too. Each day we flew with guns against them, yet did not consciously wish them dead. We wanted to defeat them, utterly and completely, but would have liked to do so without killing them. It was one of those peculiar things that cannot be explained to anyone's satisfaction, and we tended to dismiss the fact that we had to kill. But in forcing myself to consider it, I came to understand how Alex had fired so savagely at the helpless figure in the water. Alex, too, was dead. His body might still move and have its being, but his spirit had no life. It had been defeated, crushed, wiped out--perhaps by sheer terror, bitterness, strain, exhaustion: all the horrors we had to fight off more fiercely than the recognized enemy, or perhaps by something so deep inside himself, so private and so hideous that no-one could give it a name. The external enemy was, after all, just a man, and a man could be beaten with strength and with luck. But the enemy inside ourselves--the terrible fear, and the fear of fear itself--this was a demon, and demons might not be beaten by anything we could summon up, invent, or hope for. The demon had killed Alex. What was left was rotten, loveless, scarcely human. Lisa, Howard, myself: somehow we had all failed him. He had no passion to survive, no will to live. Therefore killing would be easy; it might be the only act of meaning left to him. I still held on to life--Alex had let go. But if these thoughts might explain his shooting of the German in the water, they did not seem to excuse it. It had been foul and needless...and its greatest evil was to make me hate him.

THIRTEEN

The raiders came in little bunches now: going for docks, shipping, factories. We were moved around the country, and became night-fighters for a while. I earned promotion simple by outliving my comrades; and because I was a persistently good shot I was eventually given a medal--then another. But it was too late: I had had enough. All I really wanted was to go home--but it was back to the South coast and more sorties over France. I began to think it might go on for ever. Then one day an Avro Anson landed and a very senior-looking officer stepped out. Without any ceremony he walked into the C.O.'s office and a moment later they sent for me. When the C.O. was asked to leave, I felt it could only be good news.

"Want you for a special job," said the senior officer briskly. He was a tall, grey man who looked marvellous in uniform and whose braid and decorations gave him the charsima of a visiting king. In his hands he held a buff folder and pretended to read from it. "Mosquitos," he said covertly, looking up.

"But Mosquitos are bombers, aren't they sir? I'm fighter-trained." I had meant it to convey my genuine surprise...but realised it sounded ungrateful. He consulted the folder once more, raising his grey eyes in a humourless stare.

"It says here, Dellow, that you have argued with every officer who has had the misfortune to command you." He lowered the folder, and a ghost of a smile played around the corners of his mouth. "Seems a trifle harsh, but even if it's true, it may not have been a bad thing. In any case your days of irking Squadron Leaders are over: we're making *you* one.

It's a photo-reconnaissance squadron--absolutely vital work."

"Thank you sir." I was amazed, flattered, and suspicious all at once. The posting seemed so unorthodox, and what had I done to deserve it? "I'm not sure I'm up to this, sir. I've never told anyone what to do before, and I've never even been in a Mosquito. I'm delighted of course, sir--I just wasn't expecting it."

The senior officer put his hands in his pockets and strolled about the room.

"I'm not altogether surprised at your attitude, Dellow. I was told what you were like. You are supposed to be 'quietly but persistently insubordinate.' Are you?" He gave me no time to answer. "Well, it doesn't matter if you are. I'm not looking for some boot-licking yes-man. I'm looking for a natural pilot with a lot of battle experience and a bit of dash. That sounds like you. These recce. boys need a bit of dash--they see themselves as taxi-drivers with a Brownie. That's no good. Added to that they've got the boffins on their backs, fussing about with slide-rules and bits of paper. There's a place for all that of course, but you and I know it's all really down to eyes and ears and hard experience. They've got one of the best aircraft and one of the most important jobs in the Air Force, but they need someone who'll stick their necks out for them--and his own, because this job is going to become more and more important as the war goes on. And the whole point of having someone like yourself with all his experience on fighters is that the Mosquito must be regarded as a fighter, and the squadrons run like fighter squadrons. They're very fast and very light: more like two Spitfires stuck together than your old idea of a bomber. You'll love them, you'll see."

That, somehow, was exactly what I wanted to hear. It was like the sun coming from behind the clouds. I was on course again, plain and simple, with a real flier's job to do.

"Thank you again, sir," I smiled. "I'm sorry if I was impertinent. I'm sure I can do the job, sir, and I will do it."

I was packing my personal kit, leaving the little room as spartan as it had been when I had first arrived. I wondered who would be its next occupant. Hundreds of miles away, at the other end of the country, a similar room was no doubt being prepared for me--and the men on that station would be wondering what I would be like. It was a strange thought, persisting even when Alex appeared in the doorway.

"Aha!" he said without smiling. "Sneaking off without saying goodbye, are we?"

"Oh, hello," I answered, stowing my razor. "Well, they've really got rid of me this time."

"More than Jerry could manage."

It struck me, from the bitterness in his voice, that he might actually resent my having survived for so long--but that didn't seem to make sense.

"They just keep missing me," I joked. "I don't know how." It was the signal for Alex to lose his temper.

"Well I know one thing," he snapped.

221

"You don't care about the fellows they hit. You don't bloody care, do you? You don't care about all the mess--you don't even see it!" He had stepped forward into the room and was standing over me, eyes blazing. "I know what kind of C.O. you'll make. These people aren't men to you: they're just pilots, part of a machine. You care more about the machines and all your head-in-the-clouds stuff than the poor devils who have to go up there and take a beating every day."

I put my hand on his arm. "Steady on, old chap," I said.

"Don't patronize me!" He wrenched his arm away, gasping and hectic. "You'll drive your poor bloody pilots just like you've driven yourself: until you've become some kind of zombie who's only happy shooting other people under a nice blue sky! I know why they picked you. You only care about flying--you've forgotten how to care about human beings. You forgot that the day you wouldn't take Lisa into your rotten hotel."

I squared up to him.

"We've been through all that, Alex-- and you know you're talking rubbish."

"It's not rubbish. It's the truth!"

"Well I'm not sorry to be going," I said coldly, returning to my packing, knowing perfectly well that part of it *was* true. "You've managed to ruin the war for me."

"Ruin the war for you? Your own personal show, is it? How fantastically arrogant can you get? It's bloody incredible!"

"Don't shout at me, " I growled. "I worried myself sick about you; I made a fool of myself for you; I was roasted by the C.O. for your sake--and all you can do is shoot an unarmed man in the water!"

I saw the accusation sting him sharply. It was the first time the words had been said aloud, but I carried on.

"It was a dirty lousy trick, and I saw it all. I saw every stinking moment of it...and I don't want your shame on top of my own weakness and stupidity. D'you think I've ever forgiven myself about

Lisa? D'you think I don't imagine where she is and what she's doing every day? Every raid that goes over there--d'you think I don't imagine what could happen? D'you think that doesn't turn me inside-out? I don't want to talk about it any more than you do--but I won't stop thinking about it. The only way to keep going is to make the best of it and do a decent job."

I thought for a moment he was going to hit me. Instead, he thrust his face up into mine. It was an anguished, painful face--and I realised, with a tinge of renewed shame, that whatever I had suffered in loving and losing Lisa, he had suffered more.

"A decent job," he snorted, "a decent job? You haven't learned anything, have you? You've been through all this and you haven't learned... anything!" He backed away, but I could still feel his hot breath on my chin. "This war's not about flying, it's not about doing a decent job-- it's about killing people!" He turned for the door. "Or haven't you noticed yet?"

With Alex gone, I returned to my packing, hot and angry, with the tightness of shame and fury in my chest. Clear, fresh sunlight came in through the window to tempt and to taunt me; but I wanted to be far away and doing something different. I wanted no memory of sweet things, no tyranny of the past. A scent of familiar perfume made me turn. I saw a WAAF girl smiling under her cap. She seemed to have appeared from nowhere.

"What?" I said dreamily.

She saluted very properly and said: "Your car's ready, sir." Why did they all have to be so young and pretty? "I'm driving you to the station, sir." I looked blankly at her; she must have thought I was very slow.

"Ah--yes. Right. Couple of minutes."

"Jolly good, sir." She took charge. "Let me stow this bag for you." She picked up my suitcase and stumped off down the corridor.

Here, I thought, is my brisk angel of the new order, come on worsted wings to banish all romance. Even the prettiest ones were infuriatingly sensible. Yet now she had gone, the scent grew somehow stronger. Ah, no, it wasn't the girl, it was Lisa's bottle of cologne, fallen over on the bed and spouting into the blanket like a gashed artery. I rushed to snatch it up; it slid from my sodden hands and bumped on to the floor, spilling its last pitiful drops across the linoleum. I fumbled with the stopper--too late: the bottle was quite empty. The faint, astringent smell haunted me like a song--all these years, carried through the war, and now lost in a few hectic moments. Would all things go from me like that, in a final spilling-out? Now I had only the memory of the smell, the memory of the memory. For an instant the thought of smashing the bottle flashed through my mind...but no, I carefully replaced the ground-glass stopper and gently put the bottle in my bag. I walked out of the room, leaving behind the smell of my youthful happiness. My spirits had never been lower.

The Mosquitos were based in Scotland. It was back to abominable weather, dour villages, and an airfield surrounded by miserable-looking sheep. The Mosquitos were fun, however--and now I was the 'Old Man', able to run things my way. It was not quite the serious, lonely position I had imagined. The pilots did need a bit of pushing, for they felt themselves to be out of the real war, and would gather round me like grandchildren eager for stories of the Spitfire and Hurricane squadrons in what they already thought of as 'the old days'. I told them without relish, for my breach with Alex had soured every memory. These young men had no idea of the sins which weighed upon Alex and myself--and it was certainly better to keep it that way. Soon I had them into the thick of it, and we took high-altitude photographs of targets in Norway, Holland, and along the Baltic coast. In the hard schools of a new command and difficult operations, I learned to lock away the past. The Mosquitos were a delight to fly, and we prided ourselves on being the fastest and slickest of the photo-reconnaissance squadrons. To lighten the aircraft, I had them stripped down as far as possible, and passed on an old R.F.C. trick I remembered from the Major at the Flying Club: we polished our machines with furniture wax for extra 'slip' and speed. Their gleaming finish was beyond the pale of strict regulations demanding matt camouflage for the aircraft, and it earned us the derisive nickname of *The Spit and Polish Boys*, but whenever the Messerschmitts gave chase the trick proved to be worth its weight in elbow-grease. We streaked away every time.

It was when the sorties over Germany began that I started to think of Alex and Lisa again. Of course, in a sense, I had never stopped thinking about them, but their upsetting presence had been consigned to a guilt-filled attic of my memory. As I mounted and rode the great oceans of wind, and flew through sun and rain and clouds, they had been banished with all other Earthly things;

only on the ground had I visited them as a dull worry or an impossible longing. But now when I looked down on the grey heaths of Germany, and stared far to the South where clouds began to merge with snowy mountains, I thought: Lisa is down there somewhere. I have flown so many miles, and not one of them has brought me any closer to her. When I saw the other 'planes rocking gently around me like a school of dolphins in the vast and lonely sky, I would think: Alex is so far away. Neither of them know I love them. If only there could be peace, time for me to put right what I had put wrong, time again for us to care for one another. Long ago, in Germany, I had discovered the date of Lisa's Birthday: April the Third. I had never forgotten it, had imagined her bright and happy in Spring sunshine, smiling in her clean clothes, wishing I could have given her a Birthday present. This April the Third--when nobody seemed to have any clean clothes and any smiles were grim ones--I still kept the memory sacred and hoped that somebody somewhere in Germany was giving her a Birthday present. But it seemed a faraway, innocent dream. I could not truly imagine where she was, what she might be doing, or even how she might look. Would she--once so beautiful--have been worn and ravaged by the war in the way that everything else seemed to have been? Surely not--yet I could not be sure. I could not be sure of anything any more. Then the war seemed particularly horrible and stupidly dangerous, and I wondered how long I could go on paying its appalling, wicked price.

It happened over the Dutch border. Coming home from a trip to the German factories, I flew straight into a burst of flak--my own fault: I was too low. The controls went to jelly and oil streamed from both engines; but there was no fire and somehow, miraculously, we kept on flying. Young Dickie Harrison, already divesting himself of straps and wires, was all for jumping.

"Not here, you clot," I told him.

"D'you want to be cooped up in a hut 'til the end of the war? I can't see you digging your way out and footslogging across Germany. No, you stick with me 'til we get home."

"She won't make it, boss." Dickie always called me 'boss': he had seen too many gangster films.

"Well," I said, "let's get Holland behind us while we can."

My first instinct was to put on height. More height meant more time, and more time meant a greater number of options. But would the engines take the strain of the increased throttle needed for even the gentlest climb? Well, the sooner I tried it, the safer it would be. I gingerly opened the throttles and eased back the stick. It was all right for a few seconds, but noise and judder and blacker streams of oil told me it couldn't last. Once the oil was gone the engines would seize: better throttle back again and let her slip along as best she could, steadily losing height. Dickie sat sweating beside me. The Dutch coast was visible--but after that there was still a lot of water to cross. I wondered if my number really had come up. I had certainly been lucky for long enough. Luck could not last for ever...but a pity it had to end here, now, this way.

As we crossed the coast the port engine was missing horribly and the rudder, once so slack, had now gone so stiff as to be almost useless. I could only steer by banking, and each time I did that, the Mosquito would swoop lower, down towards the sea.

"Here we are then," said Dickie excitedly. "Ever been in the drink, boss?"

"No--and I'm not jumping into cold water for you or anybody."

I had decided to stay with the Mosquito for as long as possible. Provided that nothing worsened, there was no reason why I shouldn't land her and walk away. We had had a miraculous escape, the machine was still flying, no-one was chasing us, England was coming up. There was time to reflect. If only I could keep her going and cross the coast with enough height! Everything would depend on that. Frantically, I did mental arithmetic to calculate distance and time and speed and rate of drop...anything to keep out of the sea: the cold, cruel, hopeless sea; the sea which killed so easily, which wiped everything out, which had already swallowed so many of my friends. It would not have me, not if I had any scrap of hope or strength left. I told Dickie we would just make it, then he could jump. Privately, I realized that the landing, whenever it came, would be a mess and that Dickie would have to go as soon as we crossed the coast--any minute now. It was to his credit that he sat so calmly, watching his opportunities for a safe jump dwindle with our height.

There went the cliffs! My old hunting-ground! A sweep of green, some houses, a road: Kent had never looked better.

"Okay," I said. "I've got you this far, now you can jump. There's still a bit of height."

"I'll stay with you if you want me to, sir."

Dickie was still very young.

"No. I want you back at the station in one piece. When this thing hits the ground I'll have no time for anyone."

"You're staying with her?"

"Yes."

"She'll break up! Why risk it?"

"Stop asking stupid questions and get out!"

"Right." Dickie prepared to go. "I'm off then. Here's hoping for a girls' school or a WAAF barracks," he quipped. His relief was infectious.

"Well keep away from church spires or you'll be no damn good to any of them."

"Cheerio, sir." He grinned stupidly and stumbled out of his seat to go through the hatch. I knew he had gone by the howling wind that swept up behind me.

"Might have closed the door," I muttered to the empty seat.

I was feeling better with Dickie gone, and highly pleased with myself at having got this far. But now there was no hope of reaching any of the nearby airfields--I should have loved to drop her on the tarmac and roll up to the sheds. Everything was coming very fast now and I still hadn't seen a good field. It would have to be almost directly ahead, for I could risk nothing more than the gentlest of turns--and there was nothing but twisted strings of hedgerows and short, lumpy fields running the wrong way. I was loath to cut the engines, for with them would go my last vestige of power and control. They had performed magnificently in this long slowing-down and it was tempting to keep them going-- but no, they would have to go. I switched off and disconnected everything, pulling my straps as tight as I could. Still no field! For the first time, real fear struck into me. If I piled her up now, I could easily be killed. All these years, all for nothing, and so much left undone. What a waste that would be. Desperately, in that moment, I did not want to die. "Be careful," said a voice inside me, "be terribly careful." It was somehow a woman's voice. Could it be my mother? Could it be Lisa? I pushed the ridiculous notions away. This was no time to play with the uncanny--just time to heed that little voice: "Be careful now, be terribly careful." I would be--it was all right--I was being careful. She was gliding down now like a quick, silent owl. Still no decent field! Bushes and ditches were flashing underneath with a nasty-looking clump of trees sailing towards me. A shame to smash her up now, after all this. I tried a gentle turn. Well, at least I would miss the trees. Straighten the wings now, hands ready for a quick get-out. I reminded myself to pick my legs up, remembering Ted Bailes from my last squadron losing his feet in a belly-landing like this. "Must have been bloody painful," I muttered to myself, "scraping your toes along the ground for five-hundred yards." Then I saw a lovely road swim into view just off my port nose. It was wide and smooth and straight and the answer to everything. With a surge of joy I swung the stick over: the worst mistake I ever made. I actually saw, in hideous slow-motion, the port wing being shaved off by the ground, and I heard myself say: "God! I'm going to be killed!", at the same time realizing there was no point in saying it. Then a terrible noise boiled around me and someone seemed to be screaming behind my head. A giant hand lifted me forwards and smashed me down into a blinding, shocking wall of blackness.

FOURTEEN

It was in hospital I learned the true meaning of fear: fear in the green-tiled wards, fear in the little empty rooms, fear in the white-coated whispers, fear in the long dark nights. The sharp alarms of combat were replaced by more insidious terrors. The pain was hard to bear, but worse was the ugliness and humiliation of sickness. I was not good at coping with this world of syringes, blood, and white towels. I remembered the crash-landing in perfect detail and how stupid I had been to put that wing down--but after that there was a fog of nothingness and the vague worry that I had missed or forgotten something. I gradually discovered that both my legs had been broken and one foot badly mauled. Some ribs had caved in too, and my left arm severely wrenched at the shoulder. I was a great heap of pain, a foundered ark of troubles, broken home to a mind that feared I might never walk properly or feel well again.

Dickie was the first to come and see me: bright and cheerful, his hat and gloves smelling of the fresh outdoors.

"I told you boss," he grinned, "you should have jumped with me. Never felt a thing--and there was a pub just down the road."

"Stop telling me that," I smiled weakly.

He looked me up and down, assessing the damage in his own way.

"You're a lucky devil," he said seriously. "You should have been a goner, you know. Look at the mess you made."

He produced a big blow-up photograph of the wrecked Mosquito. Bits of it were strewn along the road and the nose--with me still in it--had smashed and battered its way into a ditch. It looked as if a giant had emptied his dustbin across the fields. Dickie told me that a copy of this photograph had been sent back to the Squadron and they were putting it up in the mess with *Rich Dellow got out of this* written underneath.

There were other, less casual visitors: volunteer women with endless cups of tea and a well-known Air Vice-Marshall doing his rounds, saying 'Jolly good show' to everyone. I loathed all this, and did not respond well to the gallows-humour of bandaged tea-parties. I drifted in a sea of muddled flavours: milk, and pain, and soap, and sometimes when I coughed, the salty panic of blood. My bones were supposed to be healing, but I felt desperately weak; prey to terrible headaches and fits of melancholy. On Sunday mornings I could hear faint singing from the chapel:

There is a green hill far away,
Without a city wall…

The poignant, lump-in-the-throat words slid and folded round me like a familiar mystery. O, for a stirring battle-hymn! But no--only the mystery, bland and cool, soft and disturbing:

We may not know, we cannot tell...

And all the time, the limpid English light flooded in through white-barred windows, speaking now of Summer picnics on the grass, now of rustling walks through strewn and golden leaves; now of hectic noontide, now of mellow Blackbird-fluted evening. Then the darkness would come, breathing in at the high windows, and a solitary star peep down to taunt me with all the beauty of the World.

I rediscovered an old trick I had learned in childhood sickness: to while away the hours or beckon sleep I would imagine my bed was a bunk in a cabin of a great ship. It was not difficult, lying on my back, to sense the rise and fall of the bunk or the gentle swaying of the walls...and from this magic cabin I would build the huge black and white liner in my mind: the companionways beyond the door, the engines churning far below, the windy decks above; then the bridge, the great hissing funnels, and beyond the ship, the wide blue sea and the curve of the sky and the foreign lands which lay at the end of the voyage. Only now the trick worked imperfectly. I did not sail to foreign lands, but into fretful sleep and dreams of locked-in panic in the holds and the ship lying dead and broke on the sea-bed and hands inflicting pain around me and Lisa bending over me at the garden-party with the lights behind her hair and the bottle of wine pouring pouring pouring coldness over me and rinsing away the darkness until the World was sharp and shivery and full of light....

"You have another visitor," smiled the nurse. "Wake up now."

A tall shadow filled the room. The long sharp face, the immaculate uniform, the strange sooty smell of someone from outside...it was Alex, come like a ghost to greet me from another life.

"Hello, old fellow," was all he said as we shook hands warmly. A dull amazement spread through me.

"You look marvellous," I swallowed, almost in tears.

"You look bloody awful," he responded with a smile, "but it's good to see you."

"This is wonderful," I kept saying, "wonderful. How did you know I was here?"

"Oh, you're famous. You're the man who nurses a Mosquito all the way home, saves his navigator's life, then uses the 'plane as a ditch-digger."

"Sorry," I gurgled. "It hurts to laugh. Is that really what they're saying about me?"

"Much worse than that. Still," he added, "I'd have probably done the same. Instinct, was it, going for that road?"

"'Fraid it was, yes. No height left. Anyway, how did you get here?"

"Oh," he sat down beside the bed, "a few days leave. I wanted to see you." As he drew up his chair, I thought he looked strangely uncomfortable, as if he already longed to be outside again and was keeping one eye on the fresh blue air beyond the window and the pulse of life beyond the gate. Then I realized it was I, not he, who was doing these things. He was utterly still, absolutely himself, not uncomfortable at all, as if resting after some unseen exertion. "I say," he fiddled in his pocket, "d'you think they'd mind if I smoked in here?"

"I'm sure they wouldn't," I answered.

Alex crossed his legs. I savoured the pleasure of his lighting the cigarette. There was something magical about it, and it brought back vivid memories of our long-past but never-forgotten friendship. He was very slow and deliberate in sending a faint blue smoke into the air, and when he spoke, his voice had a new softness: not the languor of his old, sophisticated drawl, but the calm of some new inner peace.

"I went officially bonkers you know."

We both let the idea of it flutter round the room. This was 'piece of cake' talk, but invested with such terrible seriousness that I did not at first know how to take it in, much less how to respond. A kind of warmth spread through me, but there was still nothing I could say. At last the dread weight of his secrets had borne him down. I was filled with the knowledge of his torment, worse than anything I had suffered in living through the war with my weakness and my stupidity and my longing for someone I could never have. I was filled with love for my old friend.

"It wasn't so bad," he continued, brushing a little ash from his tunic. "The worst of it was they took me off general duties--well, no-one likes to be grounded, do they? Then I thought they were going to send me to some rotten nut-house, but it turned out to be a convalescent home in Hampshire: all cream-teas and lazing about. It was rather nice, actually. There was a smashing barmaid in the local pub, too; a little blonde, just your type. Of course we weren't supposed to go there. By the way," he held out his sleeve, "you outrank me now--did you realize that?"

"Good Lord, so I do!"

We laughed about that, but it was

very self-conscious. When it was finished, I said:

"Poor old Alex. You've really been through it. I had no idea..."

"Come off it," he interrupted, but there was no sharpness in his voice, "you knew very well I was going round the bend."

"It was the C.O. who was round the bend." Whatever I said would be inadequate.

"Oh, him." Alex drew once more on his cigarette. "Yes, he was a real head-case, wasn't he? They should have locked him up years ago. I wonder what happened to him."

"You don't know? You mean you're not back at the Squadron?"

"No, no. They--er--they gave me a new job after...afterwards. I'm in South Wales now, of all places." A ghost of a smile came over his face. "Well out of harm's way. How about you, anyway?"

He was over the crisis. Telling me had seemed no trouble to him, for he had confessed these horrors in his smiling, throwaway, amiable manner--a manner heightened, rather than diminished, by the torment I imagined he had suffered. Now here he was: a new and strangely disturbed man. It was not the old Alex who sat listening to my story; it was a different soul in that same lean body, a soul I could scarcely touch. It was as if great parts of him were no longer there...and I slowly realised that I was the healthy one in this room, nursing a few bruises, while Alex had been broken to the core. What was left seemed a strange assembly of remembered impressions. He wanted me to talk, and I enthused about my photo-reconnaissance missions. Suddenly, with a new coldness, he said:

"But you still haven't seen through it, have you?"

I stopped. I did not want an argument.

"No," I said flatly, "not in your way, I suppose."

He would not be put off--but where I might have expected him to be harsh and hot with condemnation, he was mild and sober.

"It's still a kind of game to you, I know. Well, I saw through it years ago; I saw through war before the war began…and I seem to remember telling you what it would be like, although even I couldn't predict how good and thoroughly professional you'd be at it. I don't think you'll ever learn now, you're just not the type--and that might not be a bad thing, at least from your point of view. I envy you in a way. It's all fun and excitement to you."

"For God's sake," I retorted, "d'you call this fun?"

"That?" he said, nodding at my bandages. "That's an accident. You'll get over it, knowing you…then you'll be back up there, doing it all again." He heaved a sigh. "You're just too good at the war. You ought to be ashamed of yourself-- although I don't suppose you are."

I squirmed.

"I am ashamed of myself, Alex, now that you mention it--but not for doing my job, for all sorts of other things: for being weak and stupid over letting Lisa go to Germany. Anyway, that's a rotten thing to say, especially to your old friend, lying here all busted up." I tried to make it sound as jovial as I could.

"You'll mend," he went on quietly, "but they won't cure your blindness. You just don't see."

I was becoming annoyed with Alex. Whatever he had been through, I didn't take kindly to this bloodless preaching. Yet I did not wish to hurt him.

"Come all this way just to tell me off, ay?" I grinned. If this joke didn't work, I would lose my temper.

"No," he smiled, "I gave up trying to reform you ages ago: too much like hard work." The danger of an argument was over, but a new grittiness had entered his voice. "They still don't know about Lisa," he said, getting up and moving over to the window. Just for a moment it was the old, determined, hard-jawed Alex. "I kept that from all of them--and it was bloody difficult, I can tell you."

"Is she all right?" I asked. "Have you

heard from her?"

"Not a thing," he answered lightly, looking out of the window. "She's still over there, as far as I know."

"Well, where else would she be?" I was shot through by doubts and anxieties. "Is she in the big house?"

"I don't honestly know," he breathed. "I rather hope not. I like to think she's gone much further South--perhaps even to the Alps--far away from all this. For all I have a German wife, I still can't imagine what it's really like out there, can you? I expect it's pretty dull really; there'll still be quiet parts of Germany you know, little towns. The family must know some safe places; she has lots of aunts and uncles in the South..."

As he spoke, I saw again the great, pink, fairytale castle clouds formed over the Danube and floating softly Northwards. I saw Lisa's bright eyes under the brim of her hat; the way she wore a scarf and walked and carried a handbag. At the same time I was filled with horror: she could be anywhere, suffering anything. All this was my fault. If only I had been strong enough to keep her safely in England, everything might have been different. Keep her! How could I have kept her? She wasn't mine to keep; nor, I suspected, was she truly Alex's either. She was her own woman, and rightly too. Men should not want to possess women, I thought, yet always do.

"...can you imagine what it's like to lose track of your own wife through some stupid war--the only woman you've ever loved? Can you imagine that?"

"Yes," I answered. "I don't know how you bear it."

"I didn't, did I?" he snapped. "Anyway," he softened his voice again, "it's not a real problem any more, Rich. It's difficult to explain, but it somehow doesn't matter so much. I've learned to live without Lisa--without even the thought of her. Doesn't mean I don't love her any more. Heaven knows, I love her-- or want to." He gave a tiny chuckle. "It's been a long time since I touched a girl...any girl. It's just that I've got used to being without her. I never thought I'd come to say that, of all things, but it's true. I haven't enjoyed it, but I have grown used to it. I'm sure she's done the same, in her own way. Easier for her, I imagine: she's got a hard streak, you know. I think provided she's away from the war, her biggest problem will be what to wear." He mimicked her soft low voice when he said 'what to wear'. To hear him made me desperately angry. How could he dismiss his long, long loving in a few hard words? How could he throw off the anguish that had made him mad?

"Don't you love that in her?" I said severely.

"Yes." He was watching something out of the window. "Anyway," he turned back to face me with a little shrug, "it's all over--things in the past."

"What's that supposed to mean?" I said bitterly. After all I had suffered on his behalf, after denying myself a closer relationship with Lisa, it was infuriating to think nothing mattered to him any more. "Don't you care about the past at all? Doesn't that marvellous time in Germany mean anything to you?"

"I care about the past all right," he answered mildly, " but I don't want it back, not in the silly nostalgic way you do. I've had to put a lot of things out of my mind, Rich: part of the treatment. Now I want a new world--without the old wickedness."

"That time in Germany means everything to me," I said, feeling hurt. "And it wasn't all wicked--it was lovely."

There was a long pause.

"Well, speaking of wickedness," he smiled, "I suppose you'll be going back to your squadron to take snaps of poor sods about to get a plastering."

"When they let me out of this blasted bed."

He sat down again and produced a cardboard box I had not noticed before.

"I want you to have this," he said, unceremoniously pulling out a paper bag. Something bright and metallic gleamed through slits in the paper. "Just like Christmas, ay?" He tore off the paper to reveal a little model of a Spitfire. It was perfectly made, and set as if banking steeply on its neat pedestal. "Solid silver," said Alex, "and the propeller goes round too: look." He spun it and it whirred expensively.

I was about to speak but he would not let me.

"There's a story behind this," he continued. "Just after you left there was one hell of a show with some Hurricanes. They were going down one after another and we arrived just in the nick of time. Oh yes, serious heroics, this one. If you'd been there you'd have got another gong. I was leading, and frankly there was nothing else to do but go straight in. We drew the Germans off--and pretty hot it was too. Blasted hell out of them--you'd have loved it. Well, a few weeks later, the Hurricane boys brought me this. Very nice of them, too: not the sort of thing you expect, is it? Go on--it's for you."

"I can't take this, Alex," I protested, full of embarrassment. "It's yours. It's quite magnificent…but no, it wouldn't be right, not after all that."

He pressed it upon me, grave and sullen.

"You've got to take it, Rich. You see, it should stay with a flying man...Oh for God's sake, you're the one who's supposed to understand these things." He looked away and drew a deep breath. "In this South Wales posting, I'm on supplies. It...it's a desk job. I want you to have the little beast."

The little silver Spitfire stood catching the light, throwing back off its mirror-polished wings all the crazy horrible glamour of a beautiful machine made for killing. I did not want it in my room, did not want to possess it at all, but knew it must stand for ever somewhere in my life: token of courage, madness, sorrow, love, and loss.

"If you don't feel you can keep this," I said gravely, "Lisa should have it--not me."

Alex picked up his hat.

"Lisa's not here," he croaked, and went out. I did not see him again for the rest of the war.

FIFTEEN

How strange the world seemed: a world without a war. Why, anything might happen now. There was a feeling that one had only to walk out into the street to begin another life. Now we were all free to do what we wanted, or to do what we could, for with this freedom came no guarantees. The world was loose and wild again, but starved and wretched too; mean and poor, with the cracks showing.

I drifted badly, for the compass of my life had been taken away and I had been set down in a ravaged country where the old maps were hardly any use. That which had destroyed so many, had made me live. Was it now my turn to die, slowly, in this dirty, broken world? Or would I be condemned to bear through life the complex guilt of war? I had ploughed the high white fields, had baked and drowned in the burning blue, lord of a drastic power; now, like a tired baby, I must learn to walk upon the sullied ground.

I had hoped for an airline job. In those days, airlines were springing up all over the place: all one needed was an old Dakota and the corner of a hangar. I knew two people who were setting up an airline in this very way, but they had no money to take me on. It would not have been too difficult for me to set one up myself, but I was tired, and somehow unwilling to take the risks I might have found exciting before the war. Now they were the source of something very like fear...and I had had enough of fear. But then I fell prey to a kind of dull fury, and suddenly I didn't think about fear any more, and wished for hard violent action without caring what it might be. I went to the pub in Soho where I knew my acquaintances--I could hardly call them friends--were plotting their airline business. There was Johnnie Baker who used to fly Mosquitos; Reg Adams, who was so tall we never knew how he used to fold himself into a cockpit; and the large, fat, foul-mouthed Freddie Lamb, who was of course known as Baa. I bought them all whiskies.

"Flush, are you?" smiled Johnnie as he thanked me.

I carried the bottle to the table.

"Not particularly," I explained. "It's just my usual tipple."

"Bloody hell," said Baa. "You never used to touch the stuff."

"Well, you can see things have changed," I told him coldly. "You can buy me another one if you like."

"Bloody hell. Talking about boozers, didn't you used to knock about with that chap with a wife in Canada? Ferguson, or something?"

"Fitzgerald."

"That's the fella. Pretty convenient, ay, wife in Canada? Dump the bag over the water and enjoy yourself. Wish I'd married a Canadian; wish I'd married anyone but bloody Pamela. You never married, did you? Lucky sod. But didn't he go potty or something?"

"Something like that. Now what about this airline business?"

"Business, ay?" Baa poured everyone

another drink from my bottle. "The boy wants to talk business."

"We're thinking of starting a round-Britain service," explained Reg.

"That sounds sensible," I said

"As boring as hell, though," put in Baa. "Up to Woolsington, over to Ringway, across to Belfast if you're lucky, then back down here. You'll just be a bloody bus-driver."

"We're not even sure if we'll get a licence," said Johnnie.

"So we made a miserable bunch, don't we?" observed Baa. "Got any money to put in?"

"No," I confessed, "but isn't that what banks are for?"

"No banker in his right mind is going to trust us, old chap."

It seemed that no bank manager did. I met Baa a few weeks later and the scheme had been dropped. He was selling second-hand cars. I don't know why so many of us went into the car business after the war, but I do know that a certain style of dress and manner was instantly recognizable as ex-R.A.F. in hundreds of garages all over the country. We had been the raciest of the Services, and were now expected to cut the same sort of dash in civilian life. The unspoken connection between motor-cars and aeroplanes seemed to provide the opportunity. Now Baa was in the car game...would I like to come in with him?

It turned out to be *for* him rather than *with* him: he gave me the job of hunting down cars to buy cheaply which he would then 'do up' and sell at a profit. They were mostly little Fords, Morrises, and Standards, sometimes a rather better Wolseley or a Riley. I went about this business all over London ruthlessly enough while he paid me on a commission basis, but I couldn't say I enjoyed it or that I liked working for Baa. I simply needed the money. I suffered his coarseness, and found myself becoming coarse too. But what did it matter? What did anything matter? Might as well make money and enjoy a drink.

At the same time my parents were

retiring and selling up the hotel. I was enormously pleased with myself when I stepped into this situation and insisted on meeting the potential buyer: Sidney Palmer, the man behind Palmer's Amusements, which were opening up arcades all along the South coast. My mother agreed that if I secured the sale, she would see I came away with a generous share of what looked like being a large sum of money. My father was kept out of all this; he appeared to be steadily drinking himself to death.

"My boy never went into the family business," my mother told Palmer at the first meeting we had with him, "No, no, he had quite a glittering career in the Air Force you know, right through the Battle of Britain, then he was seriously wounded, and decorated too. Now he's become a very successful motor-dealer. Oh yes, very superior motor-cars. He knows simply everybody in London."

"Really, Mister Dellow."

Palmer knew exactly what I was, the sort of cars I dealt in, and the sort of people I knew in London. He would turn that to his own advantage if he could--but I knew he wanted the hotel and could pay handsomely for it. He also knew that I was quite aware of his own beginnings selling ice-cream and penny-in-the-slot end-of-the-pier machines. I would turn that to my advantage. This surely marked the end of that tawdry life I had so long sought to escape: first through Alex, then through flying, then through Lisa, then through the war. Now it was ending through a fat businessman in a bad suit. I would screw the last penny out of Palmer and escape it for ever. My mother would be well off, and my share of the money could free me from Baa.

"Well now," Palmer continued, "if you strike a sensible bargain with me and let me have this old place for nothing more than it's worth, you'll be able to buy yourself and your mother a nice Rolls-Royce--or do I detect you're Bentley man? And you Mrs. Dellow: a life of ease, no more worries about a crumbling building or a lazy staff." He allowed himself a benign chuckle, like a fat shopkeeper bestowing sweets on the children of favourite customers. He gave his self-made pomposity full rein. "Moreover, everyone in the family, young and old, uncles and cousins, nephews and nieces, grandchildren, babes in arms--I'll see they all get Lifetime Passes to any Palmer's Amusement Arcade in the country. Wherever they go for a seaside holiday, they'll have you to thank for your far-sightedness. Now--what do you say?"

"I think there's a great deal still to discuss, Mister Palmer. My mother may not be familiar with the latest property prices but I know perfectly well that your original offer of four-thousand pounds is well below the true value of the hotel."

"I assure you it's generous," blustered Palmer, "positively generous. The place is somewhat delapidated, to put it mildly."

"But since you're going to pull it down and build an Amusement Arcade, that's hardly the point, is it?"

"I didn't say I was going to pull it down. Every site is different. In this case we might very well retain the shell of the building and re-fit the interior."

"I very much doubt that. We all know the building is in a very old-fashioned style: nothing like the usual image of Palmer's Amusements. You'd be crazy to pour money into it when you could demolish it and build from new. Much better spend the money on a fair purchase price."

By this time Palmer was furious. He was pacing about, looking at the floor, turning pink with rage and frustration...but I knew he wouldn't tell me what he really thought of me in front of my mother.

"Then perhaps you'll tell me--only in your own opinion of course--what constitutes a fair price for an outdated and ill-kept hotel in a not-particularly-fashionable seaside resort. And you'll have to bear in mind these are difficult times, just after a war, with a peculiar new government in office--and don't think I voted for them. No sensible businessman's going to be throwing money around. Well?"

"Oooh," I said airily, "at least ten-thousand."

We got six…but not before I had to bring an estate-agent and solicitor into the battle. It seemed like a fortune at the time, and my mother retired to a very luxurious bungalow. With my share I could have started a number of new lives, but I bided my time. I was not exactly sure what I was waiting for.

Very occasionally, I would see Alex. It must have been excruciatingly difficult for him with Lisa still somewhere in Germany and his recovery still incomplete. I wasn't much of a friend to him, my own life still in dull chaos. The money from Palmer was in the bank, but I still lived in poor rooms; the silver Spitfire on a windowsill where it caught the light and brought sharp memories.

Images of Lisa in the Germany we had once known came sweetly to me, seeming to tug at the very middle of my soul. I saw her sitting on her great white bed, holding out her arm for me to release the bracelet, smiling from the shadows of her luscious hair, the dress night-purple, colour of a dream, smiling to welcome me, to forgive me, to love me. I saw her standing against the lights of the garden-party, reaching down to pour me the wine--but that image was suffused with a sense of departure and loss and the end of our innocence and the pain of the war and I tried to banish it in favour of the first. I had loved her then as she sat on her bed, and she had loved me: not exactly innocently, or completely, or happily--for she had been engaged to Alex and I could only be the shy stranger--but more powerfully and tenderly than any other love we might have known. That had been the best love--before anything real had to be done about it. Now we were plunged into a world where actions overruled the dreams--yet the dreams came back, were pure, would not be extinguished.

When the time came for Alex to collect Lisa from Germany I did not go with him. In his old way he had arranged a meeting in London and quite casually told me that he was going over in a few days' time. I should have been beside myself with joy. This, after all, was the end of the war that had kept us all apart. It proved she was alive and able to return to England; and here was the imminent reunion of my friends, a resumption of the life so violently cast aside. Here was a chance to see Lisa again, to seek her forgiveness, to bathe in her loveliness, to free myself from, guilt by facing her, acknowledge her happiness with Alex, and go my own way at last. But all I said was:

"That's wonderful."

"But she's not very well," Alex went on. "Bronchitis, as far as I can tell, or inflamed lungs. Pretty severe, anyway, although she's out of hospital now. She had a rough time in Berlin."

"Berlin?" I was horrified. "What the hell was she doing there?"

"Well, that's a long story, Rich--and it's still not altogether clear." He began to speak as if he were de-briefing after a raid: mechanically, without apparent emotion, but I could tell he was ravaged by anxiety. "She started off living in the South, just as I thought she would, and that seemed all right while it lasted. Her aunts thought it was terribly shocking that she was married to an Englishman without being ashamed of the fact, but I expect she coped quite well with that sort of nonsense--and of course kept it quiet outside the family."

"Of course," I murmured, remembering what keeping it quiet had done to Alex, and to myself.

"Anyway, it seemed to be safe enough for a couple of years. I still haven't been able to find out exactly what she did and where she lived, but it's coming out gradually. But then she made the ghastly mistake of going to Berlin. You know her father was big in the banks over there. Well, he was called to Berlin towards the end and then was very ill himself. That's when I imagine Lisa travelled up from the South to see him."

"God--and she was there right at the

end?"

"That's it: the Yanks, the Russians, the French, ourselves--everyone converging on Berlin, and she's stuck in the middle of it. Her father died, by the way."

Alex lit a cigarette. He still smoked in that languid way, as if nothing had happened... while appalling images of what really had happened sank into my mind.

"So she was left there by herself?"

"As far as I can tell. I don't know what Werner was doing, or any of her other relations. It gets sillier still, Rich. She was captured by the Russians."

"What?"

"Well, arrested. I'm not sure why, but I can guess. With her connections she'd look well and truly on the wrong side, wouldn't she?"

"This is monstrous!" I exclaimed. "They thought she was a spy?"

"I don't know. Possibly. There hasn't been much in the way of letters--you can't be sure what's censored and what gets through these days. I think the craziest thing of all is that she convinced them she *was* a spy, but for *our* side: you know, married to an Englishman and all that. I still don't know exactly what happened myself. She got out, though--this is true, Rich--she played the piano and sang Russian folk songs to the Commie officer in charge." Alex could not resist a smile. "I don't know if she had a hand on his knee, but I wouldn't put it past her. What the hell--they let her go." I was speechless. Alex grinned over his cigarette. "You couldn't make it up if you had to, could you?"

"I can't believe it," I said at last. This was a whole new Lisa, fighting her own terrifying undercover war while we had been fighting ours more or less in the open--and with such dramatic twists and turns it seemed scarcely credible.

"But the worst thing, Rich," Alex cut in upon my thoughts, "is that she's ill. From what I can tell, Berlin turned into a stinking hole and she somehow had to survive in it. I'm not surprised she went under. As I say, she hasn't been much of a letter-writer, but I know she's back in the South now, at the big house: not as grand as in our day, but it's still there in one piece. She's with her mother, having to rest all the time, but apparently fit enough to travel. She'll be glad to get out." He reinforced the understatement by tapping a crinkled letter in his pocket, but would not let me read it. "Come with me," he said in his new, quiet way.

A riot of indecision burst through me. The offer was there--I had only to take it up and once more I might revel in her loveliness. And she was ill. She might want me, need me at last. I desperately wanted to see her, prove to myself she was all right, comfort her, celebrate her escape, help her start a new life of love and safety.

"No," I said quickly, "it wouldn't be right. You two will need to be alone."

Alex smiled and we looked at each other. I imagined Lisa nearly dying in hospital, not breathing properly--and felt my own breath rasp in my lungs. If I had had the courage to arrange her stay in the hotel when war was breaking out she might never have had to suffer any of this. I imagined her in the dangerous rubble of Berlin, walking about in a shabby coat and worn shoes when she might have been quite safe in England. I imagined her being interrogated by the Russians, and created my own version of Alex's extravagant picture of her release. It seemed ridiculous, and my mind flashed back to more solid images: Lisa in her bedroom, at the dinner-table, playing tennis, her lovely hair swinging in the sun. That was real, everything else felt improbable...but that had to be real, too. My own story in the war would have sounded improbable if I had been forced to tell it as Alex had told Lisa's. My mind settled upon the new realities. Would she really want to see me when she was ill? What could I mean to her that would do her any good now? I would not go--but should I? I had failed to help her before the war; was I now failing to help her after it? But this time she had Alex to help her--her own husband, after all. He was already on his way. Suddenly I did not want to see her. I felt empty, and did not want their love to fill me. I had no desire to struggle through an occupied country, undergo a cruel parody of that journey we had made before the war, did not wish to see what we had done to Germany, or what Germany had done to Lisa. Yet the thought of her illness was terrible to me. The thought of standing outside the marriage was worse, watching the reunion, unable to be part of it.

"Give her all my love," I said.

I might as well have made the journey, for Alex took me through it in the letters he wrote. He had flown to Düsseldorf and was now held up in the Rhineland, waiting for clearance to take a train South. He had been put up in the so-called *British Club*--social headquarters for the occupying forces and their families--and said there was nothing to do but dance with the officers' plain and horsey wives and write to me. Outside, in ghastly contrast, most of the town had been reduced to rubble: it was piled up on the sides of the streets and shattered families lived in cellars with the stench of death. On rackety walls and fences, thin paper notices were posted, advertising clothes and books. The clothes were not to wear, they were to pile on beds in place of the blankets the people did not have. The books were not to read, they were to burn to keep the people warm. The notices were also asking for news of missing persons--from what Alex wrote, Germany seemed to be full of missing persons. Then, after this letter, came a quick note to say that he had got his train. There was to be a family reunion in Bavaria; he might be months, even stay there a year. Anything was possible. I was not to count on seeing them for a long time; he'd be in touch when they came back; for the moment, they were resting in the Alps. I could almost smell the flowers and the mountain air and began to wish, with a painful heart, that I had accepted Alex's easy invitation.

Meanwhile, I had a living to make, and important decisions were forced upon me. Baa had done well and was all set to open a new motor-showroom. He took me to see it: an old warehouse in the East End. Workmen were putting in large windows on the ground floor and cladding grimy brickwork with sheets of mock-marble in the modern style. I chuckled grimly to myself. As yet I could see no large and garish sign proclaiming this was *Lamb's Motors*, but I knew there soon would be. A vile wind blew rancid smells from the river.

"Well, what d'you think, old fella? Bit of a dump but you'll be amazed what a flashy frontage will do. There's money to be made down here, ay? No bangers, mind you. This is all going to be good stuff."

"Is it really?"

"Well, the odd cheap little Ford or something just for quick turnover, and possibly one or two classy types--you know, a Rover or two, an MG perhaps, but nothing too ridiculous, no Jags or Bentleys. All good affordable middle class cars--you know the stuff that sells, that people stretch themselves for. Now if you pull your socks up, keep off the booze, and do some rooting around for a bargain or two, you'll have a decent living here, and your old chum to thank for it. Now what d'you say to that, ay?"

I smelled the river; looked into the sky. Nothing and no-one could tell me any more that such a creature as Baa Lamb should determine my life.

"I say stuff it, Baa."

His big face dropped. I enjoyed hurting him--felt he didn't deserve any better.

"What?" he blurted. "After all I've done for you? You come out of the Air Force on your uppers, you and that barmy Ferguson fella..."

"Fitzgerald."

"That's him: the one with the wife in Canada. Funny how we never saw her; never saw you with any bint either. Always suspected the pair of you...pair of bloody queers...bunch of Nancy Boys the lot of you, and bloody ungrateful into the bargain. I'll see you in the gutter before I lend you a fiver…"

"Shut up, Baa, before somebody with more sense knocks your block off. Like I said, stuff it. And stuff you."

I walked away into the raw wind.

I saw my bank manager, leased a shop in Mill Hill, put a Morris in the window, and sold it the same day. By the end of the following week I had sold another three. This was easy, and I called nobody boss. Within two months my drab existence was transformed. I had an ex-R.A.F. mechanic and a seventeen-year-old boy working for me. We took over the neighbouring shop, knocked out the windows, and installed folding glass doors. Now we could display seven cars, had room for a small workshop at the back, and I could drive around in a brand new Triumph Roadster. Fun had come back into my life.

A wonderful day came when I drove past Baa's place. Sure enough, a sign proclaimed *Lamb's Motors*, but it didn't look very prosperous. I caught a glimpse of Baa himself wandering about inside between some very ordinary-looking cars, his hands in the pockets of a not-too-classy coat. I had the cheek to nose the Triumph through the back lane and, just as I had expected, saw a pair of sagging-axled Fords waiting to be 'done up' and brought inside. If I had been going to buy a second-hand car, I wouldn't have touched this place with the proverbial barge-pole. My handsomely polished Triumph emerged on to the main road. There was nobody about. I put her into first and crawled past the open doors of the showroom. I gave a double blast on the horn, and gave Baa the old two fingers as he turned to face me. Then I laughed openly to myself and put my foot down, leaving a crisp roar in his ears. I suddenly felt that peacetime was suiting me very nicely.

SIXTEEN

Shortly after this, I married. There had been a small fire at the motor-showroom, and the insurance company sent their representative to assess the damage. To everyone's amazement it was a young woman who stepped daintily in high-heeled shoes across the splintered floorboards, poked a spanner into blackened plaster, and ran her manicured fingers over the scorched and bubbled paintwork of an Austin which had caught the flames. She was what women of my mother's generation would have called 'very forward', with no inhibitions and a loud cheery laugh. She stayed for tea, which she drank chummily out of the mechanic's mug, and soon we were talking about her parents' home in Cambridge and her elder brother who had been killed outside Tobruk. It crossed my mind to explain my stiff shoulder by the story of my having almost been killed outside Dover, but I told her nothing of that--nor did it seem to matter that I passed off all my life with a smile and a shrug and a token story of flying in the war.

"Well, goodness me. A real Brylcreem Boy at last! It must be a very quiet life selling cars after all that excitement in the Air Force, Mister Dellow."

"It has its moments," I said.

"Still, you have a nice place here." She rattled her tea-mug on a saucer which didn't fit and sat perkily with her knees and ankles together. "Is business good?"

"Good enough," I answered. "At least it was until this mess."

"Oh come now, Mister Dellow. We'll soon have you back to normal." She smiled like a doctor telling me to put my shirt back on. "Why, once this claim is through you'll be able to fill the place up with brand new Austins!"

"Really?" I said. "It's going to be that much, is it?"

"I'm looking for a new car myself," she hurried on with a toss of the head. "But mind you, it has to be a pretty little thing: a real girl's car. You might be able to help me."

"I'll see what I can do, Miss Fletcher."

We shook hands.

"Fine," she flashed me her most glamorous smile, "but you'll have to call me Ruby if you're going to find me that car."

"All right then. I'm Richard, but everyone calls me Rich...not that I am, of course."

"You will be."

We laughed and shook hands again-- but I knew we wanted to kiss each other.

It was not long before she had contrived another visit to the showroom, and was back again to see the builders repairing my wall. Soon we were meeting regularly for meals in London and for drives into the countryside of Suffolk and Cambridgeshire. Then we would spend the week-end at an inn, sharing drinks in the bar and each other in bed. She had no power to possess my past, nor had I any desire to confess it. She was entirely of the present; and her neat brown hair, her painted lips and her sherry-coloured eyes were all the more exciting for being firmly set upon the future. Eventually I found the car--a new little Ford--and had it secretly re-sprayed her favourite colour of dark yellow and re-carpeted to match. She squealed with delight when she saw it, piled me into the passenger seat, and insisted on speeding through the West End, honking the horn and waving at astonished pedestrians. The car became my wedding present to her.

Ruby and I felt free and happy together--and suddenly richer, too. She immediately put some money into the business and re-arranged all the insurance on the showroom and the cars. She said we should buy shares in the larger insurance companies, promptly sold them again--dealing in shares had hitherto been a complete mystery to me--and introduced me to representatives of finance companies so I could begin to sell cars on hire-purchase. This allowed my customers to afford more expensive cars and dramatically increased our profit. I was content to let Ruby get on with all this--she was so good at it--and to gleefully show me larger figures than anything which had so far passed through my books.   Within a few months of being married we had bought a second showroom, well out of town up the North Road at Hatfield. With its gleaming white stucco frontage and plate-glass windows, the new showroom was perfect for selling more expensive cars, and we stocked it with Rovers, Armstrong-Siddeleys, Jaguars, Daimlers, and even a couple of Citroëns brought over from France which gave an exotic look to the place. It did excellent business too. We were soon thinking of moving into a new detached house in Hatfield to be closer to the source of our new prosperity. Perhaps for the first time in my life I felt I might learn to be at ease.

At the time I had proposed to Ruby I felt nothing of any worth was likely to happen in my life without her. I had lost Lisa and Alex, come through the war, and struggled into peace with little hope and less honour. I was, as they said in American pictures, 'all washed up'. Then suddenly here was this vivacious girl all ready for me: "morning, noon and night," she winked. She too had had her difficult times, and confessed that a businessgirl's life could be desperately lonely and even dangerous without a loving man. So I was pleased and proud to love her and marry her. She promised a kind of fun even better than succeeding in business. "And we'll do that as well," she said, nibbling my nose.

I felt good because I had made her happy and released her enormous sense of fun into a secure relationship. She was a genuinely funny person with a great capacity for laughter that could cause uproar at home. Sometimes I would come in to find her in my pyjamas--"Just for a lark!" she would yell, waving to nonplussed neighbours across the street. Sometimes her best friend Delia would be in for tea--and rowdy rude schoolgirls-on-holiday teas they must have been, with the two of them painting each other's nails and doing their hair and running into the garden half naked. I would put my coat in the hall and just see Delia's bare legs scampering upstairs, Ruby tossing her shoes up after her, both of them giggling at me through the banisters, and Delia whispering "Ooh, he's a peach, isn't he?" or "I wish I had him to make tea for--he can put a bun in my oven any day." Then Ruby would slap her and there would be swearing and squealing and making-up and Delia would eventually come downstairs straightening the seams of her stockings and saying "'Bye, Richard" with her face red and a new laugh in her throat from the smutty joke she'd been sharing with Ruby. I grinned to myself when I realised I had killed people in a war, lived on the brink of death myself with foul-mouthed frightened men, seen and experienced just about everything war was supposed to throw at a man, yet could still be embarrassed by these two. I had never expected any of this--but it was glorious fun. And why not? Ruby would sing snatches from Hollywood musicals, excruciatingly badly but with infectious glee, strike a pose in my trilby; and all the time effortlessly, cheekily, and with great good humour make herself available for sex: coaxing me, teasing me, loving me. It was real love too, in a giggling, rough-and-tumble way I had never expected to find nor be able to enjoy. But we did enjoy it together. When she caught me worrying about the business or suspected me of brooding upon the past, she would dig me in the ribs, nuzzle my ear with her wet red lips, whisper "too bloody serious", and soon we would be rolling on the floor, rubbing our skin together and making laughing love.

At first I wanted to tell her everything about myself, confess everything, explain everything--then drew back from doing so. With Ruby, everything had to be new. She threw out our old furniture and replaced it. She arranged parties and filled the house with her business contacts and her insurance company friends: all of whom I had never met before and was unlikely to meet again, for the next party would be peopled by a new crowd of acquaintances. If she was not interested in her own past, she was unlikely to show any enthusiasm for mine. The few tales I told of life in the squadrons didn't seem to interest her beyond a superficial excitement which, if anything, annoyed me. I tried very hard to describe the horrors of the crash, but that ended up as a joke too, with Ruby feeling my legs with all the fascination of a schoolgirl in a Biology class, trying to find the breaks. She knew of my friendship with Alex, but quite plainly did not understand what he had suffered, nor did she seem to appreciate the depth of our old pre-war relationship. I could not blame her for this, and did not, but I spoke less and less of my former life. Although she knew the barest outline of the story, I especially could not bring myself to tell her any more about Lisa and my time in Germany, could not have her enter that sweet valley, so different from the blaring, noisome world we now seemed to inhabit. And so in the slightest, or perhaps the greatest ways, I began to deceive my wife.

One day the telephone rang and I heard Alex yelling into my ear.

"We're back!" he cried. "We're back, you old moneymaking sod! We're in a new place outside Canterbury. Come for a meal and bring a bottle. No--bring a crate!"

"Who was that?" asked Ruby, coming through the hall, her hands full with plates for the next party.

"Someone from the Spitfire squadron," I said, smiling at the baldness of my statement. "There's going to be a reunion."

"Oh Gawd," she chirped, holding up the plates to pass me. "You'll all be propping up the bar and shooting down the Germans again, twiddling your 'tashes and showing off your medals. Are you going?"

"I think I'd better," I said.

SEVENTEEN

On a cool and sunlit afternoon I drove across London and slid the long-nosed Triumph down the Dover road. The bombsites were blooming in their white and purple, and everywhere the sunlight spread its balm of peace. Even the brash unfinished buildings, gaunt and unlovable though they were, seemed for the first time to hold a promise of the new. 'We have had our fill of destruction,' they seemed to say, 'let us forget the past, let us build and grow.' The war was far away, away and behind me. How foolish I had been to nurse its terrors, to pursue its arid way of death. How foolish also to be sucked into the crass and shabby lives of men like Baa Lamb; and how narrow-minded to feel trapped by my marriage to Ruby. The future held all kinds of possibilities: here was freedom, here was life.

As soon as I was clear of the suburbs I stopped the car and rolled back its hood. Now the Summer wind came freely to me, and the hiss of the road sang of delights which only days ago could scarcely have been hoped for. I have come through, I told myself, we have all come through. The grit of wasted years is shaken off and nothing will stain our happiness now. Death and horror have been left behind; now, whatever happens, I must glory in our new-found peace.

Yellow fields slipped past me, with here and there the bright white flash of chalk flaking through thin grass. Years since I had been down this way: this was the countryside whose patchwork I had known so well from the air. The wartime airfields were somewhere on my right, but today their memories held no fascination--it was the trilling of the birds and the rich soft country smells which claimed my senses, the joys of love and friendship which filled my soul. The pale blue sky whose stars I could not see, the rustling tunnel-top of trees, each bird which flashed above and sang, each spark of spirit which leapt within me--all seemed to burn with one enriching flame and witness new awakenings.

'I shall take hold of fresh and open honesty,' I thought, half way between tears and laughter. 'It is enough that we have all survived, and that my friends can be lovers again. It is incredibly good fortune. I shall not mar it by a secret lust.'

Then I was nosing the car round the flinty walls of Canterbury and out along the straight Roman road between the orchards. Now my heart began to beat with an expectancy akin to fear, and my feet moved unsteadily across the pedals. This meeting was already too much: a meeting of ghosts set down in lively sunshine, unbearably bright. How would she be? How would she be? Farms and hedges flashed by; then a white, half-boarded house was upon me with--yes it was!--Lisa at an upstairs window waving a suntanned arm. She carried all of Europe, all of history, all of my life in that one, light, simple wave; showered it gently down upon me as I stopped the car. Uncontrollable passions burst inside my parched soul; welled up like music through every part of my being. I had no strength to get out of the car...so they came about me as I fumbled for the door: my old lean friend with his shiny hair, his lovely wife with the deep, dark eyes. She was back from Berlin; she had escaped, ill but alive; now she was here, in front of me, looking perfectly healthy and smiling merrily as if nothing had happened. Could this be real? She did look older now, for the long, girlish hair had been swept softly round her face in a more sophisticated style. It still seemed to hold, like some glorious offering of light, every colour known to Man. And, if it were possible, she was more beautiful than ever. Illness and hardship and fear seemed to have left no marks upon her--had all my anxiety been in vain? Surely she was changed, must be changed, and yes--she did look a little older in the brilliant sunshine. Yet everything about her was so delightfully familiar.

"You are safe then?" I breathed, as if by putting into words my long astonishment, its wonder might be grasped.

"Yes! Yes!" she laughed, and kissed my face. I was not ashamed to weep with happiness.

On that day, like no other I had experienced, the three of us drank in one another's presence as if, in dying, we had suddenly been offered the water of Life. We talked for hours, but not about the war, or the long separation, or the horrors of Berlin, or the madness that had stalked their love. Those things were best expressed in silence, and I could see at once that they had been stretched and broken on the wheel of intimate confession, and that, in beginning to heal, they had released a flood of compassion that was almost holy and not to be deflowered in simple talk. Of course I wanted to know the details of Lisa's time in Berlin and the fantastic tale of her escape from the Russians, but this was played down by both of them. I did learn that she had somehow convinced the Russian commander she was against the Nazis and that, through her marriage to an English airman, she had some connection with British Intelligence: a preposterous story which I could not imagine being swallowed by any Russian commander clever enough to be taking over a sector of Berlin. But it seemed I should have to believe it, and not probe too deeply into areas of experience that might still be painful to Lisa. Returning the conversation to our post-war lives, we did not even say much about Ruby, although there was some banter that I was now a married man, wealthy and successful, and when were they going to meet the woman who had tamed wild man Rich? We spoke mostly of the long journey back to England and of this house. Through talking in this way, and from the silences too, I learned the truth of separated love, and how the most wonderful thing for both of them had been this simple coming together, discovering they had both survived the destruction of that innocence which I too had shared and lost.

They had not been here very long, but Lisa had already wrought enchantment through the house. It was freshly decorated with pretty curtains and covers on the chairs. The smells of coffee and of perfume hung in every room, like the doors of a dream which opened on a youth not quite my own. For all it was Summer, a basket of logs stood in the fireplace with apples and oranges resting among them and, the final German touch, little bunches of woodland moss.

"Remember the blossom boughs?" I said, daring to pat her shoulder.

"Yes," she answered with a smile...but we did not talk too much about our time in Germany.

I sat weakly in a soft chair beside the unlit fire--in love once more with Lisa. After my joyous shock and peculiar embarrassment, I was now simply consumed with wonder. It was as if I had lived right through the war and everything else that had happened to me at an inconceivable pitch of intensity, just waiting to see her. When it had happened I could not at first quite take it in, but now, after so long, I was able to wind down like a spring and relax into the new delight of it.

I had brought Champagne but we did not open it. Alex got up to make the tea. It was curious to see him about this domestic business, not looking once at Lisa, as if he had been given a little job to do while she remained very much in charge, bringing platefuls of bread and cakes from the kitchen. He was married to her, living in the same house with her every day, making love with her, sharing everything--yet he did not seem dazzled by any of these wonders. The marvel had become ordinary to him: a new tragedy I had not anticipated... but a moment's thought told me I should have expected nothing else. I *was* dazzled--and suddenly my love for Lisa seemed the more realistic and developed, where previously I had always considered it the more boyish and ineffectual. As Lisa bent across the table, setting out the meal, I thought: 'she has grown into the complete woman'. This phrase came into my mind without my truly knowing what it meant--but as she moved about the room, and Alex continued to tell me about his new job as an estate agent and I glimpsed my car standing in the sunlight outside the little flower-boxed windows, I suddenly saw all that was light and bright in Lisa, the pure pale colours of her hair banishing all that might be dark and evil. She had matured with true grace; was older, certainly, but neither frumpish nor matronly--which, I realized with a private smile, had been two possibilities I had secretly feared. She did not look as if she had ever been a refugee; for someone who had survived the fall of Berlin and been seized by the Russians and suffered a wasting disease of the lungs, she looked healthy and serene. Most wonderful was her glowing aura; something other than physical beauty, but which a plain woman could not have possessed. Like music, she sang of all the loveliness of the world. Innocent of these things, yet wise-- her wisdom piercing me to light a life at which I had been afraid to look--she walked on Earth as a woman of the myth-worlds and of this, more delicate than flowers yet as practical as strong arms bringing food from the kitchen... right beside me, too, as effortlessly as the sunshine, and as miraculous.

At last, as blackbirds sang from tall trees across the road, I went out to the car and brought back a parcel. Inside was the little silver Spitfire.

"This is yours," I said to Alex. "I've

had it for too long--high time it was back with the right person."

"Oooh," said Lisa, intercepting the gift before Alex had a chance to reclaim it, "what a beautiful piece of work." She turned it carefully in her hands. "Where did you get it, Richard?"

This response astonished me. I was shocked she did not know, and I felt instantly embarrassed. It was as if her question--which she had asked quite innocently--had blown grim smoke into the room.

"You mean he hasn't told you about this?" I looked at Alex for an explanation, but should have known better than to find one. He was looking beyond me, trying to smile. "Oh, well," I continued shakily, "there's a great tale behind this little thing." I knew at once I should not tell it. "It, er, it was a present to Alex from another squadron. I've been looking after it all these years."

Alex turned away while Lisa put the silver Spitfire on top of their radio cabinet and, like anyone who ever handled it, spun the propeller and smiled to see it mill the air. It whirred softly to a standstill, and once more the blackbirds were the only sound... but the little sculpture looked more alive than ever, trim tail cocked upwards towards the window, dagger wings making a wicked gleam of the rich evening light.

"You have brought good things," said Lisa to me, kissing my cheeks. I was not so sure. I had embarrassed Alex with the silver Spitfire. For some reason he had not told Lisa about his rescue of the Hurricane pilots. Of course it was all so long ago--and surely they had had more urgent alarms to deal with. But now I had opened the pointless wound of his heroism, and perhaps with it all the other scars he bore. What other tales had not been told? What other dread secrets festered undeclared? And yet, in our long goodbyes at the dusty roadside, there was no bitterness. There was instead an unnerving detachment about Alex, as if he were watching all this light and happiness aware that he could never be a complete part of it. This was not the heat of his wartime madness, nor the terrifying calm of his supposed cure. A strange Winter had entered his soul. There was something else, too--something uniquely inside myself, not part of Alex, nor of Lisa. It was an old worm of shame and anger and resented guilt, turning deep inside me, gnawing at my happiness. When I had rolled up to this door, I truly had not expected to rediscover it, had actually forgotten it until the little silver Spitfire had stabbed its wings back into my memory, and with them the tormented concealment of an unconfessed murder. But now, as I waved and pulled the starter, I knew I had still not forgiven Alex for killing that German in the water.

"Right, Mister Wilson." It was a sunny Saturday morning and my customers had come into the office. "You're quite happy with the hire-purchase agreement?"

"Absolutely. You've been most helpful."

"And you, Mrs. Wilson--you like the car?"

"It's lovely."

"Then in that case," I smiled, "it's just a matter of some boring paperwork."

The Wilsons were decent people, only a little older than myself, but with the appearance of being middle-aged. They had come through the war, their house and their childless marriage intact, a secure peacetime stretching ahead. It was time for a new lease of life and a new car to go with it. I had sold them a handsome Riley, a model that managed to look stately and sporting at the same time. This one was unusual, in dove grey. Most Rileys were black. Its maroon leather seats were clean and fragrant, and my mechanic Nick had repainted the wheels and polished the radiator to a gleaming finish. I almost wished I had been buying it myself--which is the best possible way to sell a car. I was smiling to myself as I filled in the forms when Mrs. Wilson broke in upon my thoughts.

"I must say we've been very pleased with the way you've treated us, Mister Dellow. I'm going to recommend you to some friends of ours--you know," she turned to her husband, "Elsie and John." He nodded. "They're looking for another car. I know they live in Croydon now but I'm sure they'd travel this far for a good reliable car and such nice treatment. It's difficult to know who to trust these days."

"Thank you very much," I said, genuinely affected by what she had said. "It's very kind of you to say so."

Yes, the Wilsons were decent people. Surely they had no guilty secrets. Surely Mr.Wilson had not married the wrong woman; surely he did not love another man's wife; had not, through his own weakness, condemned the girl he had loved to a life in wartime Germany, capture by the Russians, and pleurisy in the ruins of Berlin. Surely he did not have a friend who had killed an unarmed man in the water, cracked up, and lied to his wife--that same beloved woman who had been forced to suffer. Decent people, honest people, ordinary people, with nothing exotic or special or peculiar about them. Happy people. I watched Wilson signing his money away to please his wife with the car, and was glad: not for Wilson's money--for if they had not bought the Riley someone else would surely have done so; such cars never 'stuck'. No, I was glad for what they had shown me: the vileness and shabbiness of deceit in my own life, which I was now determined to purge. I could be honest and decent too, despite this terrible unsettling peace, my deals with Baa and Palmer, the greed and wickedness I had seen and which had become part of me, and my hollow marriage to Ruby. From now on I could tell the truth and face it being told back to me. I filled in the form, asked Wilson to sign, and was given a glittering smile from Mrs. Wilson. Simple, happy people. They loved each other, told the truth, paid up without bitterness, and smiled when they could. Suddenly, I could be the same. A hire-purchase form lay on the desk in front of me, but I realised, between its lines, that I had been composing a letter to Lisa.

"Nick!" I shouted. "A full tank of

petrol for Mr. and Mrs. Wilson--on the house!"

When the Wilson's had driven their Riley away and Nick had gone home, I stayed in the office to write the letter. I told Lisa I had loved her ever since we first met at the big house in Germany, and that scarcely a day had gone by since then when I had not thought of her with longing. I begged her forgiveness for refusing to persuade my mother to take her into the hotel when war broke out. I told her I had made terrible mistakes in my life and feared to face the truth; now I was facing it and telling her, because she was the only person who could hope to understand, who would know that I had never wished to cause her pain or hardship, and that I bore her only love down all these years. I was delighted to find her well and safely home in England, but would regret for ever that I had failed to show my love and win her before she married Alex. These confessions were the most important words I had ever committed to paper, but they were written without art or guile, and did not seem to take very long. I looked at the letter and thought it a poor prosaic thing, far from the chivalric declaration the remains of my boyish romantic nature would have wished to deliver. But there was nothing else to say, and I was incapable of finding any other way to say even this much. I found a stamp in the desk drawer and posted the letter on the way home--before I allowed myself time to revise it or regret it or not post it at all. My immediate fear was that Alex would see it, perhaps open it for Lisa if they habitually handled or read each other's mail, perhaps see her face change as she read it and demand to know its contents, even wrench it from her in a fit of fury. But what the hell, it was only the truth. In a way it might ruin us all, but in another it might make us whole. I had not always practised the philosophy, but knew that the truth would clear the air, however painfully. One could not get lower or simpler than the truth; better to bear the pain of telling it and rebuild anew.

Certainly there had been lies for long enough.

Days went by, and of course I could think only of my letter and how it might have affected Lisa. What was she doing and thinking? How would she reply? Would she reply at all? If not, would I have the courage to write again? Had Alex found it? What would he do? And if my letter had caused chaos in that house, there was little peace in my own. Ruby was re-arranging the kitchen.

She busied herself round the room, endlessly bright and enthusiastic, amiable even when scolding me.

"...and we need a much bigger oven, Rich. Surely we can afford the best now, for all the entertaining I'm going to be doing. You're such a stick-in-the-mud sometimes: all this money and you're still quite happy living in the Dark Ages. I don't know. Are all men the same? Can you tell me that? Anyway, there are some lovely new electric cookers now, you know. Delia's just got one--I've seen it. We can't let her and that dimwit of a husband of hers have better things than us. There now," she beamed, triumphant before the re-arranged shelves. "How about a trip to the electric company next week for a brand new streamlined electric cooker?" Later, I was to realise she had been years ahead of the television commercials.

"All right," I said.

"You might sound a bit more enthusiastic about it," she chirped. "It's going to make our parties so much easier, and you'll have to learn to work it to help me out sometimes. I'm sure they're dead easy, though. If you can fly a 'plane you can work a cooker."

"All right."

At last the letter came. Thankfully, Lisa had addressed it to me at the showroom, and I did not have to intercept it at home before Ruby questioned me about the strange envelope. Alone in the office on a quiet morning, I faced my future.
Trenley House,
Canterbury Road,

Bramling,
Kent.
May 5th.
My Dear Richard,

Thank you for your long letter. I spent much time considering how to reply, and whether to reply at all, because it had upset me so much, but as you see I am writing to you now because I too must tell you the truth of how things are with me and between us.

Like any woman would be, I am flattered to think you have found me beautiful and a special person, but you must realise and accept that I am married to Alex and have gone through so much with him that I cannot be what you imagine. Our holiday in Germany was so long ago, before the war changed everything, and I am surprised that a person as sensible as yourself and one who must have seen and suffered so much is not able to accept that everything must be different now. I do not see how any of us can go back to that. I do not think we should want to. We must be practical and move forward. You are successful in your business and, from what Alex tells me, you are also married to a good wife and a clever businesswoman. You should not do anything to spoil the good life you have made. In Berlin I almost died. Terrible things happened to me and I was lucky to escape after the Russians occupied part of the city. I know what I am saying when I tell you not to spoil life; good things are so fragile.

I know you regret your decision not to let me stay at the hotel, but also I know how impossible it was for you to let me stay and I understand that it was not really in your power to decide who should stay in your mother's hotel. Since you ask for it so much, of course I do forgive you, but think there is so little to forgive and that you have been such a good friend in many different ways that it is really foolish to be so upset. You must not feel so guilty: all that was such a long time ago and we have all survived in our different ways. You have held on to your sad feelings for too long I think. You must move forward.

I do not think Alex should know about these letters, and I shall not tell him you have written to me. It would not be good for you to write again in this way, but I do not see any reason why we all should not continue to meet like sensible adult people who are good friends.

I shall always think of you with great kindness and affection.

Sincerely yours, Lisa.

My first reaction was a simple, selfish fury. How could she be 'practical and move forward' and ask me to do the same? Had she misunderstood me all these years? Had she felt nothing? How could she wipe out all that emotion in a few simple words? How could she blame me for holding on to my love when it was all that had been of any value to me? She forgave me, or said she did, yet it seemed to carry no weight, for she had dismissed my guilt as mere folly. It had not been important to her and had obviously not marked her life as it had marked mine. She had got on with the business of survival and managed it without suffering the regrets that had plagued me. And she thought of me with great kindness and affection. She had not been able to write *love*.

Then I began to accept what she was telling me. I was a romantic fool; she was a practical woman living in the reality I should have learned to face by now. I was immature and ultimately selfish--even stupid. I had no right to Lisa and no right to pursue or embarrass her. Yet I could not imagine not loving her, could not bear the thought of giving up my love. But this seemed the end of it. I should never have gambled with my secret love for her. I might have kept that, nurtured it, lived with it on the principle that something was better than nothing. I was furious with myself for having put my cards on the table and having lost the game. This really was the end of it. At least she wanted to stay friends--but the thought was no consolation. The end of it: after all these years, a war, and a marriage made in purgatory. The hardest thing of all was closing up the showroom that afternoon and going back home to Ruby.

EIGHTEEN

Alex was dead. It said so in this telegram. I took it in at once, in my quick decisive way: saw everything I should have to do and how the next few days would be and drew myself into a knot for drastic action before I let the writhing wave inside me sink me down on to a chair and the hot, thick, salty gurgling filled my throat. Then Lisa was on the telephone and the horrible story began to take shape.

I decided I had to see her, whatever might have been lost between us. I reckoned my confession would be the last thing on her mind anyway. I drove down fast and uncomfortably, not noticing the countryside or the car or anything but the blank road ahead. Suicide. How difficult it was for me to understand, even after my own depressing experiences. The stupid waste of it: to live through all he had suffered, to survive for so long against the odds, and then--just when all seemed clear for life ahead--to die. To kill oneself seemed the ultimate madness. I could not imagine circumstances in which I would do it; I only knew that I did not wish to die that way. I did not wish to die at all. Perhaps that had always been the essential difference between Alex and myself. However miserable the plight, however desperate the situation, I felt sure I would want to live, to hope for peace and beauty and all good things. Wasn't that what I was doing now, in the wake of Lisa's rejection? If that was naïve and simple, then I was glad to be naïve and simple. Yet I instinctively knew why he had done it. Life and its burden of guilt had become intolerable: he had struggled for so long, then could struggle no more. All his skill, all his knowledge, all his experience, all the myriad wonderful powers compounded together in the one man--none of these were any use against all he had had to suffer. Nothing could cancel out his terrible past: nothing but death. Had Alex heard me saying these things he might have called me hard and unfeeling and accused me of reducing complicated things to an over-simplified black-and-white. But I knew, as I smiled my grim smile, that I was right...then memories of him summoned tears again. None would come. I was dried up, full of wrath and bitterness; the iron man more fitted for life than he who could not bear its vileness, nor his own.

I took Lisa's hands--but could not kiss her. First our letters, now this. How strange to find my old desire numbed, and even the simplest affection warped by death. The house was filled with its white, bleak horror--for it was here that Alex had killed himself, here in the gas-filled kitchen. As I passed through that room I saw the ugly little cream enamel oven with its door shut blank and final, and a new rage swept through me. How could he do this? He, a man of fresh blue skies and all the natural glories we had shared; how could he fill his lungs with filthy, choking gas? It was foul--and between my pity and my revulsion crept a kind of hatred. Yes, I hated Alex for doing this. It was as much a dirty trick as shooting that German in the water. His burdens might have been greater than my own, but some of them had been self-inflicted burdens, irrational and needless. Again I wondered what he would have said if he had been able to read my thoughts. But to realise that his kind of burdens were the worst kind didn't stop me hating him. Yet hatred is a kind of love: a vigorous and passionate thing, a quality of life. One could not hate the dead: their nothingness prevented it. Oh, if only he were here to hate...and to forgive!

Lisa took me into the big warm room where, on that first day, we had all seemed so happy. The little silver Spitfire, seen like a shock, still gleamed and shone its hard, bright perfection. Yes, better to die in hot and yelling battle, soaked in fear and exultation; better still to live in warm and sunny peace, so close, so easily at hand, here in the quiet room with a beautiful woman moving in and out like someone from a dream. Why could it not have been so?

"Do you want to tell me about all this?" I said--and the saddest thing of all was that each word sounded like an insult.

She sat down: too calm, too conscious of her tiny smile.

"I didn't find Alex, you know. Those

kind people in the next house." She began to wring her hands in her lap. "If only I hadn't been away."

"You were away? I didn't know that."

"Yes, visiting some friends in London, oh, people we'd known for a while. Alex didn't want to go, he couldn't be bothered with them; you know how he could be with people. But they kept asking us to go. I had refused so often I thought I had to see them this time."

"Of course."

"I was late back...trouble with the car, you see. Not a good car..."

She was not crying, but her lips were trembling, and lines which I had never noticed before scored deeply across her eyelids. She continued her story. Quite dispassionately, as I listened, I thought: 'in the middle of all this she is still beautiful and I love her as much as I ever did, perhaps more, perhaps more than anyone has ever loved; and through all the years and all the troubles that cannot change.'

"...so you see," she went on, "I didn't

find Alex. When I came back it was all over. Perhaps that is a good thing. He always said you shouldn't look at dead people--and I have not looked at him. I still don't know really what I'm doing, what I'm saying. You realise that, don't you Richard?"

"Yes," I cradled her hands in mine. "Yes."

"Dear Richard."

There was a long pause. I moved awkwardly about the room.

"What are you thinking?" she asked. "Please tell me. Do not be afraid--please tell me."

I was going to tell her I still loved her, that I now loved her as a man instead of the gauche boy she met in Germany, that I would always love her, whatever she might have written in that letter...but could not bring myself to say such things at this moment.

"I'm wondering," I began, "I'm wondering if...if Alex ever tried this before."

She did not speak, but gave a violent

little shake of the head. What should I say now, what did she know, how much had Alex never told her? She shook her head again. I wanted to ask if she knew about the German in the water--but dared not speak those words either. It was a particularly upsetting cowardice: to realise I would probably never dare say them. I sank down, rubbing my face.

"Well do you know why this happened then? Have you any idea at all?"

Of course she had. How could she be married to him and not know? But she did not answer. However could I go on with this pointless inquisition?

"You know Alex went through a terrible time in the war," I said. "You do know all about that, don't you?"

"I am not a child, Richard."

"I'm sorry," I muttered, "I'm sorry. I just thought he might have told you--left a note or something." It all sounded so feeble.

"There was nothing," she said quietly. "I do not think Alex could take any more…and I think you know that, too. Nothing went right for him," she gave a faint smile, "not even me. I gave him everything I had, and it wasn't too easy for me either, after Berlin. But it wasn't enough. You know the war was bad for him--peace I think was even worse."

"There's no peace, is there?"

"What's that?" It was her old, brusque way of speaking English: careless, haughty, beautiful.

"I said there's no peace; no peace for us."

"That is because you will not let it come."

I looked up at the silver Spitfire.

"Perhaps you're right," I said.

"I stopped fighting the war a long time ago. Now you must."

I did not really want to talk like this. I did not want to talk at all. But I still felt compelled to discover if she knew about the German in the water.

"Well I'm sorry, but I must ask: did Alex ever mention a man called Howard?"

"Oh yes, his friend who was killed."

"Alex took that very badly, you know. In fact I don't believe he ever got over it, and he--well, he did things afterwards which I think led all the way to...this."

"Such a little thing?"

"I'm not sure the death of a friend is a little thing, Lisa."

"Even in war, when hundreds of men are being killed?"

"Especially in war, when hundreds of men are being killed."

Her hardness astonished and angered me. I was shocked by it and unprepared for any of this. Then suddenly a new fierce light seemed to take possession of her: a grim certainty, a sinister resolve. I realised, without a single word being spoken, that she did know everything, knew exactly what had happened after Howard's death, although how Alex had struggled to confess it, I could hardly bear to imagine. Then she drew a deep breath and looked coldly round the room. When she spoke, it sounded as if she were telling a story--someone else's story.

"Alex killed himself because he could not go on living after all the things he had done and all the things he had suffered. He hated the war and everything he had to do in it, concealing the fact he was married to me, killing people one after the other, taking revenge, hiding it, lying about it. Then he hated himself. A man cannot live with hatred like that. I know that is the reason. Nothing could put that right. You know it and I know it. We could not help him more than we did." I didn't think people made speeches like that: each sentence a kind of iron maxim, hammered out at me. Thus was judgment passed upon my friend--and by his own wife, too. Well, it couldn't hurt him now. Only we who lived on could suffer for it, and for him. Lisa swallowed, and her voice softened. "You are different, Richard. You could take it, I know."

"Yes," I grunted, "I could take it, God forgive me. I was always the one who was supposed to be able to take it and go back for more. I was the one who had to stay sane, keep smiling, cheering everyone up.

Nobody gave a damn if I went round the bend; I wasn't allowed to."

"But you should not be so bitter, Richard."

"What d'you expect?" I barked at her. "D'you think I enjoyed watching Alex go under? I saw the whole thing, you know. He was my friend, as much as Howard was his friend--more! Surely I don't have to tell you that!"

She watched me without speaking.

"God!" I shouted, grabbing up the little Spitfire and clenching it in my fist, waving it at her, "there are times when I hate the whole bloody war and everyone who's been in it and the whole bloody mess that's left!"

I slammed down the silver Spitfire. The noise of it rang round the room. I saw that it was quite unharmed, and that the moisture of my fingermarks was evaporating off, leaving it just as hard and clean and shiny as before.

"You cannot put any of that right now." Lisa's voice seemed to come at me from miles away, very calm and soothing.

321

Was I mad? As mad as Alex had been? "Don't go on fighting that dreadful war, Richard..." There was actually a smile in her voice, a gentle smile. "...please. And I want to thank you for your wonderful letter: it was so brave and honest of you to tell me all those things." She almost giggled. "I did know in a way how you felt of course, but it was very nice to have it written to me. I hope I didn't upset you too much with what I wrote in reply--I was just trying to tell the truth, the way you had been. It was so kind and loving of you, and I do respect you for what you told me...but you must understand my position too. The most important thing is that you move away from the war and into a new life. I have, you know--perhaps just recently. It really can be done. I care very much for you and want you to be happy in the future." I passed my hands across my face. Everything was normal again, everything was safe. Lisa was looking up and smiling--a warm smile without any grief in it. "All right?" I heard her say. "All right?"

"Yes," I answered, surprised at the sound of my own voice. "Yes--I'm sorry I shouted. I'm sorry I embarrassed you or upset you in any way. I'm...just sorry." A kind of balm descended around me. Everything would be all right again, just as she said. Of course it would. It was quite wonderful, the peace she brought; the hope, the love. Then the slow, cool facts of death slid back. But it had been a wonderful moment; truly wonderful. "Do you want me to stay for a while?" I added. "I'll stay with you if you like, if it's any help to you."

"No," she answered with another smile, "no thank you. There is nothing to be done." She was right of course, there was nothing to be done. I could imagine the atmosphere of the days to follow: they would be hectic and unreal, but they would pass, and I knew well enough how it would be when all the sympathetic friends had stopped calling, when the telephone had stopped ringing, when the last letters and telegrams had been received and answered and forgotten.

Lisa would be yet another widow; I, yet another man cheated of a friend. And everywhere life would thunder on. Nowhere would its pain be keener than in my own veins. No, there was nothing to be done. "But come and see me again soon," she added, "or I may come to London. You show me that place you have. I should like to see your business doing well."

"All right."

With such simple words are lives rebuilt... but they were only the first pathetic reachings for normality. By the time I left her, darkness was falling, and that wonderful glow which her calm forgiving smiles had brought me was quite gone. I looked up at a sky that had no colour, no light, save for the first faint prickings of uncertain stars. I felt that part of myself had been separated from me and would never come back. Before I went, she told me that when they had found Alex in the morning there was dark dried blood on his fingers where he had gashed them on the cheap oven-bottom--

trying to back out, they thought.

"It's the funeral today," I announced to Ruby as I brushed my dark grey suit.

"The tie looks awful," she remarked, and she was right. It was thin, cold, black silk: a shocking contrast to my usual ties that were broad, richly patterned ones, worn in a Windsor knot. They were my only extravagance of dress; in my circle of friends and acquaintances I had become known for them. I wished I had been wearing one for Alex, then realised it didn't matter. Nothing seemed to matter, except getting it all over with.

"You're sure you can manage on your own?" Ruby's sudden tenderness was sickening to me. She placed her hand on my arm. "I'll come along and keep you company if you like."

"I'll be all right," I smiled grimly. I did not want her there, to meet Lisa and to see her grief, or to share mine. "You don't know these people," I went on, "and there's really no need to get involved with them now. Anyway, you know the accounts need looking at this week.

Nobody does them better than you. I'll be back at the showroom after lunch, I suppose."

"I'll see you later, then. You'll need your overcoat, Rich. We've got our first frost this morning--it hasn't half come early this year. It's terribly cold."

"Yes it is."

I had never been to a cremation before--although I chuckled savagely to myself that I must have seen a few in the air. Somehow, any one of those would have been better than this. I closed my mind to such thoughts, decided to live only in the present, or imagine myself escaping into a future where these horrors would have evaporated. It was a form of cowardice, but I allowed myself to take comfort in it. It was impossible to tell what comfort, if any, Lisa was taking in such thoughts, if indeed she were thinking them, or what warmth she might be feeling from my presence at her right elbow.

Her main supporters were Alex's parents who had driven her here in their

Bentley behind the hearse and now sat on her left in the chapel. They looked very elderly and possessed a pre-war elegance and gentility that greatly upset me. I sensed what they might have suffered, not just in the last few days, but throughout the war and before it, from the very day that Alex must have told them he was determined to marry Lisa, and so driven the wedges of divided loyalties, complicated subterfuge, and appalling stresses into their once comfortable and secure lives. I wished I had known them better, and that their old age had not been riven so cruelly by their son's suicide.

As for Lisa, she was closed, silent, unapproachable in her grey, rather masculine coat, her black gloves, and the cloud of golden hair swept magnificently under her black hat. She was very much 'on parade'; I knew it was her way of maintaining an iron control. I had kissed her on the cheek, but she had scarcely looked at me. Now, as she stood next to me, I felt a slight warmth rising from her, and I was filled with desire. She was so beautiful, such a luscious golden creature of richness and of life; such a strong, vibrant presence, the very opposite of this chilly pastel-coloured chapel striving so pathetically to be dignified. Life, life, life: that was what we loved, not death, nor had we any wish or energy to celebrate death. That was why we stood so impassively. Grief was gone, everything was gone. There was no point in making a show about it. Only life was worth celebrating; and I wanted her desperately then, to share the celebration with me, warm and naked together, making love, sparking joys and colours between us, proving we were alive and had nothing to do with the white coldness of death.

The priest gave a final blessing, pressed a hidden button, and the coffin sank away. I imagined it being pushed around somewhere beneath us on its way to the furnace; the first few tongues of fire poking in through the coffin seams, fire which Alex could no longer feel nor flinch from--strange, since we were always so watchful and wary of fire in the air; then the belch of black smoke which might issue from that fake church tower I had noticed on the way in. Well, better to go up in flames than lie in wet earth; better to blow between the clouds than turn to mould. Surely we were strange animals, composed of dust and chemicals--the same chemicals which now stirred my desire for Lisa, ran it round my body, craving always for the union with her own miraculous brew. I was wildly, madly alive to the proximity of this beautiful creature of my own kind, as if she were blushing and trembling at her own vivid excess of loveliness. Although she stood as still as stone beside me, I knew she was alive in every flake and cell of her being, and I desired her deeply, craving always for that union, that blessed fire of physical love. Yet it was not so simple, so easily explained--for I saw in her the indefinable spark, the lovable spark, the spark of life itself that must be kept holy and celebrated. For the first time I saw what I truly loved in Lisa's body: not those lips, but their fullness; not that hair, but its golden sweep; not those breasts, but their delicate turn; not the body itself but the miraculous spirit it contained. I yearned to embrace her flesh: to satisfy my own, yes, but also to search for and sanctify the spirit of life that sparked between us. Life: that was what we really loved.

To leave her now was cruel; crueller than death itself. Death was, after all, inevitable. This separation was not: we might have been leaving together had it not been for a quirk of circumstances. To feel her take her delicate fingers away from my handshake and kiss was cruel. She sank into the Bentley, and I watched it drive her away. I would die loving her, as I loved her now. I would die, she would die, but our love could be given a chance to live if only we might find the courage to grasp it. I went home to Ruby. She seemed glad the funeral was over and to have me back in the house, as if she recognised a dangerous and distasteful period of my life might now have ended.

The accounts were finished, she told me. How about a night out?

A week later Lisa telephoned me, thanked me in a rather businesslike way for being so helpful at the funeral and told me, quite coolly, that Alex's ashes were now ready to be scattered. Would I come and help her? Alex's ashes--I had honestly never thought about them or what would happen to them or even that they might still exist. Now I was visited by romantic notions of having them blown away in a biplane's slipstream, perhaps over the Club field, or flinging them to the wind off the White Cliffs, down to the pebbly beach below--but in the same instant knew there would be no time or money for such extravagances or any real consideration of them. I felt they would be pointless anyway, and nobody else seemed to want to put on a show. It was to be done at the crematorium. Lisa heard my silence down the telephone.

"Will you help?" she said softly.

"Yes, of course."

Snow in Autumn: the first of the year,

shockingly early. It was only the lightest covering and had begun to thaw almost as soon as it had fallen, but a chill wind was making a slow business of it under a solid white sky. Behind the crematorium, it covered the lawn they called the Garden of Remembrance with a thin white blanket. Lisa was beside me in her grey coat again, and a silent official had just handed her the bronze urn containing whatever was left of Alex, leaving us alone.

"I don't want to," she said simply, holding out the urn to me.

She just turned away from me and I thought: 'I have to do this as well as all the other rotten jobs; I usually get them.' The urn was heavier than I had imagined and the top was loose. I was very curious about what ashes looked like, but it didn't seem right to take the lid off and peer inside while Lisa was there. There was nothing for it but to turn downwind and do the job. I held the urn by its stem in my right hand and took off the lid with my left. Suddenly my gloved hands looked strangely disembodied, like the paws of an animal on a snowy landscape. Then I flung my arm, expecting a cascade of fine dust to be blown away from me, hoping I might see faint specks of it carried away high into the sky, where I could fancy Alex belonged, at least in spirit--but at my feet fell a coarse-ground grit. I shook the urn and more ash fell out, then more and more, an obscene black smudge on the frozen lawn. I felt utterly bleak, turned in upon myself, unable to say anything of any worth to Lisa, who took my arm as we walked away and told me it would be better if we did not meet for a while. I turned my back on my old friend, and left him as bone-meal in the snow.

NINETEEN

To forget and to remember: those are the most marvellous of all human powers. How strange to sense them working, and to come through nothingness into a kind of flowering. But it was very slow, and discovered only by degrees. Lisa was unfathomably wise to keep me away from her in those first few weeks after Alex's death. I think if I had been close to her then, my love--still charged with grief and anger--might have broken us both for ever. And of course there was Ruby. Admitting to myself that I was completely in love with Lisa and that there was no going back to my struggling denial of it, I already considered myself an adulterer. I knew that Ruby would be harsh and unforgiving--and with justification. I would deserve no better from her. If our marriage was to be destroyed, I would be the destroyer. She would be terribly hurt too, and I shrank from her imagined pain and anger. Better then to keep up the sham for the moment. I had lived a lie before; could resolve to go on living this one--until it became unbearable. But I was not proud of my resolve. At the same time I became aware of a new and utter boredom. It was perhaps despicable, but was nevertheless intolerable. I eventually had to write to Lisa and ask if she would like to spend the few days in London of which she had once spoken. She wrote back and answered: *yes*. I could almost see her quiet smile in her fine blue notepaper. So I booked her into a good hotel, and we met in St. James' Park.

That afternoon, perhaps more strongly than on any other day in my life, I wished the Winter would not come. I wished the leaves could be forever green and gold...then she was walking through the Park in rich, dark, leather shoes as if, beneath her velvet hat, the world was held on threads of gold. How might she walk across a waste of years and bring, from beneath their daily snows, a spark of Springtime! And dark birds flying in the windy sky, the careless crowds of London, the roaring city traffic, all were part of the symphony of delights she brought me. None seemed to declare that she was forbidden fruit, none acknowledge the ranting puritan voice inside myself. The man-made rules of what was acceptable and what was scandalous seemed themselves to be soiled corruptions of a natural law--of which she and I were suddenly a pure expression. Then I did not fear the change of seasons, nor the march of Time which trod upon our bodies, nor the public censure which would damn our souls. If we had already come through so many horrors as individuals separated by time, distance, marriage, politics, and war, surely we could come through this together. But as I watched her in her belted skirt walk richly through the new-dropped leaves, I feared the loss of what she made me, and wanted for ever the warm-eyed harmony she brought. To forget and to remember: how simple it could be, this redemption from an existence of dreadful intensity into a celebration of ordinary things. How beautiful they were; how wonderful to find that more springs of joy gushed from life than we had thirsts to drink them.

I wanted to talk about our time in Germany, to remember it with her, to say I had never forgotten that night when Werner was driving us back from the inn and she fell asleep with her lovely golden head resting against my shoulder, when I thought I should never have any more of her, and that I had been delightfully wrong because here was another wonderful time together, stolen as it might be with Alex dead and Ruby at home, yet wonderful nevertheless, wonderful if only because of the odds stacked against it. But it seemed dangerous to talk of such things, as if the sharp sweet memories of them might pierce the fragile fabric of the present and collapse it around us, leaving us standing alone in what would look no better than a shabby liaison. So at first we spoke of terrible things, easier to speak of because they were so terrible: the war, Berlin, and Lisa's ordeal with the Russians.

"It makes a good story now," she smiled. Was it all going to be casual and throwaway? Had she come through it infected by Alex's disarming manner and his infuriating 'piece of cake' talk, making a joke of it, breezily British? Surely not. Surely it must rend her German soul, break her down, make her rage or weep; and surely I had no right to open her wounds again, to hurt her any more. Yet if it was not my fate to be her confidant, then whose?

"You mustn't talk about it if you don't want to," I said hurriedly.

"No, no," she smiled again. "it really is a good story. You'll like it," she added with the same unexpectedly cheeky grin I remembered from our time in Germany when she would slap my leg and scold me for being an embarrassed boy. Telling it would be easy to her, even as she sauntered gracefully beside me with her hands in her pockets and the heels of her perfectly polished shoes clicking expensively on the path between the trees. Perhaps I had got Lisa all wrong. Perhaps she really was tough and hard, a brawling tomboy trapped inside the ravishing body of a goddess, a rough and ready grown-up schoolgirl good at games and camping out, able to laugh her way through a war with unwashed hair and dirty fingernails. Then it did not seem very likely. Perfume rose from her in the sharp Autumn air, sunlight gilded her cheeks, showing once again those tiny lines at the corners of her eyes. No, she was utterly feminine. Clearly she was strong; but her strength would always be a natural, if unexpected, part of her womanliness.

"As you know I had to go to Berlin, although I did not wish to go. I did think it would be dangerous."

"Your father was ill," I put in.

"Yes. I don't know how much Alex told you at the time. I don't exactly remember what I was able to tell him. It was very dangerous to send letters out of Germany. My father was working with the *Reichsbank* there and he suddenly became very sick: a heart-attack."

"Oh, he didn't look the type," I said, "Too thin and strong. He seemed so vigorous."

"Ach, but you never know what is inside."

"No."

"So I went. It wasn't a good time to travel, you know, right at the end of the war, but with my family connections it was easy to have the right papers. I remember I was escorted by soldiers to a military hospital. He looked very sick but it was good to see him again."

"Yes."

"Then he died quite suddenly--easily, I think, although one can never be sure. I'm glad he died before the very end, Rich." She stopped and faced me under the cold sky. "He believed in Hitler, in the new Germany. I always knew it was impossible madness--and look what it did to us all."

"Yes," was all I could manage. She was so thoroughly sensible in the middle of shocking revelations, yet I was not sure I completely liked or trusted her this way. At the same time it was part of her magnetism--as ravishing as her looks.

"He never understood that," she continued, suddenly linking my arm and putting her hands back in the pockets of her coat. We walked on. "So clever and successful in his business and taking high appointments. I used to argue with him, when it was all starting, before the war-- but then I'm sorry to say I gave up, he was so easily part of it all. There was money; he was proud and successful with a good family. He greatly admired Alex, you know, didn't mind at all that he was English, not even after the war began. He was rather proud in a way. He had nothing against the English; admired the race. He thought we should not have been fighting you, but that we could have been allies against the Russians."

"One of those, ay?" I muttered.

"Do not be too critical, Rich."

"No, I'm not being critical. I like to think I understood your family quite well. It's just that history can make personal opinions look very dodgy, that's all."

"*Very dodgy*," she smiled, "*very dodgy*-- yes, Alex used that expression sometimes, but he was not the philosopher you are."

"No."

"Of course it was never admitted officially," she continued. "His daughter was married to an airman--that's all that was ever said."

"I'll bet that was all," I commented grimly.

Alex had the same problem--the other way round, of course. You were supposed to be in Canada."

"Yes," she chuckled, "and you know I've never even seen Canada on the films. Wasn't it all incredibly difficult?"

Again I was unsure of her manner. Was it all a joke to her, a daring game of intriguing subterfuge--or had it really given her the horrors, the way it had driven Alex mad?

"I think that's putting it mildly," I said. A few more steps of silence allowed all this to sink into my mind. "When we were flying," I told her, "we never thought about such things: you know, German families arguing about whether or not Hitler was right. But of course I always wondered what was happening to you--wondered isn't the right word, I always thought about you with a terrible worry..."

"I know," she said, giving my arm a squeeze.

"...but I never guessed any of this was going on. I thought you were well out of it down in the South."

"I was for years, Rich. This was just at the end."

"But that was the worst time, wasn't it? Anyway, go on please."

"I had no-one in Berlin and no reason to stay, but there was no way to get out either. The Russians were coming. I used to know that wonderful city from when I was a little girl, but now it made me sick. Now there was only the howl of rockets pounding at the very heart of Germany. But I no longer cared if the Nazis were winning or if the Allies were going to take it over. What did it matter? Life would be just as filthy under either of them."

"What on Earth did you do?"

"I was leaving, or trying to leave. Of course that was the worst thing to be seen doing. Suddenly there were Russian soldiers everywhere: very proud and angry, hot-headed, full of victory, like soldiers anywhere I suppose, when they have taken a city. But they were difficult to reason with. They had no love for us-- we had made them suffer in their own country." She heaved a sigh. "I was arrested when I was trying to leave. Of course I was terribly afraid they would find out what my father had been."

"Of course, yes." I suddenly saw the whole thing: how fatally dangerous her situation must have been. Yet it still sounded like an adventure story. She was making it sound that way, chuckling as she spoke of her interrogation, a glint of cunning in her eyes, pleased with herself, turning her face up to mine for a kind of approval. That was it: she was pleased and proud, arrogantly proud of having escaped so craftily. It was a deep and sudden insight into her character, unexpected and surprising, but it took me only a moment's reflection to realise I should have known she had been always been like this. She had said she despised the Nazis and argued with her own father, she was saying now how close to death and torture she had been at the hands of the Russians--yet somehow I knew it had all been a kind of game to her, the game Alex refused to play, the game which he had accused me of playing as I flew in the war and survived it, but which was in reality beyond my limited reserves of cleverness or bravery. It had not been beyond Lisa. She had played it like the adventuress she truly was, with a silky panache. Foul and debased as it was, she had played it and won, through her looks and her cunning and her incredible good luck, but mostly, I guessed, through her diamond-hard core of crafty ruthlessness. Now I knew why she could laugh. It wasn't humour, it wasn't even relief, it was a mad glee--of the sort I had known as I took off in a Spitfire, flicked her long nose through a cloud, and turned to put myself between the sun and my target. I thought I had forgotten all that, but found it lived again in Lisa. It was wicked, but infectious if one understood her soul... and with mixed feelings, I found that I did.

"You flew rings round us all," I grinned, "and managed to keep your feet on the ground at the same time."

"I was just lucky," she said, gripping

my arm, but I knew it was more than luck as she told of her interview with the Russian Colonel. "At first I thought I was going to be raped," she said quite blankly, as if *raped* could have been *shot*, *tortured*, or *released*: just one of the options at the time, "but it seems they thought I was too important for that. Of course I spoke no Russian, and kept talking in English, thinking that might save me. Some of the soldiers might have thought I was English, I don't know, but of course the Colonel knew better. He knew exactly who I was, with all my papers on his desk. I was terrified, yes, but I knew I had a chance with this man. I was so lucky, Rich. They had taken over a hotel on the Friedrichstrasse and his office was a salon with a piano. There was a guard at the door but I sat straight down at the piano-- it seemed the natural thing to do, even there. He asked me what I was--I think he meant what I was politically--but I said I was a piano teacher. 'Play then,' he said, and I played some Russian folksongs." She hugged me and winked. "Lucky I

346

knew some Russian folksongs, ay?"

"Not half!" I grinned, and could not resist kissing her on the cheek. "This is incredible. I don't know that I can believe it all," I laughed aloud.

"Oh come now Richard," she smiled, "you have to believe me. It is such a good story and I am telling it so well. It's such...what would you and Alex have called it?...such *good stuff*."

"It's very good stuff!" I smiled. "Come on then."

"The Colonel said: 'You are lucky. Normally we shoot fascists.' 'But Colonel,' I said, 'I am not a fascist. I am married to a courageous English airman who is fighting on your side. That can easily be checked if you contact your English allies. Then you will take me at once to the British Sector.'"

"Bloody Hell--you dictated terms to him?"

"In a way. It was necessary not to appear frightened."

"So you made all that up and told him you were a spy for the British?"

"No, my dear Richard, that is exaggerating it. That's something Alex told you, is it? No--but it's true I allowed him to think in some way I might be working for the British."

"Amazing. Absolutely amazing."

"Then he said: 'But how can this be? Your brother was with a Division in North Africa. We understand he is a good German soldier.' I said I was not able to choose my brother or his politics, but that I had chosen my husband and was loyal to his country. I said also that you would not respect me if my brother were a bad soldier. That impressed him."

"Well, it would."

"But I knew he was still going to have me shot--perhaps not immediately--but deep down I knew that is what was likely to happen. He did not believe I was a spy for the British, of course he didn't. There was no evidence of that--but in the end he had no time to check anything, there must have been more important things for him to do. He despised me for being a German, and he suspected me of being a

Nazi whatever I said, but he was forced to admire my courage. Perhaps I knew that because I have always lived among soldiers. I think he decided it would do him more good if he made me a problem for the British and he suddenly telephoned someone; I heard him speaking in perfect English. I was locked up for two nights in a filthy room, then the British came and I was arrested all over again...oh, a very pompous little Major, he wouldn't have listened to my piano-playing: you and Alex would have hated him. I think I preferred the Russian. I don't know what the British believed either, but of course I told them the truth. At last I was driven into the British sector--but by this time I was sick. I thought it was just a painful cough but of course it was pleurisy. I nearly died in hospital there--and I was so afraid I would be caught by my own lies, that the British would think I was a German spy. I knew they could check about Alex but that would not prove anything. As far as they would be concerned I would be a Nazi from a Nazi family. I knew I would have to escape them and get back to England, or at least to my home in the quiet part of Germany. Well, I was terribly weak and must have looked half dead, but I just walked out of the hospital one day with the cleaning women, wearing a scarf round my head and one of their overalls, it was so easy."

"Good God!" I exclaimed, "This is pantomime, Lisa. I can't believe it. You just walked out of some British military hospital in the middle of Berlin like Mister Toad in *The Wind in the Willows* dressed up as a washerwoman!"

"It's you who is making it pantomime, Richard," she laughed. "And you must not tease me. I have not read that book, but I know what you mean. You must face the truth, Rich," she said cheekily, snuggling an arm into my waist and smiling up at me again. "British soldiers walking about the corridors, two guards on the door: good Corporals, both of them, looking straight ahead thank God, Military Policemen in Jeeps outside--all outwitted by one sick woman," she laughed. "Will you men ever live it down?"

"I still don't know how you managed it," I said as soberly as I could, but I was disturbed and excited by her story with a thrill I had not expected. I admired and loved her more for it, felt sorry for her, felt personally involved in her adventure just by being told it, yet was sickened by it too. It was plunging me back into the tensions of the war--albeit shockingly unexpected ones and different from those I had undergone--but with the same rancid odour of fear. Yet with it came that crazy glee: the simple, brutal business of war; for people like us, so much easier than shadowy, complicated peace: that most unpalatable of truths which no-one dared admit these days.

"I was very sick of course," Lisa was continuing her story. "I had to live somehow, and find a train to the South. I had very little money with me, no extra clothes, no medicines--but inside I was strong. I slept for two days I think in a cellar and ate some old potatoes there. I was lucky it was warm weather. I grew a little stronger; I realised I was not going to die. Can you imagine how joyous that was? I was going to live, or at least not die of my sickness. Now I only had to leave Berlin and I would be safe. That of course would be most difficult of all. I had just enough money for a train ticket but I had not any papers. It was easy enough to move around the ruined parts of the city but I knew once I went to the station I would be stopped. I became hopeless again, Rich--do you know how that feels? I had to eat, I was spending more and more of my little amount of money on bread; I had to buy an old coat from a poor clothing shop, something I could travel in and look a little respectable so I would not be picked up by the Military Police in my hospital worker's overall. But the worst thing was, I was dirty. I smelled dirty, Rich. That was horrible to me; and my hair was filthy; and there were bites on my body, from the louse you know, and I thought I am not going to die of my sickness but I'm going to rot away instead, be eaten by dirty things and die of hunger and go rotten. A time is supposed to come when you don't care any more, but I did care... do you understand me, Rich?"

"Yes," I answered, horrified by what she was telling me.

"Then one day my shoes broke. That is when I cried, I think. I remembered myself as a little girl coming to Berlin for a holiday treat and walking along the *Unter den Linden* in smart black shoes and little white socks and now here I was in the same city standing barefooted on the broken pavement. That felt really terrible, you know--and I remembered my mother once telling me I had such pretty hands and feet, and I looked down at them and they were so dirty and painful. I felt almost naked without my shoes and knew I could never pass out of the city if I was so ragged and barefooted. That is when I had the idea to cable my mother and ask her to come and rescue me; it was not possible to telephone, of course, and I could not write a letter. Oh, I didn't know if it could be done, but I had to try. I begged some very old shoes from a woman selling clothes and went to the post office. I expected soldiers to be there and that I would be arrested or that the telegram man would ask me for my papers, but no, it was all so easy. I could have done it days before. I wrote I was terribly sick and begged her to come, told her where I would be. I imagined she would have tremendous problems with papers and with moving through the British sector, but in three days she was there. I nearly died with shock when I saw her coming towards me with Military Policemen beside her--but she had been to the hospital and told them who she was and who I was and I was arrested again and put back in hospital."

"My God--all over again?"

"In a way, yes--but this time the British seemed to know the truth about me and Alex and didn't want to hold me prisoner. I'll never be sure exactly why-- and you say you find all this difficult to believe, well so do I, even now. But it is true, they were sending me out. The nurses cleaned me up and cut my hair very badly; then another officer, much more kind than the first, told me off very sweetly for escaping and causing such trouble, issued me with a new kind of pass, and told me to take my mother-- some kind of saint, he said--out of Berlin and not to come back."

Suddenly it was Autumn in London again, rich and warm. Lisa's coat with the warm brown fur at the neck and cuffs was anything but austere. Other women were looking at her with what I took to be surprise, perhaps mixed with disgusted envy. But in those moments I loved her more than ever, if that were possible. The end of her incredible story, told in her curious chuckling way, moved me not to anger or horror, and I was now beyond surprise. It moved me to greater love and admiration, that so much more than the already wondrous mixture of loveliness should be inside the warm body and the rich coat which swung beside me. It came to me that if I had once, as a boy, loved her beauty and fallen helplessly under her spell, I now loved her soul, and loved it as a man should love.

That first evening I took her out for a meal. It cost a small fortune--which could still be spent in Austerity London if one knew where to go--but it was worth every penny to see her smile, to feel free and happy and slightly drunk again. We indulged these appetites without guilt, for now we were not ashamed to talk about anything...and it was over this meal that I told her, for the first time in plain language, that I loved her. She smiled slowly and looked down, like the coy girl perhaps she never had never been, then looked straight into my eyes and told me she had known anyway-- "for years and years and years." We raised our glasses to the admission, and in a way, I had never felt less secure. I felt the world might explode around me; at the same time I wouldn't care. But I knew I was happy. Things which until today would have been unspeakable were now our common stock of reminiscence and of laughter. I learned many things over that long meal: among them that Werner had become an armoured patrol commander and had been decorated in the North Africa campaign.

"Ah, Werner and his motor cars. That old Mercedes of his would fetch a good price today. If he was over here, he could have gone into business with me!" We laughed especially loudly at this. "Well, I'm pleased he found a way to keep driving, even through the war."

"I fear he has grown fat," Lisa chuckled again. "You would not recognize him."

"Werner fat? Impossible."

"I tell you it is true. He is an industrialist in Frankfurt: too many meetings, too many lunches."

"You've kept your figure. You're like a girl."

"More dinners like this and you will have me as fat as Frau Zeller!"

"Ah yes, old Frau Zeller...and those cakes. Heavens, those cakes. I can taste them now."

"I loved her like a grandmother. You understand. My mother and father were always away. People I loved have always been away."

"I understand."

This came after the brandy and signalled the end of our high-spirited little celebration of admitted love. We were back to our quiet, half-guilty, half-joyous dream-world of astonished pleasure in having found each other so tolerant of its enormity. Then we spoke of her long years in Bavaria, before she had gone to Berlin and again after she had been taken home to convalesce, an exile in her own country.

"That is how Alex felt here," I said.

"It makes me realise I am only coming out of it now, only now. It has taken so long. You will think me hard for saying this, but I think Alex dying is part of it; I think I might never have come out of it if Alex had lived." Did that mean she had never loved him, that he had blighted her life with his madness, that she was pleased to be free, and with me? Surely it could not be so devastatingly simple, so horribly convenient. I was ashamed even to think it--yet could not help but think it. "It's taken so long," she was saying. "Nothing was right for years, was it, all the way through the war and after it. You have helped me so much."

"It's you who have helped me--without knowing it, I think." I said this lightly, easily, with only part of me aware how important it was. Such is the way with all the greatest confessions.

"Do not think me so innocent!" she laughed. "I know about life, Rich. I have no illusions about it. All one can do is make the best of it, and if one gets a bit of happiness along the way--well, that's not so bad. But one pays for everything--everything."

"How very true," I said, a little wounded, "but how very hard. Anyway, you've done your paying."

"Yes," she softened, "I think I have."

I hurried on, choosing to ignore the truth that *I* had not yet done *my* paying.

"I have forgotten everything but you," I told her

She laughed delightfully.

"Liar," she chuckled, taking up her wine. "You know that isn't true."

Her eyes were very brown. How could they be so dark, and her hair so golden?

"Let me say then, you are all I want to remember."

"That is not true either, Rich: you want to remember your flying, and the good comradeship in the war Alex used to tell me about, and some other things too I expect--but I forgive you for it."

She clinked her glass against mine and smiled at me. Suddenly, I felt as I had felt in Germany before the war, when this long adventure was just beginning: happy, under a kind of spell, above all free, whatever responsibilities might lurk at home. Once again in my life, it seemed that anything could happen; that a new unashamed lightness had taken hold of me. Why resist it? Life went on, and might soon be over. Love her then, and love her completely. It would be so beautiful and so perfect and so simple: a consummation of all these years--years which would have been survived and spent for nothing if the love were now denied. Allow it then, welcome it, glory in it. To love could be no sin. The sin would be in *not* loving, in denying it, in hiding its simple wonderful truth. Love her then, completely--and leave Ruby. There was little enough left in our marriage. It had not taken long to sicken, surely a measure of its weakness. This would be its death-knell. There were no children to suffer, and Ruby would have little to complain of. What she really loved was the business and the money. She could have it, and be well provided-for. Anyway, I thought, if I had ever fallen in love with Ruby, it had been truly a fall. This was the opposite: Lisa and I were rising into love. I was still able to think like that--after all the muck and of terror of the war and the shabby peace--and was glad.

The meal was finished. Lisa put on her hat in a gesture so innocent and girlish that it was almost painful to behold--for here was the woman I had loved all these years and would always love, as simple and happy as a child, as powerful as a goddess. Outside, the London trees were losing their leaves, the year was old. As I put her in a taxi and it carried her away, I wanted all these partings to be over--no more waving hands and slamming doors and separations. Yet I knew that neither of us were ready for each other's love to be suddenly transformed from this long suspended animation into a daily waking life, shaking off the mysteries, becoming a third entity born of an ordinary togetherness. It was a certainty that gave no comfort, for to have found her in these wintry days after Alex's death was like the precarious gift of fire in a frozen desert; and to lose her as another Spring began would be unthinkable. How should I endure all the tender green, or bear to watch a flying cloud above the town? Where might I rest my head if not against the exquisite thunder of her heart? How should I ever face another woman if her perfume rose like this in chilly air? Yes, I had risen into love with Lisa, and now could not tolerate the possibility of any fall. If I had to go graceless through the dirt, stoned by Ruby's disgust, I should surely do it, and crawl through shameful tunnels towards the light of fulfilment.

The next morning--oddly free of these considerations as I left Ruby painting her nails--I drove to Lisa's hotel and met her coming out. She looked younger than ever in a cream-coloured headscarf. We laughed and took each other's hands and I kissed her. She seemed to be in a tomboyish mood. I looked at the sky--the grey clouds parting.

"Just enough blue to put a patch on a pair of Dutchman's trousers," I told her as we set off for a walk in Hyde Park, chuckling at the old service expression. "It's going to be a lovely day."

It did turn bright and blue, with a wintry sun pouring down on London. The brilliant light deepened those little wrinkles at the corners of her eyes, but I thought her more beautiful for having been through the fire; her spirit refined, her soul enriched and more mysterious. She took off her scarf, letting the sun warm her face. Her hair was an endless fascination to me, the way it curved and was full of colours, like a profusion of tiny flowers in a field of wheat. Red, blue, white, green, black: all were there when the sun brought them alive. There was a perfect double curve from her creamy brow to her neck: a swaying curve more beautiful than any captured by the artists of the world. This, I thought, would have been impossible to paint. When I told her so she laughed and said that Titian might just have managed it.

We went for lunch, and as the afternoon closed in, I asked her what she was going to do.

"I shall give piano lessons," she said.

"What--nasty little boys and horsey girls?"

"Very probably. But I already have two charming pupils. One of them shows real promise. He is only nine years old but has already composed something. Not

Mozart, but a good enough simple theme and variations, you know."

"Oh yes, I know about those," I smiled. "That's where you take a perfectly good tune and ruin it with a lot of fiddly bits."

"Richard," she laughed, "don't play the Philistine so badly. Alex had no ear-- but you have soul."

"If you say so."

"Well, I can't predict a great future for him or any of your pupils. They will all fall in love with you be and be hopeless pianists."

We spoke long of her piano-playing, and of how I had always been enraptured by listening to her. Here it was then, the time of music and of love--not quite as I had imagined it in the middle of the war, but here certainly enough: by turns jokey and heart-rending. How curious life could be.

We went for tea, like sightseers taking a break. We shared a kind of magic: one moment frenzied, the next utterly calm. Sometimes it was as if we could not bear to look at each other any longer and had to say something to break the mood, glancing out of the café window then letting our gaze meet again, easily, without guilt or anxiety. We had been children in Germany, now it seemed we were much older but happier for it. There was the constant streak of sadness that this had not happened earlier, that the crazy middle of the Century had somehow intervened, but that hadn't been our fault, had it? We laughed when we actually said this, or something like it. What fun it was to be adults.

"Tell me about flying, Rich," she said with real enthusiasm. "You were very good, weren't you?" She saw me frown and bite my lips a little. "Not if you don't want to," she added.

"Oh I want to--I want to tell you, of all people. I loved flying and still do. I just wish I hadn't had to fight a war at the same time. But the horrible truth about flying in a war is that you don't know what you're doing--you just do it...or that's how I seem to remember it.

Sometimes you just do it because it seems the right thing to do, sometimes because you're scared out of your wits, but mostly because, well, you're just doing it. Doesn't sound very exalted or clever or heroic, does it? Still, I don't have to tell you what was horrible about the war."

"You could take it up again: civil aviation."

"Yes, I thought about that straight after the war--lots of us did. I knew one or two chaps who were trying it."

"You still could," she persisted. "You could be a bush-pilot in Australia."

"You know," I answered with a somewhat boggled mind, "that is something which honestly would never have occurred to me in a thousand years."

"Well," she grinned, "it has now. I hear there are all sorts of opportunities out there. Don't they call it the land of opportunity?"

"You mean I could end up as a kind of flying doctor, delivering babies and taking tonsils out in places I can't even pronounce, and missing kangaroos when

I come in to land?"

"You are hopeless, Rich," she laughed.

"Well, I'm not sure I'm right for civil aviation now. I'm afraid I fell in with the wrong sort of people and made money out of cars instead. Should've stuck to aeroplanes, perhaps...but then I'm not sure I would have met you again...I mean not in the same way, like this."

"Richard," she looked with downcast eyes again, smiling slowly, "you would have."

"Yes, Darling, I would."

At last, on that darkening evening, I fulfilled an old promise and drove her out to Mill Hill to see the first motor showroom. It all seemed glum and shabby, and the ownerless cars looked like pieces of other people's lives piled up incongruously in my own. I knew she did not like it, and as we wandered through the upper rooms where tins of paint and batteries were stored and tyres lay in dusty heaps, I wanted to be far away from all this, have no connection at all with the hollow life to which I was returning with

Ruby, and be somehow back in Germany with Lisa, where pink and grey and yellow clouds rode up across the forests from the Danube and the Alps. I knew of course that such dreams were unlikely to be fulfilled, and that we only had the future: a future that now seemed very uncertain. Only hours ago it had been fresh and inviting and worth taking every risk for. Now the future frightened me: it was swallowing us up as I drove her back through Canterbury down long, unlighted roads. What I really wanted was there never to have been a war, and I think I told her that as she sat warm and silent in the seat beside me. She did not answer, and as we neared the house, I felt like someone standing naked in a cold wind. I kissed her once, twice, three, four times too often at the door--then saw the tiny glint of tears upon her cheeks.

"You must not come in," she whispered. "You must leave me please, for just a while. You will be able to understand?"

"I think so. But I love you more than

anything."

"I know."

I drove back to London chilled and sullen, once more upon a journey when all I wanted was to be at home with Lisa. Home: the word rang hollow in my ears. I was not driving home, but to a bleak and loveless house, to a cheated wife and her false welcome I did not deserve, to a loveless night. And Lisa was locked up alone, miles away. I could still not be sure how she loved me, how she could return my love, or if we might ever have a solid future together. Could anything we shared be truly ours? We had travelled through our lives to this amazing rendezvous; found not ourselves, but different people. In some ways we would have to begin again, to learn to love each other afresh, and to cope with the reality of love. For the moment she had refused me; for the moment I was married to somebody else. If everything was going to be melted down, something might be forged anew--or the destruction could just as easily be left as it was, a useless lump of molten lives. Only the little silver Spitfire, whose gleaming wings I had seen briefly from her door, had any sureness of form in a chaotic world.

TWENTY

Lisa and I did not meet for months, but we became lovers in our letters. If this sounds quaint and old-fashioned, it is also true. We realised we were allowing ourselves to meet in the only country where lovers such as ourselves might feel free, which some would call the country of the soul. In these happy weeks I wrote as if I were at the other end of the world, telling her stories of the car business and how London was looking. I was not afraid to return to the theme of my long guilt over rejecting her at the hotel, and she forgave me as many times as I mentioned it. She wrote of Alex and the terrors he had to face after his breakdown and then gradually share with her after her return from Berlin. She wrote of his suicide; I wrote of the happy youthful friendship we had shared before the war. I confessed the details of my disenchantment with Ruby and the rapid deterioration of our marriage into a barely tolerable business arrangement. She wrote that she understood me and loved me and thought me the gentlest lover any woman could wish for. I wrote to tell her she was more than a man deserved. She always replied on the thickest, creamiest paper I had ever seen and I learned that this was German paper, somehow cherished through years of loss and violence and now reserved for me alone. I kept her letters in a black steel box at the showroom in Mill Hill, not daring to leave them at home. Mill Hill might have been the poor relation of my glossier showroom at Hatfield, but it was where Lisa had walked that last night of our London idyll and her presence would forever haunt my feelings for the place. Apart from that, Ruby was frequently in the Hatfield office but rarely at Mill Hill. The black box looked severe, but it contained warmth and sweetness and understanding which I had never known before, and I would often stay late in the office, open the box, and read the letters like a boy in love for the first time. Then I would see that they were born of a stolen love, and had nothing to do with the innocence in which I had first loved Lisa--but they were, against all the odds, happy letters.

But they could never be enough. I knew Lisa was a strong, passionate, mature woman, a woman of action, and I had already denied my own desire for her too long. I would tell Ruby everything and leave her, walking away at last from my life of lies. I felt like a surgeon raising his scalpel for the first incision. The skin looked healthy, but terrible cancers spread beneath. I would hew them out. There would be pain, but we would have our cure. But just as I drew myself up for this task, the scalpel was snatched from my hands and used against me.

"You've been writing letters to that bloody Nazi woman!" This was my greeting one evening when I returned to the house. Here it was then: I was undone--but I did not feel released or glad. I felt guilty and full of shame, exactly how Ruby wanted me to feel. "Well? Deny it if you can. You can't, can you?"

"No I can't. I occasionally write to Lisa." I drew a great breath. "We are very close, and loving friends."

"Very close? Loving friends? Is that what you call it in German?" Somehow she was not as wild as I had often expected. She had planned this response, thought it out for a long time after some inexplicable discovery of the box.

"But believe this if you believe nothing else," I continued. "Lisa is anything but a Nazi."

"I don't believe anything you tell me," said Ruby coldly. She was quite businesslike--no rage. "I've known about you and that bitch for a while. You're not a very clever adulterer, are you, keeping sickly love letters in the office? But then what more could I expect from you? You do realise she's been seducing you all this time since your barmy friend topped himself, don't you? You do realise you're acting like a stupid child, falling for everything she says and does? No you don't, of course you don't. It's amazing what a bit of blonde hair can do to a man--something any fool can get out of a bottle. Or is it the funny accent? You're as soft as a piece of shit. I'm amazed she puts up with you at all. She should try being married to you."

"She will, Ruby. I am going to leave you."

"Oh really? A decision?"

"I was going to tell you. Now you have read the letters I *am* telling you."

"Well that's just fine, isn't it? You leave me slaving away here, running parties for your friends..."

"They're your friends, Ruby, not mine. I've made it very clear I tolerate these people rather than like them. You're the one who wants parties."

"And what do you want? A quick bang with your Nazi woman in the back of a car in the showroom? I wondered what you got up to working late at that place. You, the boss, supposed to be

375

'working late'--it's pathetic. You've got other people to do that for you; you've got me doing it for you behind the scenes--and a good job too. You don't know one end of a balance-sheet from the other. Anyway, you wouldn't come home at the proper time if you wanted to. It's me you're avoiding, isn't it? You're either too busy with her or to ashamed to face me!"

"I'm not going to deny I love Lisa. You have the sort of life you want here; you can keep it. I am going to leave you Ruby, because our marriage means nothing. I don't hate you, I'm actually sorry for you. I'm not doing any of this to hurt you."

"Any of this! Any of *what*?" she screamed. "What *is* going on between you and that bitch?"

"You seem to know it already. But it's nothing you would understand. We're not *sleeping together* if that's what you mean, we're not *having an affair*, if that's how you'd put it. But I do love her, and she loves me. It's been terribly complicated for years--but at the same time it's simple enough. In a way there's nothing simpler. We love each other. I owe you the truth, I was going to tell you it anyway, and that is the truth."

"Oh, so now I suppose you feel high and mighty telling it. You feel strong, don't you? Honest and manly, doing the right thing, at last finding the courage to come clean--you sanctimonious bastard!"

"Well I wouldn't be the first man to stray from a greedy wife with nothing in her head."

"How dare you? You're just being selfish, and that's all you've ever been. I'll make you suffer for this. You say you built up this car business, but you know bloody well it would never have taken off without my ideas and my business contacts and the money they've brought you. You can bang away with your bloody Nazi 'til you're blue in the dick and I'll turn a blind eye to it, but if you dare leave me and dismantle this marriage I'll pull the plug on your lease and your insurances and more than half your precious car business just won't be there. Yes," she blazed triumphantly, "while you've been strolling about London with your beautiful spy, I've actually been doing some work. I've turned this business into a limited company--and I'm the Managing Director. I'm also the majority shareholder. You do understand what that means, don't you? You, lover boy, you're just an employee. Shall I sack you, or keep you on in some delightfully menial position?"

There, just there, came a memory of her wit in happier times, a flash of when I thought I loved her for her bright-mouthed sarcasm, which now could only be cruel, which I had made cruel--and which I never wanted to hear again.

"You can do what the hell you like. I'm leaving you."

"You'll have no job and no money."

"I don't care."

"Yes you do."

"Well if I care so much about my wealth and position, how d'you know I won't go into partnership with Freddie

Lamb and set out to ruin this business of yours you're so proud of? It could be done you know, buying up the right places, spreading a few nasty words about in the trade; it would be tough enough for a woman on her own without Baa and his boys putting the frighteners on you."

"Oh no," she sneered, "Don't try to be clever with me. You're bent double with scruples. I know damn well you've worn the King's Uniform and the Old School Tie and what that sort of nonsense means to you. You wouldn't use my methods."

"You have no idea how far below them I've already fallen," I reflected sadly. "Before I ever knew you I betrayed a trust and denied a greater love than ours, and I caused Lisa the kind of suffering you should be thankful you've never even dreamt of. I know you're angry and full of condemnation because I've failed you as a husband--and you can despise me if you like. I've been unfaithful all right, but not how you imagine. But that's not something you'll have to put up with any more. I'm leaving you, Ruby."

"You're not--because you know what'll happen. You'll be back in the gutter, a piece of failed wreckage from the war, drinking yourself to death. Remember I picked you up out of all that."

"You've got a funny memory."

"Well, I made this business anyway, and you've lived very nicely off it. I put you on your feet, got you away from those drunken wasters you called your friends, I made you worth something, you weak stupid bastard, and this is the thanks I get. Well I don't care about that-- but you will. 'Cos if I drop you you'll be right back in the muck you came from. You'll have nothing. And d'you think the beautiful spy will want you then? She'll scrape you off her shoe like the piece of shit you are. No no, you want to keep her, you want your romantic little outings in London, your soulful chats in Hyde Park; so you'll stay with me and keep this marriage going in front of our friends and when they've all gone home you can be my little odd job boy round the garage-- and you'll bloody well like it too."

"Have you quite finished?"

"Yes I've quite finished--with you. But you haven't finished with me. Just remember that the next time you fancy a bit on the side with Old Blondie. Now shove off--and don't bother coming to bed tonight either--not that you've ever been much fun there. You're as passionate as a block of ice--or does the Ice Maiden like that sort of thing? If she comes to me I'll tell her how to get more joy out of a brush handle."

Winter sunshine crept into Lisa's house, alive with the smells of coffee and perfume and the fresh Kentish air I had brought in upon my coat.

"See what a present I have brought you."

She opened the slim parcel I had wrapped so carefully; the crackle of its paper was echoed in the fire, where new logs blazed. It was a record of Mozart's Clarinet Concerto.

"Ah, we will have music again."

She did not say it lightly, but as if she were already sunk into a dream of memories. She put the record on her gramophone, and as the divine music soared and breathed around the room and frosty light sparkled in upon the pictures, we knew we had arrived in a new territory where we would make love, would strike the spark which had glowed for so long in our separate bodies and which was now flaring to its glorious and inevitable union. We were most tender, but fierce; deliberate, but gentle; reverent, but laughing. If once my weakness had caused her to suffer, now my strength brought her pleasure. The old sins were forgiven, and she came to shrive me in sweetest fire. Once again it was a time of music and of love, and there had been no better. We rested together, her skin most wonderfully alive in the bronze and golden firelight. She said nothing, but I heard her smile as she cradled her head against my shoulder. The scent rising from her hair carried with it all my joys and yearnings, and she seemed almost to sleep, enfolded like a child in my arms. Being with her made nonsense of all strife and war, of all ambition and of fear. It was all that mattered; all that ever had or ever could matter. Yet we did not say these words or any others like them. I had told her everything about Ruby; now I would leave that tragedy behind with all the others, and come to her. Words were not needed; the touches of our skin were our speeches, declarations, poems, prayers, and promises. We listened to the music, I held her, she rested on my shoulder. In our simple human contact were banished all the empty years.

We dressed again in the early darkness and she brought out bottles of German wine. They were rich and foreign-looking, slim and brown, with the colourful labels I had not seen since that Summer which already seemed a lifetime ago and was still a life apart. The wine was crisp and sweet, cold and magnificent; the essence of those distant hills and that distant time, powerful, potent, full of history and of life. We lounged on the settee and drank the wine lustfully. It transformed the little English house into a crowded wooden inn, a palace on the Rhine, a hunting-lodge in deep forests, a castle in the Alps. The Winter moon rolled up across the window, the frozen stars were hot and winking at the walls, pulsating in a firelit haze...and now strange music raved and roared in my head. It was Lisa! Incredibly, it was Lisa, sitting bolt upright on the settee, singing that heroic song I had not heard since she and Werner had sung it in the storm. God--that had been all our lifetimes ago! Her voice was loud and deep and unrestrained. She took lungfuls of air, her breast heaving, arms waving. She sang not at me, but beyond me, as if to an audience of ghosts behind my shoulders. Blood seemed to drain into the very middle of my body and be stirred up into an anxious froth of love and terror, joy and shame. It was unbearable. Things not to be expressed in words or deeds spun through me. They could only be expressed in music--and here it was, the loud and poignant music of my very soul and hers, the raging whisper of memory made shockingly real. Of course the song could not be finished, of course she had to sink against the cushions, burying her mouth in hot, cupped hands. Anguish seized my heart and ran through me like a madness. Soon my own hands were very wet with her warm tears, and I was soaked with grief and tenderness.

"You should not cry," I croaked. "You should not cry. We can be happy. We can be happy together."

These words forged iron in her soul. It struck through drunkenness to beat me down.

"No, no, we can't be happy," she dried her own face, "do you not see? Don't you see what you and I and all of us have done makes happiness impossible for us together?"

"I don't understand at all," I said. "I love you."

"Oh yes, yes, yes," she softened, and fresh tears glistened in her eyes. "I know that. You do not have to tell me that--but I want you to tell me that, always. And I love you: I'll say it a thousand times if you don't believe me."

"Let us always be lovers then!" I seized her hands. "Why not? It's what we want. It's what we are!"

She took her hands away.

"We cannot always have what we want or be what we are. That is the child in you, Rich, the child that Alex saw in you. Alex is too much with me."

"Is that the reason?" I said it bluntly to the fire. "Alex is dead."

She sparked up, dry-eyed.

"But his memory is too strong. Do you force me to be cruel? I cannot love you properly yet because of him."

She stood up, whole unto herself. I could not reach out and touch her.

"Alex is dead," I repeated. "Will you live the rest of your life as a nun because of that?"

"No nun has had the times I've had." A faint smile came to her lips, but vanished again. "But I am not good for you, Rich. If you leave Ruby, you lose everything you have built up since the end of the war."

"Oh for God's sake--let it go! I don't want it, I don't need it. She does not hold me by that! Haven't I told you? You and I together--that's all I want now."

"No, I am bad for you. Look at me now; all you will see is an ageing woman, and your old friend's widow. And I make you destroy things. There has been enough destruction."

"There is just no need for this," I said helplessly, staring into the fire. "We can have everything together."

"But not yet, darling Richard." She came up to me, and very tenderly put her arms around my waist. I knew then that it was hopeless. They were the arms of comfort, no longer the arms of passion; the arms of a friend, not a lover. "It would not work for us yet. We have been friends too long. Please, let us stay friends." She heaved a sigh, oddly like a baby turning over in sleep, resettling herself. "Come to see me in Germany." She patted my cheek in a strangely masculine way. "Come when you are sober."

I was shattered. I saw that her eyes were red and full of woe, but that a strange smile had also come back across her face.

"You're going to Germany? To live there?"

I was empty, I was burnt-out.

"Yes," she answered, letting her arms fall from my waist. "It will be best, I think." She drew a new breath. "Come and see me, my darling. Come and see me years from now when everything is settled and you want…you want an old friend."

I caught sight of the little Silver Spitfire, glinting and flashing its hard, sharp light behind her. She saw me looking at it, suddenly went over to pick it up, and placed it cold and solid in my hands.

"Please take this," she said.

Something like revulsion crept through me.

"I don't really want it, Lisa. Alex won

it. I don't deserve it."

The truth was I never wanted to see it again, to have it stalking my loneliness.

"All the same, please take it." She pressed it firmly into my grasp.

"Why must this thing keep coming between us?" I muttered. "It's been back and forwards too many times."

"But please take it--for the sake of all our memories."

"I'm trying to put those memories behind me, like you once told me I should."

I would be hard, I would be determined, I would not be moved.

"I want you to take it." She looked at me with those brown eyes. "Somehow, it should not come to Germany."

"All right then."

I shoved it into the big pocket of my coat and felt a great tiredness, like age, wash over me. It seemed I was beyond regret or anger. As I walked out into the frozen night clenched like a fist around me, I did not look up at the stars. I did not wish to see the splendour of the sky.

TWENTY-ONE

"So the Nazi bitch won't have you, eh? But I will, by God I'll have you! I'll have you running round working your arse off--and there'll be plenty of work to keep your mind off lower things. Fletcher's Motors is about to expand. You'll be delighted to hear that I've bought up a string of old garages and I'm going to turn them into new showrooms that'll make the Hatfield one look old-fashioned. We'll be rich--richer than ever; there'll even be a few pennies for you to spend on stamps for your love-letters. And don't think you won't be writing them, 'cos you'll be stuck here working for me; there'll be no dirty-weekend trips to see the blonde bitch, not now…because you're a coward. I used to think you were brave, just because you went through the war in a fancy aeroplane. But you were just lucky. You're a coward, you've always been a coward, and you'll stay with me because you're still a coward--and because you've got nowhere to go.

The Nazi bitch won't have you, and I can't say I blame her; but I'll have you--I'll have you exactly where I want you, day in, day out, working in my business the way I say. And if I hear one squeak out of you I'll drop you back in the gutter. You'll be back working for that bloody villain Lamb flogging Standard Eights up a back lane in the East End. And that little silver statue you had the cheek to accept from your barmy friend--we'll keep that right here in the lounge, so you can look at it every day and remember what a coward you are and how better men than you were shot to pieces trying to do something for this country while all you've done is screwed a bloody Nazi."

Some of this happened much as Ruby said it would. Over the next two years she did indeed buy the old garages and turn them into profitable motor-showrooms on the main roads North of London. The house in Hatfield was relentlessly improved, and rang to more parties where she became known for lavish food and lavish drink and peals of lavish laughter. These parties became increasingly difficult for me to bear as the stupid drunks became more predictable and the laughter more vacant. I made a dull truce with Ruby, which she would have called submission, but not for one minute did she relax her offensive. I would have left a thousand times, but knew that Lisa was not ready for me--because I was not yet ready for Lisa. I still had not crawled out of the last tunnel.

I began to know at last what I should have to do, and what Lisa had so subtly been trying to teach me. Of course I should have to renounce Ruby and the shabby life we led--but that was easy, had already been accomplished in an effortless moment. Only the husk of it was left. But I could not step out from it until I had achieved a greater and more complex renunciation: I should have to renounce war, utterly and finally, and renounce everything it had made me. I should have to stop looking at the silver Spitfire and remembering the soaking terrors of battle--and its cruel joys. I should have to learn to look into the sky, watch the magical streak of a new jet against the burning blue, and not wish to be back in a warplane. Like the old knights at the end of their quests, I should have to throw away my sword and let my armour rust--but not to become a hermit, rather to live in the real world and grasp it as it spun around me. I should have to let Alex die from my being as he had died from life and was still dying from Lisa, and let grief mature into the same peace she would teach me to embrace as tenderly as my beloved.

Meanwhile, the whole world seemed to be changing. We had a new decade and a new Queen. I watched her on the newsreel coming down the steps of the B.O.A.C. airliner to be greeted by the three ministers: she was a slender girl at a poignant moment, but pretty, serene, and vivacious--and suddenly the future could be like that too. The following year London went wild for the Coronation. The crowds in the decorated streets, the neo-medieval additions to Westminster

Abbey, the flags, the gleeful children visiting from all over the country, even the excitement of our neighbours who had bought themselves a television set for the event--all these seemed to signal a joyous rebirth, and it was impossible for even the most cynical person not to be drawn into it. It re-awakened a curious sense of history in myself, a vision of how the world could suddenly look in one direction, of a people no longer lost. But at home with Ruby no new age had dawned, nor could it.

Apart from my longing for Lisa, I had utterly tired of my life, and tired of Ruby's inexhaustible march towards better things. The better things for which I yearned were quite unknown to her, and with each bright-lipped laugh I stepped further back from wanting to explain them. I longed to breathe a cool fresh wind from off the sea, to catch a glimmer of mountain snow, to leave behind the silly and the petty. I was overwhelmed by a mysterious glimpse of truth, discovering the pointless vanities of domestic misery.

The call which at one time or another must torment all men, now stirred me. I thought I recognized it from the days of my excitement in flying and from my manic lust for danger in the war, but it was not so. It was not a lure of danger, a lust for the so-called poetry of adventure which can itself be debased. It was a sudden knowledge that the sordid thrashings of unhappy people could be transcended, that a man need not live like this. At last I should head for the abyss, plunge in, and wash off the grime of wasted years.

Lisa's old idea that I might become a bush-pilot in Australia now teased my imagination. It brought smiles of outrageous adventure, of a wild scheme suddenly made feasible. Surely it would not be difficult to find a job out there; I could fly almost anything. I'd start off in Sydney or Melbourne, but Queensland and the Northern Territories were the places to be: still wild country with enormous distances. Mail, provisions, visitors: everything went by air. I couldn't fail. And I would be swallowed up in a vast new country where nothing of the old life mattered. That was the true opportunity in that land of opportunity, as Lisa had called it.

Lisa. Surely she would not come. I could not imagine her so far from Europe, so far from her heartlands...and yet, she was brave and adventurous. Perhaps we *could* go together. But no, if I went to Australia it would have to be alone; alone into the abyss. And now I longed for escape more fervently. The years were passing at a shocking speed, the run of my own life was overtaking me. I must do it, and soon. And this longing grew from being part of my life until it became life itself and built a cold, calculating purpose to which, at length, everything became subordinate: a hard core of desire in a great white void of want. A day dawned when I could tolerate the emptiness no longer. The business of leaving came easily. I told no-one, put none of my affairs in order. The truth would slide out soon enough...let it come then, how and when it would. Packing my bags for Germany, I felt I could already hear the sound of singing, and see the fairytale castle clouds ride up from over the Alps. I would be there in time for Christmas. Then there would be her Birthday, with the Spring beginning, and I would be able to give her a Birthday present in her own country, and kiss her, and wish her well, and hold her, and be held by her, and know that the terrible years had not passed in vain. I took the silver Spitfire and turned it in my hands, but did not pack it. Instead I left it gleaming cold upon the bedroom windowsill. It would at last go from me, and I should no longer think of death or war or heroism or cowardice or glory or shame or all the other things I had thought about for so long. But it was with genuine happiness that I remembered Werner and Alex, the flying and the sunshine, the lost and the forbidden. Staring down into the empty garden, I could already feel the warmth of Lisa's hand and catch the rising perfume of her hair. Beyond the distant roar of traffic I could hear the Summer cooing of the pigeons, and sense the faint and thrilling music of the South.

THE END

Printed in Great Britain
by Amazon